P9-CDI-823

Acclaim for the Legendary MICKEY SPILLANE!

"Spillane is a master in compelling you to always turn the next page."

—*New York Times*

"There's a kind of power about Mickey Spillane that no other writer can imitate."

—*Miami Herald*

"Satisfying...its blithe lack of concern with present-day political correctness gives it a rough-hewn charm that's as refreshing as it is rare."

—*Entertainment Weekly*

"A superb writer. Spillane is one of this century's bestselling authors."

—*Cleveland Plain Dealer*

"Spillane's books...redefined the detective story."

—*Wallace Stroby*

"A wonderfully guilty pleasure."

—*Tim McLoughlin, The Brooklyn Rail*

"A fun, fast read...from one of the all-time greats."

—*Denver Rocky Mountain News*

"Spillane...presents nothing save visual facts; but he selects only those facts, only those eloquent details, which convey the visual reality of the scene and create a mood of desolate loneliness."

—*Ayn Rand*

"A writer who revolutionized a genre [with] heavy doses of testosterone, fast action, brutality and sensuality."

—*Publishers Weekly*

"Sexy and frantically paced."

—*Chicago American*

"Salty and satisfying...will hit like a slug of Old Crow from the bottom-drawer bottle."

—*Buffalo News*

"Machine gun pace...good writing...fascinating tale."

—*Charlotte Observer*

"Simple, brutal, and sexy."

—*Kansas City Star*

"If you think he has lost his touch or drained the well, read this one...the new one is better than ever. If you are a Spillane fan you will enjoy this one more than anything done before. It is fast-moving, easy reading, and has the greatest shocker of an ending."

—*Albuquerque Tribune*

"The socko ending is Mickey Spillane's stock in trade, and never has he done it with greater effect...Sensational."

—*Buffalo News*

"A swift-paced, pulsating yarn...which very definitely shows that Mr. Spillane still has control of his fast ball, plus a few sneaky slow ones for the change-up."

—*Springfield Daily News*

"Need we say more than—the Mick is back."

—*Hammond Times*

The only thing I heard was the night sounds. It was still the same old night for me—nothing had changed. You had to walk the streets to really know what the city was all about, though what you learned would probably make you sick.

And I was learning that I wasn't alone.

I'd heard the strange noise, like muffled clicking of heels, behind me. I thought nothing of it at first, then it got louder. I walked faster and the noise ceased.

But when I slowed down, I heard it again—real close. On a stretch where the streetlamp was out, I came to a complete stop, spun around, and met him face to face.

In the night I saw the flicker of the blade...

OTHER HARD CASE CRIME BOOKS BY MICKEY SPILLANE:

DEAD STREET
THE CONSUMMATA *(with Max Allan Collins)*

OTHER HARD CASE CRIME BOOKS BY MAX ALLAN COLLINS:

QUARRY
QUARRY'S LIST
QUARRY'S DEAL
QUARRY'S CUT
QUARRY'S VOTE
THE LAST QUARRY
THE FIRST QUARRY
QUARRY IN THE MIDDLE
QUARRY'S EX
THE WRONG QUARRY
QUARRY'S CHOICE
QUARRY IN THE BLACK
QUARRY'S CLIMAX

DEADLY BELOVED
SEDUCTION OF THE INNOCENT
TWO FOR THE MONEY

The LAST STAND

by **Mickey Spillane**

PREPARED FOR PUBLICATION AND WITH AN INTRODUCTION BY MAX ALLAN COLLINS

A HARD CASE  CRIME NOVEL

A HARD CASE CRIME BOOK
(HCC-133)
First Hard Case Crime edition: March 2018

Published by

Titan Books
A division of Titan Publishing Group Ltd
144 Southwark Street
London SE1 0UP

in collaboration with Winterfall LLC

Print edition ISBN 978-1-78565-686-6
E-book ISBN 978-1-78565-687-3

Design direction by Max Phillips
www.maxphillips.net

Typeset by Swordsmith Productions

Printed in the United States of America

Visit us on the web at www.HardCaseCrime.com

For the Spillane "satellite" writers—
Earle Basinsky
Dave Geritty
Joe Gill
Charlie Wells

CONTENTS

THE LAST STAND

MICKEY SPILLANE AT 100
an introduction by Max Allan Collins

In July of 2006, at the age of 88, the last major mystery writer of the twentieth century left the building. Only a handful of writers in the genre—Agatha Christie, Dashiell Hammett, and Raymond Chandler among them—achieved such superstar status.

Spillane's position, however, is unique—reviled by many mainstream critics, despised and envied by a number of his contemporaries in the very field he revitalized, the creator of Mike Hammer had an impact not just on mystery and suspense fiction but popular culture in general.

The success of the paperback reprint editions of his startlingly violent and sexy novels—tens of millions of copies sold—jump-started the explosion of so-called "paperback originals," for the next quarter-century the home of countless Spillane imitators, and his redefinition of the action hero as a tough guy who mercilessly executed villains and slept with beautiful, willing women remains influential (*Sin City* is Frank Miller's homage).

When Spillane published *I, the Jury* in 1947, he introduced in Mike Hammer one of the most famous of all fictional private eyes, and one unlike any P.I. readers had met before. Hammer swears vengeance over the corpse of an army buddy who lost an arm in the Pacific, saving the detective's life. No matter who the villain turns out to be, Hammer will not just find him, but kill him—even if it's a her.

Revenge was a constant theme in Mike Hammer's world—*Vengeance Is Mine!* among his titles—with the detective rarely taking a paying client. Getting even was the motivation for this hard-boiled hero.

This was something entirely new in mystery fiction, and Spillane quickly became the most popular—and controversial—mystery writer of the mid-twentieth century. In addition to creating an eye-for-an-eye hero, the writer brought a new level of sex and violence to the genre. He was called a fascist by left-leaning critics and a libertine by right-leaning ones. In between were millions of readers who turned Spillane's first six Hammer novels into the bestselling private eye novels of all time.

Since then, Hammer has been the subject of a radio show, a comic strip, and several television series, starring Darren McGavin in the 1950s and Stacy Keach in the '80s and '90s. Numerous gritty movies have been made from Spillane novels, notably director Robert Aldrich's seminal film *noir, Kiss Me Deadly* (1955).

As success raged around him, Mickey Spillane proved himself a showman and a marketing genius; he became as famous as his creation, appearing on book jackets with gun in hand and fedora on head. His image became synonymous with Hammer's, more so even than any of the actors who portrayed the private eye, including McGavin and Keach.

For eighteen years, well past the peak of his publishing success, Spillane appeared as himself (and basically as Hammer) in the wildly successful Miller Lite commercials, alongside his "Doll" (Lee Meredith of *The Producers* fame) and overshadowing countless former pro athletes.

Alone among mystery writers, he appeared as his own famous detective in a movie, *The Girl Hunters* (1963). Critics at the time viewed his performance as Hammer favorably, and today many viewers of the quirky, made-in-England film still do. Virtually an amateur, Spillane is in nearly every frame, his natural charisma and wry humor holding him in good stead beside the professional likes of Lloyd Nolan (Michael Shayne of the 1940s Fox movie series) and Shirley Eaton (the "golden girl" of *Goldfinger*).

The Girl Hunters wasn't Spillane's first feature film—it wasn't even his first leading role in one. In 1954, John Wayne hired Spillane to star with Pat O'Brien and lion-tamer Clyde Beatty in *Ring of Fear*, a film Mickey co-scripted without credit, receiving a white Jaguar (the car, not the cat) as a gift from producer Wayne.

Mike Hammer paved the way for James Bond and every tough P.I., cop, lone avenger and government agent who followed, from Shaft to Billy Jack, from Dirty Harry to Jack Bauer. The latest Hammer-style heroes include an unlikely one—the vengeance-driven *Girl* of *Dragon Tattoo* fame—as well as a more obvious descendent, Lee Child's Jack Reacher.

Now, on the occasion of Spillane's centenary—he was born March 9, 1918—I am pleased to team up with Hard Case Crime to present readers with a very special birthday present: two previously unpublished works, one from near the start of his mystery writing career, the other the very last novel he wrote, finished within weeks of his passing.

The manuscript of *A Bullet for Satisfaction* that I found in Mickey's files is somewhat mysterious. Typewritten on his distinctive yellow paper—like almost everything among the unpublished, unfinished material—a section of the short novel is similarly familiar in being typed in Mickey's usual single-spaced format (it saved paper and "looked more like a book").

Two other sections, however, are double-spaced. A number

of partial Spillane novel manuscripts were indeed double-spaced but on white paper, presumably prepared by a typist to be sent in to Mickey's publisher to indicate that contracted-for work was underway. *Satisfaction* was the only example in the files that appeared to be rough-draft material, typed on the yellow paper Mickey preferred (he found it easy on the eye and immediately identified a manuscript as unfinished), but partly utilizing double-spacing.

And although the short novel had a beginning, middle and end, it lacked Spillane's usual edits. Mickey liked to claim he never rewrote, but that was an exaggeration—he typically tweaked word choice in pen and replaced paragraphs or even sections with typewritten inserts. A number of the later Hammer novels I wound up finishing gave me alternate versions of entire chapters—*The Goliath Bone* (2008) had a dizzying number of first chapters for me to choose from and eventually combine. The lack of edits on *A Bullet for Satisfaction* suggests it was set aside early in the writing process—and yet was a more or less complete draft. So why was it abandoned?

Of course, it's not automatically mysterious to find unfinished but substantial material in Spillane's files. Over the past decade-plus since Mickey's passing, I have completed six Hammer novels working from 100-page beginnings and other materials (characterization and plot notes, sometimes roughed-out endings), and another six from shorter fragments (usually around 30 or 40 pages, again sometimes with other materials).

In addition, I've completed *Dead Street* (all but the final three chapters by Mickey) and *The Consummata* (again from a 100-page start). Also, a number of Hammer short stories, gathered in the collection *A Long Time Dead* (2016), have been developed from smaller fragments.

Mickey frequently walked away from an in-progress novel

when another project took over his interest. In the last years of his life, he frequently moved from one novel manuscript to another (*Goliath Bone* and *The Last Stand* being his final projects, though he also considered *Dead Street* active). He often had a different novel going in each of his three home offices.

As you will see, *A Bullet for Satisfaction*, written in tough-guy first-person, has the themes, plotting techniques, melodramatic characterization, hard-breathing sex, and violent action so characteristic of Mickey's earliest work. Obviously written no later than the mid-'50s, *Satisfaction* seems almost a compendium of Gold Medal Books-era *noir*—a rogue cop, a corrupt town, sleazy bars and night spots, crooked politicians, a good girl or two, a bad girl or two, a friendship damaged by betrayal, and Spillane's trademark vengeance theme.

The existing draft had a number of inconsistencies and rough patches, as well as a risible subplot about Communism that required me to go beyond simple editing into Spillane/Collins collaborative mode. But *Satisfaction* was certainly something that with a bit of work Mickey could easily have sold to one of his regular magazine markets, *Manhunt* or *Cavalier*. So why didn't he?

One possible clue is that the manuscript may date to the period around 1952 when Spillane was dealing with his religious conversion to the Jehovah's Witnesses. The only Hammer novel he published around then was *Kiss Me, Deadly* (1952), which finds the writer struggling with the sex and violence elements expected of him. He may have shelved *Satisfaction* because it would have gotten him in trouble with his newly adopted church.

It's also possible that he was working on it with one of his group of satellite writers, ex-military buddies who gathered around their successful friend in the fifties. Charlie Wells,

Earle Basinsky and Dave Geritty all wrote and published crime novels with Spillane's help, both as a mentor and as a conduit to such publishers as Gold Medal, Dutton and Signet—Spillane provided cover blurbs for all three writers. Another satellite writer, Joe Gill, a pal of Mickey's from comic-book days, became a prolific magazine contributor and comics scripter, including the very Hammer-like 1960s P.I. feature, *Sarge Steel*.

Wells and Basinsky published a pair of novels each—the former, *Let the Night Cry* (1953) and *The Last Kill* (1955); the latter *The Big Steal* (1955) and *Death Is a Cold, Keen Edge* (1956). But only Geritty had a substantial career, publishing eight novels under assorted bylines ("Garrity," "Dave J. Garrity," "David J. Gerrity") and ghosting two celebrity autobiographies. In Geritty's sole private eye novel, *Dragon Hunt* (1967), Spillane loaned out Mike Hammer for several cameos and let his friend re-use the basic plot of the final daily continuity of the comic strip *From the Files of...Mike Hammer* (1953–1954), which Mickey, Joe Gill and artist Ed Robbins had written.

Of the satellite writers, Geritty seems the most likely to have had a hand in *A Bullet for Satisfaction*. But the manuscript clearly is a child of the early '50s, and Geritty did not get a book published till 1960 (*Cry Me a Killer*, Gold Medal). It seems more likely Mickey censored himself for religious reasons, and put the novella aside.

But for the purposes of this volume, *A Bullet for Satisfaction* provides a sharp, revealing contrast with Mickey's final completed novel, *The Last Stand*. Together these companion pieces bookend Mickey's extraordinary career.

A month or so before his passing in the summer of 2006, Mickey sent me *The Last Stand*.

We spoke on the phone and I told him what a kick I'd gotten

out of it. He was happy with the book—happy to have finished it, under the circumstances, but overall pleased, though he told me of a few things he'd like to touch up "if he had the time." (My contribution to the novel has largely been carrying out Mickey's instructions.) He then turned his attention to his final Hammer novel-in-progress, *The Goliath Bone*, calling me days before his death and asking me to complete it for him, if necessary.

Around this time, he also told his wife Jane that there would be a "treasure hunt" after he was gone, and to "give everything to Max—he'll know what to do." Jane reminded him that I was not a Jehovah's Witness, and Mickey said he understood—I would not be bound to leave out things that might displease his church.

My wife Barb (with whom I write the *Antiques* mystery series) and I joined Jane in the treasure hunt that took us to all three of Mickey's offices in Murrells Inlet, South Carolina. The files were extensive, as I've indicated. We sat in the Spillane dining room with a feast of manuscripts before us, each of us combing through our stacks of pages, occasionally one of us crying out, "Here's a Hammer!"

Included, of course, was Mickey's final completed manuscript —*The Last Stand*, not a Mike Hammer. After much thought, and some input from Hard Case Crime editor Charles Ardai, I decided to put it aside, with the centenary in mind. My immediate priority was to get the unpublished Mike Hammer material out there—Mickey had only published thirteen Hammer novels in his lifetime—as well as the two other substantial unfinished crime novels, *Dead Street* and *The Consummata*. My current Spillane project is completing the earliest manuscript in the files, *Killing Town* (Titan Books, forthcoming 2018), the first Mike Hammer novel, preceding even *I, The Jury*.

The Last Stand represents the culmination of the final phase of Mickey's writing life, in which he was more interested in adventure than mystery—although from the beginning, Spillane heroes had been two-fisted adventurers, and all of his work contains elements of mystery and crime fiction. His two published books for pre-adolescents—*The Day the Sea Rolled Back* (1979) and *The Ship That Never Was* (1982)—reflect that bent toward adventure, and his love of the sea. His final published novel, *Something's Down There* (2003), similarly reflects his enthusiasm for boating and deep-sea fishing, with Mike Hammer replaced by the evocatively (and similarly) named Mako Hooker.

The Last Stand is a wonderful chance to spend some time with one of twentieth century America's greatest storytellers in the mellow twilight of his life. In it, he celebrates his love of flying, much as *Something's Down There* celebrates the sea; he allows his imagination to soar, as well, while keeping it grounded in the reality of the down-to-earth story he's telling.

Mickey's final novel provides a coda to his larger body of work, and is at once atypical and typical. His hero, Joe Gillian (named for satellite writer Joe Gill) is a tough, confident man, very much in the tradition of Hammer, Tiger Mann and other Spillane protagonists. His story, however, is told in the third person, where the Hammer canon (and the vast majority of the writer's fiction) is in vivid first person. Here the prose is spare but occasionally poetic, and dialogue drives the narrative.

In these pages, Spillane returns to his recurring themes of male friendship and male/female companionship. It is easy (as someone once said) to see Hammer's friend Pat Chambers in Gillian's friend Pete, and Hammer's life partner Velda in the lovely Running Fox. The bad rap Spillane gets as a supposed misogynist overlooks the obvious: the women in his fiction are usually strong, powerful and smart, every bit the hero's equal.

That Joe Gillian bonds easily with the Indians of an unspecified "rez" is no surprise, either, as Mike Hammer's friends were often among the outsiders of society. Nor is the modern-day Western aspect of the novel inconsistent with Mickey's view of Mike Hammer as an urban gunslinger. The Mick's interest in Westerns is also evident in the unproduced screenplay he wrote for his friend John Wayne, which has led to the posthumous novel *The Legend of Caleb York* (Kensington Books, 2015) and several sequels.

Also present, not surprisingly, is the dominant theme of Spillane's fiction—vengeance. But in *The Last Stand*, it's the brute called Big Arms who craves revenge, not hero Gillian, who is a man of a certain age at peace with himself, looking for neither trouble nor riches, though the love of a good woman does hold appeal. Crime-fighting and mystery seem almost to have to seek Gillian out, though seek him out they do.

Gillian's very masculine but non-aggressive view on life reflects Spillane in his final years. The Hammer of *Black Alley* (1996) is definitely a laid-back version of the character, which pleases readers who have followed Hammer's journey over the decades, but can confuse those who only know the hate-filled young investigator of *I, the Jury*. Like *Black Alley*, *The Last Stand* is a barely concealed rumination on coming to terms with aging.

Not long after his home was destroyed by Hurricane Hugo in 1989, Mickey and I sat one evening in the makeshift tiki bar he'd built in his backyard. Mickey spoke of his anger at those who had looted his home in the aftermath of the storm. I saw in his eyes the burning rage of Mike Hammer and he held his hands in front of him, squeezing them into fists. He told me what he would like to do to the thieves, then his fists became fingers again, and he said, "But I'm not like that anymore. I don't do that now."

Perhaps not surprisingly, when I spoke to him about *The Last Stand* on the phone, he said to me, "You know, I really like that Big Arms." If a voice can have a twinkle in it, his did. With that big-kid quality he often got when he spoke of work he'd done that had pleased him, he said, "I really like that character." Not Joe Gillian, but Big Arms, who haunts the good-natured pages of *The Last Stand* like Mike Hammer's ghost.

Max Allan Collins
May 28, 2017

A BULLET *for* SATISFACTION

by **Mickey Spillane**

and **Max Allan Collins**

CHAPTER I

The Belmont Hotel was really jumping. Everything had happened so fast. How could just one death raise such a commotion? Maybe it was just this mid-size city. Maybe it was the way people reacted to these things. Or maybe he was just a damn big man, so that any way you looked at it, something big had happened, and big things have to be handled in a big way.

We pushed our way through the mob. The reporters didn't waste any time making the scene, looking like flies seeking a dead animal to light on as they headed for the stairs. A couple of uniformed police were having a hell of a time keeping the press boys back.

I walked up to the policeman in charge. "Where?"

"Upstairs, Captain Dexter. Second floor, room 224."

After answering me, he removed a handkerchief from his pocket and wiped the sweat from his forehead. I motioned for one of the detectives with me to take over, to give the guy a break.

We skipped the elevator and took the stairs. When I opened the door of room 224, my partner Fred Jenkins was already there handling things. He walked up to me and gave me a tired smile.

"How's it coming?" I asked, already knowing the answer.

"Not much to go on yet, Captain. It'll be a tough one. The guy had his share of enemies. Any of them could've taken him down. He was a big one, all right."

He'd said a mouthful. Mayes Rogers was a big name in politics around here—he'd made it to the top, and on the way ruined quite a few. A lot of people would have liked to see him put underground, and maybe they had good reasons.

I pulled out a cigarette, stuck the flame of my lighter to it, and drew in the smoke. For a minute I watched some of the boys make an inspection of the room and then motioned for Fred to come back over.

"What you got so far?" I asked, as I pushed a chair over for him.

"Just that our local representative was found with a bullet in his head," Fred said. "Chairs were overturned and things scattered all over. It could've been a fight. Looked like there was a party going on, because there's a record player over there and there's crumbs and empty whiskey bottles on the floor. No one downstairs knew of a party, though. In fact, they didn't know Rogers was in his room—they thought he was out."

I walked over to the bed. Rogers was lying several feet from it, blood on the lower half of the bed and on the pillow on the floor. The rug was bloody, too, which made it look as if he'd tried to run. Or maybe been dragged.

The medical examiner came in and began his job without even giving us a glance. I looked over to where a man was sitting with a blank expression glued to his face.

Fred said, "That's Bob Bacon. He's the one who found Rogers."

Our eyes met. He glanced at me, barely nodded, and then away. We had exchanged nods before, at the courthouse, but that was about all.

I went over to him. "Captain Dexter, Homicide. What time did you find the body?"

"I went out with some of the boys. Mayes was supposed to go with us, but decided to stay in his room at the last minute.

Said he was tired. We came in around nine and I went back up. That's when I found him."

"By the looks of things," I said, gesturing around, "it seems he had a party. You didn't know anything about one?"

He shook his head and ran his fingers through what was left of his thinning hair. "No. Like I said, he was going out with us but changed his mind."

"Was he alone in the room when you last saw him?"

He nodded.

"Was anything bothering him? Did he give an explanation why he didn't want to go?"

"He didn't seem bothered. He just said he was tired and decided to turn in early."

I glanced over at Fred. "You said no one downstairs knew he was in the room. *Somebody* knew he was in this room and blew his brains out. Did you talk with the elevator operator?"

"Yeah," Fred said. "Took an elderly couple to the second floor. That's all. We checked them out. Nothing there."

The room was hot and sticky and I could use some fresh air. I went to an open window and stared out at the lights breaking up the darkness—cars, buildings, streetlamps. After I'd filled my lungs with the night, I said to Fred, "Fingerprint boys finished?"

"Yup."

Fred had just got the word out when the medical examiner came over with his usual twisted expression that might have meant the victim was killed with an axe or maybe just died in his sleep. He held up a crumpled piece of metal.

"A .45, Captain. One bullet in him, one in the wall."

A .45 makes the kind of noise not easily ignored—even a silencer has trouble keeping it down. Fred knew what I was going to ask him. "Anybody hear a shot?"

He shook his head slowly. "We checked all the rooms in possible hearing distance. No one heard a damn thing."

"Rogers has a wife, right?"

"Yeah. His second. First wife and two kids were killed in a car accident shortly after he was elected."

"He won twice, so someone must've liked him." I turned away without giving Fred time to comment. When I got to the door, the flash cameras went off and I took one last look at the corpse without a face. Then I closed it behind me.

Daybreak found me in my office—a kill like this doesn't allow you time to sleep. The report of the murder was on my desk and reading it took no time at all. When I finished, I tossed it over to the sleepy-eyed younger detective sitting across from me. Fred read it as quickly as I had.

"Well?" I asked.

He threw me a puzzled look and shrugged.

I said, "Someone had a beef with Rogers and settled up, which doesn't narrow it down for crap. This whole damn thing points to nothing."

"So where do we start?"

Now I shrugged. "I didn't get enough from Bob Bacon last night. Maybe he wasn't in the best mood to spit out the answers I wanted to hear. Must be quite a shock to see a good friend stretched out on the floor with a slug in the face."

"You know where to reach him?"

"I'll find him," I said.

Bacon was a politically active attorney I'd seen a few times in court. He was fairly new in town and until now I'd no reason to talk with him.

He was sitting at his desk, fumbling through papers, when he saw me walk in. "Find anything yet, Captain?" he snapped before I even shut the door.

"That's why I'm here, Bob. Trying to get a start."

I dropped my weight into one of his chairs while he stuffed his papers into a drawer.

Bacon was going to let me speak first. He sat there wearing a flat look that was hard to read. He was barely middle-aged, but his nearly bald head and serious face made him appear older.

I asked, "How close were you to Rogers?"

A bittersweet smile erased the blankness. "I'd say I was his closest friend. I backed him in the elections, and I've been at his side ever since."

"Then you'd know if anyone had anything against him."

The smile vanished and a shrug preceded his reply. "You got me there, Captain. Mayes was a popular guy. That's why this is such a big shock to me."

"You can expect a man in his position to have people who didn't like him. Who even hated him. He was a public figure, and a powerful one."

"Like I said, Captain, I don't know anyone, offhand, with that kind of grudge against him. If so, I was unaware of it. And Mayes would surely have told me."

I sat there quietly while my eyes picked up on a slight tremble of the chin. Bacon wanted to say something, but couldn't get it out.

Finally he blurted, "Mayes has a wife. *Had* a wife. She lives outside a small community called Drake, not far from here. Know it?"

I nodded.

He said, "She might know something Mayes never told me about. Wives know things."

"Yes they do." I filed that in the back of my mind and said, "What was Rogers doing in a hotel, with a wife in Drake?"

Another shrug. "We had a meeting there, some of his staff and me, and it ran late, so he decided to stay over." He paused for a second. "After the meet, some of the boys decided to go out for a late supper. He was going to come along, like I said, but he changed his mind. Said he'd had a long day."

"Did you stay in the hotel?"

"No."

"What made you come back?"

He paused again. "I went upstairs with some of the other boys, and just stopped at his room to say good night."

"Who was in the lobby when you and your friends came in?"

He thought that over, then said, "To tell you the truth, I don't believe I saw anyone. Not even anybody at the desk."

"There were bottles and food on the floor. Mayes never mentioned a party?"

"Never. If he was throwing one, I didn't know about it. He just said he was going to bed."

"Maybe he had a circle of friends outside of work he liked to party with."

"If so, I couldn't tell you who that'd be."

"Well, someone knew he was in his room—someone with a .45. I guess you know they don't make a small bang. Somebody should've heard it—there were two shots."

His eyes narrowed. "The room next to his and several on down the hall belonged to some of the men at the meeting. I guess most of 'em were out."

I reached into my shirt pocket and pulled out a pack of cigarettes, lit one up. "About his wife."

"Like I said, she lives in Drake."

A small farm community ten miles from here.

"You told me that much," I said.

"I really know very little about her. Only met her a few times. At political meetings mostly. Occasionally I'd see her when I stopped by his house."

"Anybody live there but Mayes and his wife?"

"No. But I understand her sister has come to stay with her for the funeral and all."

"How did Rogers and the sister get along?"

He blinked at my left-field question. "Normal relationship, I guess. Sister visited them off and on. Sometimes stayed with Mrs. Rogers when Mayes was on a prolonged business trip. Not too much difference in their ages, the sisters."

Suddenly his expression shifted.

"I just remembered something," he said, sitting forward. "There *is* a guy who had something against Mayes. Arnold Moore. His brother, George, was after the nomination in Mayes's first election. George dropped out of the running. Arnold accused Mayes of pressuring his brother out and said, and did, some crazy things."

"Interesting. Know anything else about him?"

"He's a mechanic at Anderson's Garage. A bachelor, lives with his mother. That's all I know about the guy, except that he's got a hair-trigger temper."

"I'll have a talk with him. But the widow first."

"I for one would love to see you find the son of a bitch who did this."

I stood up and so did he and we shook hands. He added, "If I can be of any more service to you, drop by."

I thanked him and left.

Drake seemed to be a peaceable place, a *Saturday Evening Post* cover come to life with its green trees, singing birds, and a storybook downtown. Just outside the city limits, I spotted a farmer in coveralls at a curbside mailbox, reading a letter. I pulled over and he looked up with a friendly smile.

"Excuse me, sir," I called from the car. "Would you happen

to know how to get to the Rogers place? That's Mayes Rogers?"

He studied me for a moment, then raised one of his well-used fingers and pointed.

"Turn left at the crossroads and follow the road for a quarter of a mile. Trust me—you won't miss it."

I thanked him and headed that way.

I drove for what I thought was a full quarter of a mile and then down a dirt road. I was about to think the friendly farmer had given me the wrong directions till I saw the name Rogers on a mailbox at the bottom of a hill on top of which a huge white plantation-style mansion nestled. I mashed the gas and cut up into the long, steep gravel driveway leading directly to the front yard.

Only one car was parked in front of the house—a bright red Cadillac. I killed the engine under a large oak tree, hopped out and got a breath of the country air. After a couple of moments of just staring, I walked up to the porch and rang the doorbell, twice.

A good minute passed before a tall, hulking butler in full livery opened the door. Handsome in a vaguely British way, he wore a proud look of distinction that made me stare too long.

"Yes, sir?" he said, polite but with the expression of a guy staring at a shoe he'd just removed only to find he'd stepped in something.

I flashed him my badge and said, "I'd like to talk with Mrs. Rogers."

The hulking figure stepped closer and the stern look on his face didn't change. My shield impressed him not at all.

"Mrs. Rogers is asleep." That was all he said. The condescension on his face and his heavy masculine tone said the rest. I leaned closer, our bodies nearly touching.

Through my teeth, which weren't exactly smiling, I said, "You tell Mrs. Rogers that I'd like to talk to her concerning the death of her husband. I'm sure she'll be interested."

"Mrs. Rogers is asleep and left word *not* to be disturbed."

I was about to knock Jeeves on his can and out of my way when a female voice stopped me.

"What's the trouble, Marsh?"

Marsh said, proud of himself, "This police officer is here to see Mrs. Rogers. I informed him that she is unavailable."

"It's all right, Marsh. They're bound to come sometime."

A new expression came into Marsh's face, a sort of deference. He stepped aside.

She moved to the door and I could see her now—every lovely inch of her. She wore a simple blue dress over complicated curves, and didn't seem to mind my staring, because she only smiled. She held out a hand for me to shake and I did.

"I'm Ginger Bass, Mrs. Rogers' sister. She's asleep now. Maybe *I* can be of some help. Come in, please."

I went in, gave my hat to the butler, to give him something worthwhile to do for a change. I followed the Bass woman into a well-appointed living room off an entryway larger than my apartment.

She gestured me into an overstuffed chair. She sat down on the couch and still seemed not to mind that my eyes were going over her like they had a search warrant.

And she was nice to look at. I'd guess she was in her early thirties and her blonde hair wasn't from a bottle. Her apple-cheeked face had a smoothness that nonetheless showed depth, with plenty of natural expression.

She tugged down her skirt—like that was going to stop me from appreciating those well-tanned legs—and folded her hands in her lap. "You're from the Gantsville police?"

"Captain Dexter, Homicide. We've gotten off to a rather slow start on this case. I don't like to bother Mrs. Rogers at a time like this, but obviously it's necessary."

The sister shook her head. "Doris hasn't been well since she received the news of her husband's death. If you want to question her, I'd suggest you come back in a few days—"

"I haven't got a few days to wait for answers. I need them now. Might be you could help."

She sat up, eager to pitch in.

I said, "You knew Mayes Rogers well, didn't you?"

"Quite well," she said with a nod. "I visited Mayes and Doris now and then. You see, I live alone, a couple of little towns over, and they were nice company for me. Mayes was always a gentleman, very much a sincere, decent person. I really don't understand how anyone could have done such a thing."

"Do you know if anyone has ever threatened him?"

"No."

"Any problems?"

She gave that a quick thought. "Business or political ones? No."

"That implies other problems."

"Well…personal ones, yes."

"It's important you be frank."

"…between him and Doris."

"Could you be more specific?"

She gave me a glance that said she wasn't sure she would respond, but then she did: "Mayes had his women. He was much older than Doris, but that didn't keep him from having his women. He had a certain charm. Doris was extremely upset once, when gossip spread about Mayes and the Banner woman."

"What Banner woman?"

"Jean Banner. Very high society, at one time anyway, and a notorious flirt but....Doris threatened to leave Mayes over it, and that was the last of Jean Banner in his life. I'd say that was their biggest problem."

"How would you rate the marriage otherwise?"

She shrugged. "Okay."

"Okay?"

Then she came out with it, sighing, "When they got married, she worshiped the ground he walked on. After a few years of...wedded bliss? She started taking him for granted. Or maybe it was the other way around. She had wealth and everything that went along with it. Everything except a husband who loved her." She shook her head. "Frankly, Mayes was more in love with himself than Doris. That was the only thing about him that I disliked. In other respects, I would say he was a very good man."

I said bluntly, "I'd like to talk with Mrs. Rogers now."

She hesitated a second, lips tightening, then stood.

Her voice was soft now, as if she might wake her sleeping sister otherwise. "I'll go see if she's awake. Really she doesn't sleep. Just cries. I guess it's good for her to cry."

She left the living room and walked into the adjacent entryway, where I could see her start up the second-floor stairs, each step measured, careful.

I smoked a cigarette down to the filter and was reaching for another one when I saw them coming down the stairs.

And Mrs. Rogers was every bit as much the looker as sister Ginger.

Her hair was raven-black and fell freely to her shoulders, wide shoulders for a woman, but there was nothing masculine about the figure beneath the pale yellow dressing gown. Her head was bent slightly and Ginger was leading her down, saying something softly. When they reached bottom, I stood and went out there to join them.

"Mrs. Rogers, I'm Captain Dexter from Homicide. I do apologize for this intrusion. If it will not be too much strain, I'd like to ask you some questions."

She forced a smile and nodded.

After we all found our seats in the living room, Doris looked at me, her eyes wavering, tears forming. "Who could have done such a terrible thing! Mayes never hurt..." She buried her face in the palms of her hands.

I sat back while Ginger gave her sister a handkerchief and tried to calm her.

Finally Doris said, "I'm sorry, Captain...Dexter? Dexter. I... I don't know what to say."

"Just take your time. Take it easy and if you can't answer a question, I'll understand. Did your husband ever have any serious disagreements with anyone?"

"Yes, he had them. Who doesn't, in his position? But everyone he dealt with ended up liking him. He was that kind of man. And he himself *never* carried a grudge."

"Did he seem at all disturbed during the last days you spent with him?"

She swallowed hard. "No. I'd say he was his usual self. Mayes didn't let things bother him like most..." Then everything she'd been holding back exploded. Ginger made a useless attempt to calm her and I knew our talk was over.

Ginger guided her sister gently back upstairs and fifteen minutes passed before she returned. She sat back down on the couch and said, "It was too much for her. It'll be some time before she can really answer questions."

A funny expression tightened her face and she stared blankly at the ceiling. "I want to help you, Captain. Help you *and* Doris."

"I'd appreciate that."

"Captain Dexter, I feel I can talk to you honestly. There's something about you that I like. Something tells me I can trust you."

"Feel free to say what you think is best, Miss Bass—or is it Mrs.?"

Her turn to smile had come, and she did a nice job of it. "It's Miss. Does that surprise you?"

I risked a grin. "I don't consider it bad news."

"You see," she said, still smiling, "I admit to having doubts about men in general. I almost married one, once upon a time, but he, uh…wasn't true to me, to sound old-fashioned about it."

"I'd say he was a fool, Miss Bass."

She blushed just a little, just a nice deep pink of her cheeks. Then her voice took on a touch of hardness as she said, "I suppose what I saw between Mayes and Doris hasn't encouraged me to seek any…relationship. Their lives have been mostly separate ones. Doris is a very nervous and sensitive girl, and Mayes did things that upset her, as I mentioned."

I just listened.

"I went to a party Mayes held here after the last election," she said, her eyes staring past me into her memory. "All kinds of people were there and most of them were pretty high. Then women began drifting in, and they weren't the wives, either. The party turned into…something wild. What you might call… well, it was an outright orgy. Most of it was going on in the bedrooms, but…things were going on."

She paused there and gave me time to let it sink in and I nodded for her to continue.

"That night Doris got a good look at what some of the important people in Gantsville really were like. Especially Frank Graham, the District Attorney—he was drunk and he was bragging about having 'access' to all the money that anyone in the party would ever need."

I knew Graham some. We'd tangled a few times when he was reluctant to prosecute a case I'd made. But I wouldn't call us enemies.

She continued, "Frank didn't know I heard him. I was in the kitchen nearby and I could hear him. He was telling someone about people in the Syndicate who could be 'friendly,' in return for just a little cooperation. He said they already owned half of the state house, and only good things would come of it—if we looked the other way on certain matters, the schools and roads and everything a community might want or need would be provided. He mentioned some names. Names I'd seen in the papers. Gangsters, Captain."

I took in a deep breath, let it go out slowly, and asked, "How do you know you can trust me, Miss Bass?"

Her laugh seemed half-hearted. "I guess I have to trust somebody. I don't believe Mayes was part of any of that, or if he was, he hadn't anticipated where it was going. These are the kind of things that start out small and get bigger. Many times they end up in murder. This time, maybe…Mayes' murder."

"How long ago was this party?"

"Less than a year ago. Shortly after the election."

"What were some of the names of these…'gangsters'?"

She told me. They were names I recognized, all right. So would you.

"Any others, not so familiar?"

Her frown held both thought and fright. "Graham kept mentioning 'Shark.' I got the impression that Shark is a person. That it was a nickname or code name or something."

If she was playing straight with me, this could break apart the local political machine and spill everything I had suspected over the years. What she had overheard revealed one real sweet filthy mess. It was politics as a racket in league with other, bigger racketeers.

At the door, I thanked Miss Bass.

"Could you make it 'Ginger'?"

"I'd like that," I admitted. "And my friends call me 'Rod.' "

"Goodbye, Rod. Don't be a stranger."

"Not likely," I said.

CHAPTER 2

The sun was winking at me through my partly closed shades. I forced myself up and made a big breakfast. After putting on a freshly pressed suit, I was ready.

Things were going to light up today.

Frank Graham was somebody I'd always tried to leave alone. As D.A., he held a high position and he had powerful friends and the press in his pocket—a certified big deal. But this time I just couldn't steer clear of him.

My insides were a hard tight knot as I walked into City Hall and up the long flight of marble steps. I skipped the regular procedure involving the okay signal with the secretary and walked right into the D.A.'s inner office.

For a big shot, Graham was a stocky little guy, five bucks worth of man in a hundred-dollar suit, sitting behind a big mahogany desk the good citizens paid for. For all the stacks of papers and file folders in front of him, he didn't appear to be doing anything but puffing on a cigar that should smell better, considering its likely one-dollar price tag.

When he saw my face, he made a nervous gesture with one hand, and gave me a broad smile that showed off teeth so white they had to be caps or choppers.

"Captain Dexter, just the man I hoped to see today! How's the Rogers case coming? Any developments?"

I took a chair opposite him. "Getting hotter all the time. Finding things out every day."

His smile curdled and he squirmed in his chair, but he managed, "I appreciate you keeping me up to date. I hope I'll be prosecuting Mayes' murderer one day soon."

"You and Rogers were good friends, I take it?"

"Oh yes."

"You even got together socially, I understand. Went to parties together and such."

His smile recovered, but his forehead frowned. "Time to time, sure. What are you driving at, Rod?"

I settled back in my chair and stared at him for a good long ten seconds, then said, "I'm driving at you being one of those rotten apples we hear so much about, Graham. You know—in the barrel?"

His fat face reddened and his neck muscles bulged. "What the hell—"

"Spare me the indignation, Graham. You might be a big man to some, but to me you're nothing but a fat slob with your hand in the till. You know, I'm torn between throwing you in the can or just messing you up, real pretty."

The color drained from his face. He sat there huffing, as though he couldn't get his breath. "You must be out of your mind to think you can talk to me that way. Retract what you're saying, and apologize, and I'll write this off to overwork."

"No apology, Graham." I stood and threw him a lopsided grin and leaned across his desk as he sunk lower in his chair. "You have all the inside information. You can point me to the right people, because you are not the top of the ladder, but you know who's on the rungs above and below you. You can help me clean up this town into something worth living in. You play ball with me and you can come out a hero."

It was a hell of a gamble, but I'd convinced myself it was a good bet.

But Graham was still red and huffing. "You have no right to burst into my office and make wild accusations this way!"

I stood straight. "Fine. Then I'll just continue my investigation of the Rogers murder and go anywhere and everywhere it leads me. And before I'm through with you, you'll be doing plenty of talking."

That was all. I walked to the door and slammed it behind me.

I'd really shown him, hadn't I?

Two days later, I was in my apartment, stretched out on my bed, drunk. You think of nice things when you're drunk. Things seem kind of funny, sometimes. Even when you're depressed.

The D.A. was a powerful man. You'd think I'd know that, right? But he was even more influential than I thought. The lousy goddamn bastard.

I took a long swig from a pint whiskey bottle, and when it hit bottom, I tossed it on the floor and cursed. I tried to get up, but something kept me glued to the bed. So I cursed again.

The drink had taken effect. Visions danced in front of me and I swore at all of them. I couldn't make them out and that made me even madder. A sick feeling was eating away at my stomach, and I tried to vomit. But the only thing that came out was more cursing.

I was dead, a thing of the past. Three days ago I was a cop. Now the cop was gone. What was left? Nothing but a thirst for booze, quenched by a bender, and vengeance, which I'd quench a whole other way. And when you're playing a game like this, there's only one way to play it, and that's a hell of a lot rougher than they do.

They were going to die. Every last one of them would feel pain and I would receive satisfaction by watching their expressions as I pulled a trigger.

The morning crept up on the night and overcame it. The taste of last night's whiskey still in my mouth, I showered, dressed slowly, and skipped breakfast. There's only so much a stomach can take.

Now I had no set rules to follow. I could do what I wanted without fear of losing my job or my badge because they were both gone. My gun had been taken away and the right to use it, too. So what! There were other guns in the world.

Up the steep gravel drive to the big white house, I found the door unlocked. I went in, not rousing the tall butler, and found Ginger Bass watching TV in a room down the hall. I knocked on the jamb, for good manners' sake.

She looked up, surprised but not startled. She was in a pink short-sleeved sweater, blue capri pants and her bare feet.

"Captain Dexter…Rod! Come in." She seemed to like seeing me there—she even smiled, though I must have looked a mess despite my best efforts. There was a trace of sympathy in her expression as I tried to smile back.

I said, "I had to see somebody. You came to mind."

Her voice was almost a whisper. "I read what happened in the paper. I don't really understand."

"Oh, they left the really good parts out."

She got up, turned off the TV, returned to the couch and patted next to her for me to sit. "Tell me."

Something inside made me want to laugh, but all that came out was a grunt. "The honorable Frank Graham put me out of commission. I went to his office, laid things on the line, and he blew his stack. His version got in the papers. Nobody was interested in mine. Anyway, I'm out of a job."

"It's awful, Mr. Dexter," she said, shaking her head. "Such a miscarriage of justice. And it's my fault! It was what I told you that—"

"Miss Bass. Ginger. The fault is mine. I handled it with all the finesse of a guy with ten thumbs, a tiny brain and one big temper. You wouldn't have a cup of coffee handy, would you?"

We went into the kitchen and had coffee. I drained two cups

before she finished one, and when I reached for a cigarette, she placed her hand over mine, her fingers pressing deep into my flesh.

"The other night when I said I thought I could trust you," she said, "I meant it. I'm sorry you lost your job, but I'm glad you're not involved in this thing anymore. It's something big and dangerous, really something evil."

"It's not over, Ginger. I'm not a cop anymore, true. At least not legally. But I'm going to find the killer and expose everyone messed up in the racket."

Her forehead tightened and she breathed heavily. "Why? Is it really worth it?"

"Yeah, it is. I didn't go into police work so guys like Frank Graham could get rich doing business with the Syndicate, while others like Mayes Rogers get killed for not playing along."

"But aren't you risking the same thing happening to you?"

"Not the same. Mayes wasn't shooting back."

She removed her hand. "You make me wish I hadn't said anything."

"Stop that. I would have found out on my own. How's Doris this morning?"

"I checked on her an hour ago. She was still in bed, and not sleeping…as usual."

"I know this is tough on her. She needs time. But she has plenty of it and I don't. My big problem is getting someone to believe me, and taking action. No one in a public service job will stand up against Graham."

She was gazing at me in that strange little way women have when they're so damn seductive without trying and I stood, lifting her up and pulling her close to me. She responded and I knew all the things she had told me were true, not just about

Graham but her own loneliness and pent-up desire for something real, something lasting.

I kissed her, barely letting our lips meet, and when I tasted the moist sweetness of her lips, I pulled her tighter against me.

Her breathing was heavy but she got it out, like a bittersweet nothing in my ear: "Don't keep after this thing, Rod—it's not worth it. Go start over somewhere. Maybe I could… Rod, I'm *scared* for you."

I held her out to where I could look in her lovely face. "It's got to be this way. If I run away, I'm not a man anymore. They can take my badge, but not who I am."

"But where will it end? When you've gunned them all down? Then will you go out for more? Those gangsters, maybe? And be alive at the end of it?"

What she said hurt me. She meant that I wasn't a cop anymore and there was no use pretending I was anything but a hate-filled thing. I shook it off and kissed her again.

Then I said, "I need to talk with Doris."

She shook her head. "You can't, Rod. Not now. Please trust me."

"So I'll talk with her later. When she's up to it. Where's that butler character?"

"Marsh?" She smiled. "His day off. If he were here, he'd never leave me in here alone with you, with the door closed. He's very protective of both Doris and me."

"Good that someone is," I said. "But everybody needs a day off."

I took her by the hand and led her back to the couch. Soon the thoughts of killing became lost as I let my mind turn to better things, like the whisper of fabric and whisk of zippers and the soft warmth of flesh.

*

The fat man was in his office going through papers and when he saw me at his door, he gave me a half smile that burned me up.

"You wanted to see me?" I said.

"Good!" the D.A. said. "You got my message. Have a seat, Mr. Dexter."

I did so, sat down, and returned his half smile. "You're very good, Graham. I have to hand it to you. Suddenly my performance reviews for the last year reflect what a lousy job I've been doing. I get shown the door with only the vaguest references getting in the papers about the real reason."

He folded his hands. "Maybe you'd like your job back. Maybe those performance reviews were a...clerical error."

"How would that happen?"

"You would agree to limit your investigation into the Mayes Rogers murder to...non-political avenues. You would stay out of my business, and away from political matters that are of no concern to you. It might even prove a profitable decision on your part."

"Always room in the barrel for one more apple?"

He frowned. "Think about it. You have twenty-four hours to make a decision. Now get out."

I got up and moved to the door, then turned back to him. "I don't need twenty-four hours. Here's my decision—I'm not through with you. I'm going to get you and your entire crooked bunch. I may wind up in jail, or dead, or maybe even get my badge back. But you, my fat friend, will be over. That I guarantee."

Graham stood up and shook a pudgy fist, his voice a sharp squeal. "*Get the hell out!*"

I said, "I was just going," and closed the door behind me. Suddenly I felt better.

Soon I was sitting at a booth at the rear of a bar near City Hall, drinking alone but not overdoing it, strictly beer, and watching an overaged broad trying to get money out of a drunk. She was doing her best to get her night's earnings without going to bed with anybody and the man was too drunk to realize it.

The woman was still hounding the drunk when he walked up to my table, kicked a chair out, and sat down. The drunk's name, by the way, was Fred Jenkins.

"Fred, old buddy," I said, "where you been? I thought the boys from the PD would've sent me a food basket by now."

"How's unemployment?"

"It's a breeze. They working you hard?"

"Damn right. They brought in this new captain from Capitol City to take your place. He's trying to make an impression."

"You still working on the case?"

He nodded. "But not getting anywhere. Why do you want to know?"

"Why do you think? Let me clue you in, Fred. Rogers' sister-in-law shared some interesting things. She overheard Frank Graham blabbing his mouth at a party Mayes threw last year. Seems his campaign contributions include some big ones from a very shady source."

"...Syndicate?"

"That's one name for it."

"Dangerous stuff, my friend. I mean, Jesus, Rod—you don't even pack a gun anymore. Stay out of it."

"You really think I could do that?"

"Hell no. You're as bull-headed as they come and you'll fight this thing to the finish. I know this is a hell of a thing for a cop to say, but I'll say it anyway. *Get yourself a gun.*"

"Now there's an idea."

Fred got up, kicked his chair back under the table, and looked down at me. I knew what was going through that mind of his.

He raised his hands in slightly drunken surrender, and whispered, "I'll get a piece to you. A rod for Rod. I just hope you won't need it."

I put a hand on his arm. "So long, Fred. Tell 'em hello at the office."

He said he would and stumbled out.

I got a little drunk myself, but nothing to compare to yesterday. When I met the night air I felt somehow refreshed, all the hate inside me cooled. Maybe I had the beer to thank, or the thought of that gun Fred would get me. Anyway, I walked, with nowhere in mind.

The only thing I heard was the night sounds. It was still the same old night for me—nothing had changed. You had to walk the streets to really know what the city was all about, though what you learned would probably make you sick.

And I was learning that I wasn't alone.

I'd heard the strange noise, like muffled clicking of heels, behind me. I thought nothing of it at first, then it got louder. I walked faster and the noise ceased.

But when I slowed down, I heard it again—real close. On a stretch where the streetlamp was out, I came to a complete stop, spun around, and met him face to face.

In the night I saw the flicker of the blade, the darkness unable to cover that up, or his gleaming white teeth that rictus-smiled. He made a dive at me, swiped me across the sleeve with the blade, and jumped back waiting for the next move.

This guy wasn't a killer—a killer would've made a quick play out of it. This boy thought he was real cute. He made his move again and I met him with the palm of my hand across his mouth, cupping his chin, shoving him back. He spat blood and tried it again, and this time I let him almost make the swipe before I dropped and kicked up, into his gut with the flat of my shoe.

He went down choking and when he hit the sidewalk, I kicked him in the ribs a few times to make him stay there, and he started puking.

I got a good look at his face. He was olive-complected, maybe Italian, skinny, slight, in a dark suit with a black shirt and a white tie and pointed patent leather shoes. Like I said, cute. He still had the knife in his hand but he wasn't paying any attention to it. I kicked it from his fingers and brought him up by the shirt front, a few buttons jumping ship.

I said, "Okay, pal. Let's talk."

His mouth was hanging open and he didn't even seem to know I was there. I slapped him and he squinted at me, then faked the goddamnedest smile you ever saw, like he was daring me to do something about it.

So I belted him in the gut and he doubled over.

While he was losing the rest of his supper, I stepped into the nearby alley and picked up a discarded piece of an iron pipe and brought it back over to him. I yanked him up by one arm and let him get a close look as I held the pipe in front of him.

"Ever see somebody wiped out with one of these?" I asked conversationally. "The good thing is, you pass out after two or three good ones, and you're dead with the next couple."

"Now...wait...*wait!* I was..."

"You were what?" I tapped him gently on the noggin with the pipe. His face went blister white.

"*Please!* Please...come on, you win. You win."

"What, is it a contest? Who sent you?"

He shook his head. "If I talk, I'm dead."

I made a click in my cheek. "Tonight's just not your night, boy. You lose either way. But with me, it'll be sooner. Now, who sent you?"

He just shook his head again.

I tapped him with the pipe a little harder this time.

"*Okay!* Okay…but I ain't one of them. I'm strictly smalltime. They…they offered me two C's to tail you and cut you up a little. Just a few swipes with the knife."

"Who's 'they?' "

"*They* is him. There's one person and he calls the plays. When he talks, everybody shuts up and listens. He's big, man—big in size, big in how's he hooked up."

"His name, buddy. Say it."

"All I know is, they call him Shark." He started whimpering. "They'll *kill* me if they find out!"

"Nobody's going to hear it from me. But I don't like knife jobs. Maybe I should do your friends a favor."

Tears were making their way down his face and he was trembling like he was having a fit. He had failed and then spilled and if it got out, he would have to face the jury, and they would give him a death sentence.

I had one more question for him. "Where is this Shark character?" I'd been a cop in this town for a decade and never heard of him.

He shook his head, a sob still lodged in his throat. "Who knows?" he said. "He moves around."

"Did I mention I didn't go for knife jobs?"

His lower lip quivered. "Try Morgan's. Shark owns the joint now."

He sank to his knees and covered his face with his hands and really broke down—he had that much fear for who sent him. If this Shark was such a powerful character, he should be ashamed, sending an excuse for a man for a job like this.

I walked away, tossing the pipe with a metallic clunk, and left him crying on the pavement, praying for a mercy that wasn't likely to come.

CHAPTER 3

The shrill ringing of the phone woke me from a disturbed sleep. I was glad to hear Ginger's voice.

"I've been worrying about you," she said. "When you didn't call me, I thought something might've happened."

"It did, but I'm fine. I got jumped by a punk who didn't know any better. Guy called Shark hired him—a name you've heard before."

I heard her breath catch. "You're scaring me."

"Don't be. Now things will begin to tie up."

"When are you coming over?"

"Soon, baby, soon. But first I got some work to do. In the meantime, see what you can squeeze out of Doris, if you can."

"Do my best."

Nearing eleven that morning, I turned my Ford down a street that took me to a rough section of town I knew all too well. Everything was pretty quiet, but would be hopping by nightfall.

Morgan's Lounge was probably the biggest nightspot in this district, and just respectable enough for a hood to operate out of safely. Too early to stop by, so there was time to kill.

I ended up at Larry's Place, a hole-in-the-wall I frequented when I was down here. I dropped myself at the bar and, a ways behind the counter, spotted a little chubby bartender with no hair and a red face.

I leaned over and said, "Boo."

"*Rod!* Rod Dexter! Where in the happy hell you been keeping yourself?" He handed off a pilsner glass to the other bartender, trundled down and reached over to give me half a hug.

I gave him half a smile back. "I been around."

"They still workin' you to death? I hope nobody said there's trouble in here. This joint's always been cool."

A feeling came over me that almost made me wish I hadn't come in. "Larry, I'm not with the force anymore."

His sad look made me feel even worse. He started to say something but I beat him to it.

"Forget it," I said. "These things happen."

He drew two beers behind the counter. We drank them without talking and, when I finished, I said, "I can use a little help."

"Name it." We walked over to a booth and Larry told his fellow bartender to bring us over a couple more beers.

"I might be through as a cop," I said, "but I want to go out in style. I'm working on something that's as big as hell and twice as dangerous. I don't want to get you involved, not directly, but I need some answers."

He nodded, his smile saying there was nothing I could spring on him that would faze him.

"Who is this Shark character?"

The smile left his face. "Big is right. Shark's a guy with big ideas, for sure. But nothing good."

"What kind of ideas?"

The back-up bartender set the beers in front of us and Larry gave him time to get out of earshot.

Then he said, "He's buyin' up politicians like he's picking out steaks at a meat counter. I don't know too much about the details, just what I pick up from chatter in here. I get the feeling he represents big interests from Chicago who want to own this town."

"He ever come in here?"

Larry sipped his beer. "Naw. We're too smalltime for him. Some of his boys come in occasionally. He bought old Jake Morgan's place down the street. I hear he paid quite a sum, too. Held onto the name to keep under the radar. Otherwise a copper like you woulda heard."

"Ex-copper. How long has he been in town?"

"Not long. Doesn't take long, though, for money to buy a foothold."

"How do I get to meet him?"

"Believe me, you don't want to."

"Don't figure I'm tough enough?"

"Nobody's tough enough when they're dead." He shrugged. "If you gotta, just go over to Morgan's. You'll find him there, if you can squeeze through his wall of bodyguards."

I grinned and finished off the beer.

As I slipped out of the booth, I said, "Keep your ears open, buddy."

"Will do, old friend."

"See you around."

So soft I could barely hear, he said, "I sure hope so."

I killed the rest of the afternoon at a show. The movie was one of those extra-long spectaculars with guys and girls in short skirts and lots of swords and plenty of gore and no plot other than some patched-together history lessons. After I got out, I walked until eight.

By that time, the nighttime foot traffic, with plenty of upright citizens slumming, had started filing into Morgan's and I made my way in with them.

Shark evidently hadn't made any changes to the place—same large room with low ceiling and little light but lots of fake black leather and chrome trimmings, plus mirrors to make it seem even bigger. It was as noisy as usual, people talking, a small combo playing jazzed-up standards, and glasses clanking.

I quick scanned the room—a couple of swarthy men leaned at the bar trying to make a pimple-faced bottle blonde wearing a tight black dress that she spilled out of like two too many grapefruits in a bin. The men must not have gotten what they wanted out of her, or vice-versa, because they walked away grumbling. Maybe the price wasn't right.

I spotted an empty stool at the bar, sat down, and gave the waiter my order of beer. When he threw a foaming mug in front of me, I threw a bill down, and he swept it up, gave me a going over like I was too young to buy it, then tossed me my change.

The combo was playing at a steady beat and I drained my glass, thought about a refill, but changed my mind when I spotted them. Three men walked slowly out of a small room at the rear. They took a seat in the middle of the room and a waiter brought them drinks. I let my eyes stay on them, trying to get a good look at their faces, but the place was too damn dark.

I slid off the stool and crossed the floor. On my way there, I studied the tall man seated between the obvious bodyguards. He had the kind of face only a mother would love, or maybe not even her. It was a long thing with sharp angles off of which flesh drooped.

I went over and jerked out the only vacant chair at their table and shocked the hell out of them by sitting down. I knew it was him. His stone-faced bodyguards on either side were itching for me to make a move or just say the wrong thing.

Shark knew who I was, too. I could tell by the way he eyed me. He was half-grinning, but his dead black eyes, like his namesake's, told me the full story. Shark was a hard man. Age had slowly crept up on him, but his skeletal frame retained signs of muscle under a sharkskin suit that I guessed was a trademark.

His dark high-cheekboned face leered at me, the way some guys do a dame.

I didn't like the silence, so I said, "Name's Dexter."

He didn't speak, but deliberately held out his long, lean hand. Just as deliberately, I took it, and felt his power as he returned the squeeze. His face sucked in and he broadened his smile.

He sat back and, in a thin, sharp voice, said, "I've heard of you, Mr. Dexter. You made the papers. Disgraced after years of such a good record. Shame."

"Goddamn shame."

What came out next was almost a laugh: "You're a very interesting man, Mr. Dexter."

"How so?"

"Most people in your position would get out of town, since nobody here's likely to hire you. Or are you looking for work on my crew?"

"No. I just wanted to tell you not to insult me again."

His eyebrows raised but the expressionless eyes stayed the same. "When did I insult you?"

"When you sent a boy with a knife to do a man's job."

Shark's smile curled at both ends. "Looks like I should have sent a man with a gun."

"Be my guest. But make it a small caliber."

"Why's that, Mr. Dexter?"

"It won't hurt him so much when I shove it up his ass."

I nodded to them, got up and split.

Next time they would play it tougher and smarter. There would be no rules—I wasn't a cop anymore. I was playing in their league now. I would have to outsmart them, and set them up for the kill.

And it was going to be a pleasure.

*

I slept hard that night, and didn't wake up till almost noon. After a shower and shave, I went out for the paper. I picked it up along with a box the mailman had left. I tossed the paper on the couch and tore into the package.

There it was.

Just like old times—Fred had done what he said he would. I gripped the handle of the Police Positive .38 and it felt good, a part of me that had grown back.

I reached into a desk drawer for a holster I'd kept, and slid the gun in. When I snapped it onto my belt I felt almost normal again. I had been a cop just too long, I guess. Without that .38 on my hip, I felt naked.

I was about to reach over for the paper when the phone rang.

"Rod—it's Larry. There's a doll in here who looks real hot. Like she walked out of a men's magazine. She came in with some of those boys we were talking about. You know the ones. She's still here, drinking. Interested?"

"You bet. Don't let her leave."

I hung up and made tracks for downtown.

Larry's had a little kitchen in back and the place had a modest lunch crowd munching on burgers and the like. I was hoping she'd still be there, and I wasn't disappointed—she was sitting alone at a little table and Larry nodded from behind the counter in her direction.

She was drinking a cocktail and blowing a kiss on a cigarette. She didn't seem to notice me edge over to her table. I was going to use what little charm I had stored up on her, and maybe it would work.

"Mind a little company?" I asked. "You look lonely."

She removed the cigarette from her red-lipsticked lips and they smiled a little, like she was expecting me—she nodded to the chair across from her.

"Lonely isn't the word for it," she said, when I got situated. "There's another word—sick."

"You look well enough to me."

And she did. She was a brunette who made magic out of a white silk blouse and black pencil skirt, aided and abetted by nylons and black pumps.

"Rod Dexter." If it meant anything to her, she didn't show it.

"Jean Banner."

Jean Banner. The name echoed in my mind—the woman who'd almost ruined Mayes Rogers' marriage!

I stayed cool, outwardly at least. "I always liked the name 'Jean'—simple, pretty." I waited for a reply but all I got was a smile. "You on your lunch break?"

Her eyebrows lifted. "If so, I'm drinking it."

"No offense meant. A smoke and a drink, that's one of my favorite lunches. Where do you work, Jean?"

"I'm at Morgan's. Sometimes I hostess, most times I sit at the bar or with certain customers, and look pretty."

"You're good at it."

She laughed and finished her drink. "What do you do, Rod?"

"Unemployed. They laid me off at the office—they tell me I'm insubordinate."

"Sounds like my job." She took the last draw from her cig and buried it in an ashtray. "Did you have to jump when somebody snapped their fingers? That's what makes me sick." She frowned at me. "What was your last name again?"

"Dexter."

"Dexter...Dexter...I've heard that name somewhere lately. Sorry. I don't have a great memory."

"Let's go someplace that's real quiet, and I'll jog it."

She wet her lips, made an unladylike gesture with her tongue, which was followed by a nodding yes.

"I know a quiet spot by the lake," I said. "Kind of secluded. It's a bit of a drive, but I have wheels. There's a place where we can rent suits for a swim. Okay?"

"Sounds nice."

If she was for real, that made me a heel. And if she wasn't, I was a sucker. But either way, it might be fun.

The breeze off the water wafted against our faces. Jean and I were stretched out on a blanket by the lake and for a moment I forgot all about what I was really after.

"Nice not to work," she said, extending her legs full length and raising her arms toward the sky.

I told her I thought the same.

"I hate my work," she said. "Did you hate your work?"

"Not really. Tell me about yours. Anything good about it? Exciting maybe?"

"Well…you meet all kinds of people. That might be exciting to some, not to me."

I rolled over on my side, facing her, and she came to me without giving me the time to make the first move. I felt her lips press hot and sticky against my mouth and her tongue went exploring and in that one second I knew how Mayes Rogers has fallen.

I pulled gently back away from her, not saying anything, just looking down at her lovely form. Some girls look like hell in a bathing suit. This one had all the extra flesh in the right places and the curve of her hips swept down to a pair of legs that belonged on a calendar.

"Rod…would you think less of me if…if I asked you to love me?"

Like I needed any encouragement.

I bent down and drew her to me. She fell back on the blanket and I kissed her, then pulled back.

"It's all right," she said softly. "Go ahead."

But I shook my head. I knew that if I didn't stop now, I never could. So I gave her a look that let her know it was over for now. She sat up, leaning her elbows.

"What?" she asked.

"Who exactly is Shark?"

A look of abhorrent shock came over her, then her face turned a deep, burning red, her brown eyes wide with sudden hate.

"You *bastard*!" she screamed. "*You're* the man they *want*! You *used* me to…"

"It's not like that," I said, but it was.

She came off her blanket at me and dug her nails into my shoulder and I covered her face with a hand and shoved her back on the blanket. She leaned back, the pale imprint of my fingers stark against the red of her face, and said, "Dirty bastard…"

"Cool it. No one's going to hurt you. And I could have had you, right? But I didn't. A 'dirty bastard' would have."

"You…you could get me beaten. Or killed!"

"No one knows you're with me."

She'd cooled down some, but the distaste was still clearly written on her face.

"They'll kill me," she said, with terrible calmness. "They've killed before and they'll kill again."

"Like Mayes Rogers?"

She sucked in breath; let it out. "I don't know. They don't discuss business with me. They *use* me. Like you did."

"Almost did. What was Shark's relationship to Rogers?"

She shook her head. "I don't know. They had *something* going. This Rogers was a real big shot, you know. Shark wanted power, and Rogers wanted something in return. They got together and talked. That's all I know. I swear it is."

"Any idea if it worked out?"

Jean shook her head once again, the brunette hair tousled now. "I don't know. I do know they became enemies over something, and any terms they'd come to…unraveled."

"What about Frank Graham?"

Her upper lip curled in a sneer of a smile. "Our esteemed District Attorney? I know him. He's Shark's best buddy."

I studied her. "How would you like to get out of this mess?"

An eyebrow arched. "Would people in hell like to get out?"

I took one of her hands and squeezed gently. She looked at me and found a smile.

"Not necessarily," I said. "Some like the heat, and the company. But we can get out, if we play our cards right. You see, I'm going to nail Shark. He's already tried to mess me up once, and he likely made the call that got me fired. So—what can you tell me about him?"

She considered that. "No one knows much about him. He's from South America—Brazil, I think. His father was a big man down there, in their version of the Syndicate. Shark came to the U.S. and started high up in the Chicago branch."

It was a takeover of a town, all right. Superficially, Gantsville would thrive, new schools, freshly paved streets, even churches. But crooked wide-open casinos and whores and drugs and loan-sharking would flourish unchallenged.

She sat up and leaned in, a hand finding the bare skin of my arm. "I was once somebody, Rod. Society page. Beauty contents, talent searches, movie offers. Not anymore. Mayes Rogers ruined me." She covered her face with her hands.

"Go ahead," I said. "Get it out."

I meant for her to cry, and she did, but she was also talking: "I had a baby. Mayes Rogers' baby. I…I put it up for adoption. He gave me money but wanted nothing more to do with me."

"The world is a big, dirty place, doll."

Jean caught her breath, between sobs, and asked, "You... you're going to kill Shark?"

"Him, at least."

"Forget...about them. Take me somewhere. We'll start over."

"It's a little soon, isn't it?'

"Not with what we're facing. We can start out together. If it doesn't work out, we'll each have new lives without the Sharks of the world in it."

"There are sharks everywhere, baby."

The night swept down on us, a crying girl who had been dirtied and had nothing to live for, and me, a man who had only one thing to live for—the deaths of others.

I pulled Jean down on the blanket and we picked up where we left off, passion and animal instinct and tenderness and urgency combining to wash everything away in a moonlight that made us both pure again, for those moments anyway.

The night made a switch with morning. I'd just dropped Jean off at her apartment, and—since I didn't get any sleep last night—I thought several hours of shut-eye might do me some good.

It took me a half an hour to drive to my apartment and when I left the car in the parking garage, I was tempted to use the front seat of my car to sack out. But finally I went on up, picking the paper up from outside my door, then sticking the key in the lock.

When I opened the door, I saw him. I made a fast play for my gun and he'd have been dead if he hadn't groaned, "Rod... buddy—it's *me*!"

Some things the eye can see that the mind can't take in immediately—things you can't possibly picture even though you're standing face to face with them.

He was sprawled in my easy chair, his head bent back. His face was a bloody mess, mouth open but the only thing coming out were garbled words and a trickle of blood.

"Fred!" I ran to him. "What the hell happened?"

He shook his head slowly and closed his eyes. But he got it out. "They…were pros…worked me over…good." He stopped there, closed his eyes, and kept them shut.

Someone had beaten the hell out of my old partner, and like he said, the beating was thoroughly professional, the kind that does just enough damage to make you feel like you're dead, or make you wish you were.

I rushed to the bathroom and returned with a wet washcloth. Fred was trying to move when I got back.

"Take it easy, kid! You aren't shot, are you?"

He shook his head and groaned again and I touched the wet cloth gently to his face, soaking up some of the blood that had already dried.

"Keep still and don't move," I said.

Then I went into another room and put a call in to his wife, telling her not to worry. She insisted on coming over but I talked her out of it. Right now Fred wasn't a very pretty sight.

I came back and he said, "Thanks for calling her."

"She's phoning a medic. He'll fix you up. Can you talk?"

Fred managed a nod. "I was…driving over here…almost here…when all of a sudden…a car ran into the back of me. I got out, mad as hell, and…they jumped me. One had something… smashed my arm with it. I reached for my gun… couldn't get it before something hit me across the back. Probably a…a tire chain. They worked me over until…till I blacked out. When I woke up…somehow…somehow I crawled the rest of the way… made it over here."

"You've been working the Rogers case."

"Started where…you left off."

The doctor took his time getting there. But once he did, he gave Fred one look and said, "We better get an ambulance over here. This man needs to be in a hospital. Where's the phone?"

I showed him and he made the call. Then I called Fred's wife back and told her he was being admitted. She could thank heaven she wasn't a widow, or her children orphans.

Around noon the next day, I went to the Mayes house to see Ginger, just to let her know I was still alive, if nothing else. I admit I felt like a louse, having been with Jean. The lovely blonde was watering flowers when I pulled my car up the drive.

"Rod! I thought you might be dead!"

I got out of my Ford. "How's Doris doing?"

"Better," she said. "Able to discuss things now, a little."

Doris was sitting on the couch when we entered the living room.

"Morning, Mrs. Rogers. Good to see you up."

"Thank you," she said. She was still in a dressing gown. "Why not call me Doris from now on? I'd imagine we'll be seeing a lot of each other, till this matter's resolved."

Ginger and I took chairs opposite the couch.

I asked, "Have the police been to talk with you?"

"Only once, but I wasn't well enough to answer any questions."

"Homicide department? Fred Jenkins maybe?"

She shook her head. "No, uniformed."

"I doubt if they'll ask any more questions."

"I'm sorry about you losing your job, Mr. Dexter."

"Make it Rod. I should've seen it coming. Kind of begged for it, actually."

The room had an air of thick silence about it. Doris sat straight and firm, hands folded in her lap, never showing expression.

Good-looking though she was, the black hair lustrous and long, something about her made you feel uneasy. Even figuring in what she'd been through, she seemed humorless and solemn, compared to Ginger.

"Our best suspect is an out-of-town gangster they call Shark," I said. "Fred Jenkins, a friend of mine at Homicide, was badly beaten last night. Doris, I'm sorry, but we need to go over this again: did your husband seem troubled or apprehensive about anything before his death?"

"No. If anything was bothering him, he never showed it or told me."

"Are you familiar with this Shark person?"

"Only what with what Ginger has told me."

"Then you know enough. Shark is going to sit back and see if I get anywhere. At some point, probably sooner than later, he'll try to have me killed. He's already tried to scare me off."

Shaking her head, eyes narrowed, Ginger said, "All this violence…I'm *worried* about you, Rod."

I didn't respond to that, instead asking Doris, "What about Arnold Moore?"

That name had been stored in the back of my mind for Doris, when she was up to it.

A sickening look came over Ginger's sister's face. "He's a very tough man. His brother was supposed to run against Mayes, who somehow convinced him not to, and for some reason Arnold felt his brother had been given a raw deal. He went as far as to threaten Mayes physically. But nothing ever came of it."

"I don't think he's connected with this, but again, who knows?" I stood. "I'll see you later, Doris. Maybe Moore will put up with an ex-cop asking him questions."

✲

Everybody was at work at Anderson's Garage, except a tall, frail-looking guy standing beside a Coke machine doing nothing. I walked up to him and said, "Looking for Arnold Moore."

He scratched his head stupidly and pointed over to a black Ford from under which a man's legs stuck out. I told him thanks and waited around the car until the man rolled himself out.

He was a large, stocky guy with a crew cut and a bulldog mug.

"Rod Dexter," I said, looking down at him. "Spare a couple minutes to answer some questions?"

His face lit up and he dropped his wrench to the floor, got to his feet, and with his right hand wiped dirty sweat from his unshaven face.

"Why not?" he rasped. "I could use a break." He took a half-smoked cigar from an ashtray on a nearby workbench, used a kitchen match to relight it. He pretended the cigar was his focus, but he was looking me over. "Ain't you the one who got bounced from the cops?"

"I'm the one. Mind answering some questions about Mayes Rogers?"

His round face took on a nasty smile. "Now, there's a guy who got what he deserved."

"That bad, huh?"

"Badder than that. He was a certified louse who hid behind other people when the going got tough. Maybe it's against the law to kill, but exterminating rats is legal, so I think it's okay to get rid of some of the vermin that make up this crummy world. Mayes Rogers, for one."

"I heard your brother almost ran against him for the nomination."

The mechanic raised both eyebrows and sent dark spit to the floor. He followed that up with some choice obscenities, finally saying, "The bum didn't give him a *chance* to run! I don't know what that bastard did, but he changed my brother completely." He shook his head. "And, hell—my brother coulda beat him! And Mayes Rogers *knew* that."

"Rogers have any enemies?"

"Besides me, you mean? Hell yes! Plenty."

"Name a few."

The question drew a blank stare that made him look silly. "Well, I don't know offhand. But he had 'em, all right. My brother's a bookkeeper at City Hall, and a damn good one, too. Maybe you can get more out of him on this subject than I ever could."

I nodded. "I'll give it a shot. Thanks for the time, Mr. Moore."

The cigar was riding a corner of his mouth as he let off a nasty grin. "You ain't a cop no more. If you're tryin' to clean this crummy town up, some...well. You want some help, let me know. Like if you need to borrow a wrench or anything."

Then he ground the cigar under his heel, and got down to slide back under the Ford.

When I got to City Hall, I hurried up the steps. I spotted a few old ladies taking a coffee break and walked up and asked, "Excuse me—where might I find George Moore?"

One lady with a face that had been pretty since childhood answered, "He's in room ten."

George Moore was much older than his brother, and a lot more dignified—suit and tie, glasses and mustache.

"Excuse me," I said. "Mr. Moore?"

The gaunt little man straightened and said, soft-spoken, "That I am, son."

"Rod Dexter."

"Oh?" He looked at me curiously, as though the name made

a small dent in his memory. "What can I do for you, Mr. Dexter?"

"You can tell me about Mayes Rogers."

His eyes perked with sudden interest. "Personal information?"

"I'll take anything I can get."

"We never had much direct contact. He wasn't the sort of person I'd...cultivate."

"That why you were going to run against him in the election?"

Moore stopped shuffling his papers a moment and put them on the desk, making a neat pile.

"I thought the time had come to try to move up in the world," he said, then gestured around the file room. "But let's face it—this is about the extent of my capabilities."

"I've talked to your brother. He doesn't seem to have any love for Rogers."

"Arnold got a little sore when I dropped out. He certainly would've loved to see me go after that nomination."

"Bad enough to want to kill Rogers?"

He shook his head. "Arnold always had a bad temper, but he would hardly go that far."

"How far would he go? He *did* threaten him."

"That never amounted to anything, really. I merely lost interest in running and Arnold didn't understand." Moore stuck the last of his papers in a desk drawer and shut it. "Arnold is a good man. A bit wild when he drinks. But don't bother trying to pin anything on him—you'll get nowhere."

"I'm not trying pin anything on your brother."

"I'll take you at your word, sir. But if you're checking up on people, try the deceased's good friends and associates."

Friends like Frank Graham and Bob Bacon and maybe a man called Shark....

He asked, "Is there anything else?"

"Did Mayes or those friends or associates you mention pressure you out of the race?"

Again he shook his head. "I just didn't have the support, Captain. Yes, I know who you are. Who you *were.* I simply didn't have the clout or the monetary backing to make a run worthwhile."

At the hospital, a friend at the desk let me in after visiting hours to see Fred.

My ex-partner, his face bandaged and swollen like he'd stuck his head in a beehive, was reading a magazine and didn't notice me at the door.

"Honey, I'm home," I said.

He tossed the magazine on the bedside stand and pretended to be cross. "About time you came by."

"Tell me you feel better than you look."

"Doc says I'll live. Wish I felt that way. Man, did those sons of bitches beat the crap out of me. At least the department okayed my sick leave."

"Yeah, great guys." I pulled up a chair. "I checked out the Moore brothers."

"And?"

"Arnold's just a working stiff with a temper. If he'd killed Mayes, it would have been a long time ago. And George is a milquetoast who got rolled over by the political machine."

"Speaking of which—you meet our new representative yet?"

"That was fast. Rogers is barely cold."

"Not local rep, state rep. You remember Brinkley resigned, when he got sick? Well, they replaced him."

I shook my head. "Who with?"

"John Graves." He must've seen my reaction. "You know him?"

"Yeah," I said slowly. "We go way back."

That perked him even more. "How far?"

That was when a nurse came in and politely told me to scram. I said okay, told Fred I'd catch him later, and went down to the lobby to find a pay phone.

It rang five long times before she picked up.

"Ginger, can you meet me downtown?"

"Sure," she said. "What's up?"

"Maybe I could just use some sensitive female companionship."

"I'm glad I rate," she said. "Where?"

"Dixon's Coffee Shop on Main. Shake a pretty leg."

At Dixon's, I staked out a booth and ordered coffee. I was on my second cup and third cigarette when Ginger rolled in, pretty as hell in a yellow-and-white frock.

She came over and looked down at me. "Tired of coming to my place?"

"It's your sister's place. Maybe I wanted a little privacy."

"A coffee shop is privacy? Sounds like I'm in for a very good time."

I smiled, gestured for her to sit down, and signaled the waiter. He brought her a cup and refilled mine. I let it cool while I drank in the warmth of her.

Ginger said, blowing her coffee before she tasted it, "How's your friend Fred?"

"There's some men who aren't easy to kill. He's one." I picked up the cup and let the hot stuff go down.

"Something is going to happen, honey. I can feel it. I've seen too many kills in my lifetime and I know the feeling. Here's the thing—I don't want you around when the action starts. So I want you to steer clear for a while. I'll keep you posted. But I want you safe."

"I like hearing a man say that, Rod. More than I ever thought I would."

"Now don't get sweet on me, baby." I meant it kidding, but the look she gave me, I realized I'd hit a nerve. And seeing that look in her eyes, and feeling what it made me feel, I realized that maybe there was something here it wasn't good to kid about.

"You worry me, Rod. You do know I…I care about you, don't you?"

"I feel the same about you, baby."

She kept her face down, not looking at me, and I placed my hand over hers and grinned at her. "Hey—they won't get me. I hate them more than they hate me."

That made her laugh, but no joy was in it.

Next morning, after Ginger was on her way back, I stopped by Larry's. The chubby little guy was in a booth shoveling in his breakfast courtesy of his own short-order cook. He stopped eating and signaled me over and offered me a bite to eat. I passed that up and settled for coffee and a hard roll.

"So what's new?" I asked.

He wiped egg from his mouth and said, "That dame you went out with. She was back here this morning. Looking around for someone. You, maybe. But she didn't say."

"I better check her out. She alone?"

"Yup. Like I said, waiting for somebody who didn't show."

I watched Larry shovel in the last of his eggs. I thought back, a long time ago, to when Larry wasn't too well off. He got mixed up with some young hoodlums that hit a filling station. Cops brought them into the PD and I happened to spot a chubby kid with a clean face and no leather jacket standing out like a sore thumb among a bunch of would-be James Dean crumbs. He was crying. I talked with him, put in a few good words to the sergeant, and he got off light. He still thanks me for it. Not with words, but with favors.

I got up from my seat and thanked Larry, then left.

Jean Banner lived in a rundown apartment building that had sneaked its way past the health inspectors, a long way from the society page. I knocked twice on the door and, when it opened, a girl Jean's age slithered her curvy body over, not properly concealed under her nightgown.

"Who's calling?" she asked. She was a little shopworn but still a hot number, though her eyes chilled.

"Jean Banner in?"

"Not now she ain't." She batted her lashes at me and I felt sick all of a sudden. Little Jean had an outright prostie for a roomie.

"When you expecting her?"

"Around five. You ain't by chance that Dexter fellow she's been yappin' about, are you?"

"I'm him."

"I thought she said you was good-looking."

I had to smile. "To each her own."

She thought it over. "You ain't my type."

She meant I didn't pay.

I started to turn away and she said, "Told me to tell you to come back at seven, if you stop by. That's seven at night, mister. Sounds like you two got something going."

"Maybe I'm her type," I said.

She smirked and shut the door on me. I could swear I heard her slither off.

At seven I was back, and this time Jean answered, in a pink silk blouse and red skirt. She said nothing, just waved me in.

Something was wrong. I could tell it by her eyes. But I was already inside before I saw the guns.

"Hold it right there, Dexter," somebody said.

They moved into the light—only two of them. One was a dark-complected guy with pockmarks and a twisted smile. The other was a grinning Bob Bacon.

"The trap has finally sprung," he said. The balding attorney tried to look tough, but it was a phony act, just like he was.

The other one grabbed Jean. She tried to break away and he slapped her until she was still. He was dead—he just didn't know it yet.

Bacon shoved the gun in my back and shoved me toward the door. Jean followed me with her own gun-in-the-back escort. Down on the street a black Chevy was waiting for us. Bacon pushed me in the front seat and the other guy climbed in the back with Jean.

Something made me want to ask a foolish question. "Where we headed, fellas?"

Behind the wheel now, Bacon smiled and let a slow, rumbling laugh come deep from his throat. "What have you got against a little joy ride, Dexter?" He laughed again. So did the guy in the back.

Killing them would be a pleasure.

Bacon put it in gear and took off. He was having fun. "We're going to take you to a place where we'll make sure you don't interfere anymore. The girl, too."

"Go to hell."

"What a coincidence! That's where we're headed."

I was sitting there thinking about how stupid they were. Bacon knew my .38 had been taken from me on my dismissal. But he hadn't thought I might have another—they hadn't even bothered to search me. It was so goddamn funny, I almost burst out laughing.

We finally made it to the place he had in mind—a small shack on a dirt road somewhere out of town, on a stretch I didn't know. You couldn't even see the road. Yes, it was a good place for a killing.

"Get them out!" Bacon ordered his stooge. He flashed the gun by my face to let me know he still had it and I said something nasty to him. The pockmarked guy at the back poked his gun in my neck and told me to get out. I did.

I followed Jean into the shack with Bacon breathing down my neck. Bacon gave me a shove and I pivoted around and clipped him under the chin. I was about to show them the surprise in my hip holster when the other guy, behind me, sapped me and I was on my knees.

I saw Bacon's foot coming but the only thing I could do was curse it. It caught me above the forehead and I felt like I was scalped. I made a dive for the blurry figure that was someone's legs, missed, and fell face down on the floor.

Somebody laughed.

By the time things came into focus, they had Jean tied, her hands bound behind her back. She was kneeling, as though saying a prayer.

And I saw what he was about to do.

The pockmarked stooge ripped the blouse from Jean's back. She wore nothing underneath. You never saw anything more beautiful or ugly. The bastard smiled and licked his lips.

He eased down, never letting his eyes leave her, and picked something up—a steel chain.

He balled half of it in one hand and brought it down across her back. She cringed but made no sound. The next blow sent her on her stomach. I wanted to make a play for the .38, but Bacon had his eyes and gun on me the whole time.

The third blow of the chain made her mouth and eyes open wide and her body quivered. By the fifth one it didn't matter. She was dead.

The beautiful woman had been turned to bloody pulp and the two sadists loved it. They must have because they looked at their handiwork too long, and Bacon's eyes shifting to her gave me the chance I wished had come sooner.

With what I had left in me, I rolled across the floor and before they could get off a shot, I had already put three slugs into the stooge's face, making holes that added oversized pockmarks to a hideous array, spattering brains on the shed wall behind him, while another of my slugs caught Bacon in the arm and spun him like a top, losing his gun on the trip.

The shyster panicked when he got a look at his friend's bullet-ridden face and made a break for the door. I let him almost get there before I put one in each calf. He screamed and made a rattling thud when he hit the floor on his face.

I managed to get up. Bacon looked back me, his face a distorted thing punctuated by the round whites of his eyes and the screaming blood-bubbling hole that was his mouth.

I had one bullet left in the .38 and it had to count. So I stuck the nose of the gun against the bridge of his nose, between his eyes, which crossed comically as he reflexively tried to see what was about to happen. His scream was cut off when I pulled the trigger, collapsing the upper part of his face, which filled with blood gushing from somewhere, the life draining from him. The only bad thing was how quick he'd gone.

I felt sick as hell. Not from what was left of these clowns—the attorney with the caved-in forehead, the pockmarked stooge slumped there with what had been inside his head dripping down the wall behind him. No. It was what they had done to Jean.

I would have held her in my arms if it would've done any good, but she was just meat now. I couldn't even look at her. I didn't have it in me. I made tracks for the door, hopped in the Chevy out back, and got away, leaving hell behind.

CHAPTER 4

It was almost daylight when I got home. Everything was beating away at my brain as I fumbled for my keys and unlocked the door, exhausted as hell but wondering if sleep could come with my nostrils twitching with the cordite-tinged stench of death. I opened it, cursing back the tears for that poor dead girl.

Ginger said, "Hi," softly, turning it into three embarrassed syllables somehow.

I switched on the light and when I saw her I breathed deeply—she was stretched out on the couch, propping herself up on her elbows, barefoot, her blonde hair tousled, her face free of make-up but lovely as ever, her shape only hinted at under my terry bathrobe, cinched at the waist.

"I told you to stay away."

"Sorry," she said, in a clipped, hurt way.

"Sorry back at you," I said, sighing. "How did you get in, anyway?"

"Your super believed me when I said I was your girl and wanted to surprise you."

I could see why he had, but I'd been negligent not to tell the guy not to be so free and easy with my security.

Even though I was sick to my soul, aching physically and emotionally, I smiled. She eased herself up and came to me, and I took her in my arms.

"Rod..."

"Yeah?"

"I waited all night for you...to hold me. Just hold me."

I held her.

*

The super made it up to me by loaning out the furnished apartment one floor up for me to get some sack time without worrying about getting murdered in my bed. Ginger hadn't slept much through the night, waiting and anxious. While I'd have preferred to get her well the hell out of town, Ginger insisted on heading back to the nearby little community of Drake to be with her sister at the Rogers place.

Meanwhile I had things on my mind, including some follow-up questions for George Moore, the guy who almost challenged Mayes Rogers in the last election. Something there wasn't sitting right. His address was in the phone book and I headed over.

I pulled to the curb across the way and down half a block, switched off my headlights and shut off my engine. I staked the little bungalow out for forty minutes and three cigarettes, and then I saw him.

Still in a suit and tie from work, George Moore was leaving his house, walking as though late for something. The auto mechanic's smaller brother got in his car in the drive, backed out and sped off. I waited a few seconds, then followed.

He sped up. Maybe he guessed someone was tailing him. I eased off the gas and let him move way ahead—so way ahead that I lost him.

But I played a hunch and it paid off—I drove to Morgan's Lounge and his car was parked at the rear of the club with the employees. That was hardly the place to question him or to risk a confrontation right now. So I headed back to his place and returned to stakeout, like I was still a cop.

Three hours and change went by and I had almost dropped off to sleep when his headlights roused me, and this time if he hadn't spotted me, he was blind. He pulled into his drive, got out, walked to his door and shut himself in.

I sauntered up to the front stoop, rang the bell, and when he opened up, he smiled as politely as if I were expected, and invited me in.

I found a chair in a modestly furnished front room and started in: "A few unanswered questions, Mr. Moore."

He sat across from me and shook his head. "Mr. Dexter... Captain Dexter...please make this brief. I feel I've answered enough questions already, and after all, you have no official standing."

I ignored that. "You made a remark the other day about Mayes Rogers and his friends, and his associates. Flesh that out a little."

"I don't care to go into any further detail. You want to pursue it, pursue it. But I don't want to get involved."

"You're already involved, Moore. I tailed you to Morgan's tonight. Don't bother denying it."

His eyes flared behind the glasses. "Are you insane, man? If you want to get yourself killed, that's your affair. Leave me out of it."

"The D.A. and that lawyer, Bacon, were friendly associates of Mayes Rogers. But what about a guy they call Shark?"

He was trembling now. I had him.

I said, "*You're* a friendly associate of Shark's, too, aren't you, Moore? You checked in with him tonight. Why?"

He said nervously, "I'm not in that thing. I just...somebody told him you'd been to see me yesterday, and he called and ordered me in. To explain. I said I hadn't told you anything."

That was true enough.

"Tell me now," I said.

He nodded and wiped the sweat from his brow. "It's money from Chicago. They're buying the town and Shark is their man, and D.A. Graham is *his* man. Those that play ball will profit handsomely, everyone else is out. I'm handy to them because I have a spotless record. I can juggle books and make one person look crooked when he isn't, and another look honest when he's not."

"So eventually everyone in local government of any standing is in the Syndicate's pocket."

He nodded.

"What was your reward to be?"

"A special election. I'm to take Mayes' place."

Like he'd always wanted. Poor little fool had visions of grandeur.

"And of course," I said, "you've kept this from your brother, who thinks you're a great guy who got screwed over."

He nodded again, looking like he might bust out crying.

Moore had told me all he knew. I didn't care about any other names—with Bacon gone, I was only interested in those other two bastards, Shark and the D.A.

I got up and was heading out, but Moore had something else to say.

"Mr. Dexter…Captain…believe me, I didn't know these efforts would include murder. Dirty politics is one thing, but wholesale homicide is nothing I bargained for, even with somebody like Mayes Rogers."

"I believe you."

He swallowed, his eyes swimming with tears. "I might as well tell you this also," he began. "These people have done something I want no part of. Shark has brought in a man to do his dirty work—a professional killer. He's supposed to be very good at what he does."

"I appreciate you sharing that."

He nodded. "Think what you will of me, but I don't believe in murder."

"Well, you're in bed with people who don't just believe in it—they revel in it. So take my advice and pack a bag. Get out of Gantsville."

But I doubted he would—even if he could. These slobs had made a little man feel big, and now he'd traded his integrity for the privilege, never realizing the price tag might be death.

I left the pad upstairs to go back down to my apartment to raid the fridge. I had hauled the six-pack of Pabst out when the knock came to the door.

With my hand on the .38 on my hip, I cracked the door and peeped out at the two men. Two uniformed cops. I knew them both well.

"Rod," one said as nicely as he could. "We hate to do this, but we have orders to bring you in."

"What for?"

"Suspicion of murder."

"What the hell you talking about?"

"George Moore," he said.

That hadn't taken long.

"Give me a minute," I said, and shut the door on them. I removed the holstered .38 and put it in drawer of the stand by the door. Maybe carrying a gun without a license was small stuff compared to murder, but why court trouble? I got a sports jacket out of the closet and a tie. Made myself presentable.

When we got to the station, I was taken to an empty office that smelled of sweat and fresh paint. I recognized the office because it used to be mine.

A guy who was clearly a plainclothes cop walked into the room, a stone-faced character built like a construction worker and about as humorous as a preacher at a funeral. I'd never seen him before.

"I'm Captain Culp," he said.

"I guess you know who I am. They tell me George Moore was murdered and I'm a suspect."

"That's right, Mr. Dexter." He rested half of his ass on the edge of my former desk. "Witnesses saw you leave the Moore house shortly before he was reported dead."

Shark must've known I was there last night. He'd had Moore killed to throw the blame on me. I was really getting to them.

I asked, "Who reported the death?"

"I'll ask the questions."

"I've got more right to ask a sensible question than you have pinning a false charge on me. Your so-called witness wouldn't be an anonymous phone tip by any chance?"

He was getting steamed. I knew his game, probably better than he did.

He asked, "Why were you at Moore's house last night?"

"Who says I was? Neighbors? If so, give me a lineup and have them pick me out. Come on, Culp. You have to be a better cop than that. I'd hate to think they gave my office to a moron."

His eyes tightened and he reddened a little. "You are inches away from a jail cell, my friend."

"I'm not falling for your crap because you haven't got any evidence. Book me or spring me. Because if you throw me in the can, I know a lawyer who will tear you to shreds." This poor excuse for a cop suddenly had the damnedest look on his face. He'd received his instructions from somewhere and now didn't know what to do with or about me. At least he had enough sense not to get rough.

"Okay," he growled. "But don't think you're getting away with anything. I'll drag you back in here as soon as I've got enough to put you in a cell."

"Captain Culp?"

"Yes, Mr. Dexter."

And I made a suggestion that was physically impossible, but his reaction was fun to watch. I left the station, refusing a lift back, and walked to a cab stand.

Hate was boiling up inside me, but satisfaction was, too—they were getting very damn nervous. The people in this city who were inviting the Syndicate in were getting scared. Who could say what I'd expose? Or who I might kill next? Nobody had the balls to act, afraid of their masters and afraid of me, afraid they'd get the same thing Rogers got, or Bacon. They might think they were little gods now, running this town or soon to. But they were just humans. And humans die.

In my borrowed apartment, I slept till noon again, decided to get up, and went back to my own pad and downed breakfast. I was about to shave when the phone rang. It was Ginger.

"Business this time, darling," she said. "Doris came across some papers that belonged to Mayes. Interested?"

"Sounds worth the trip. Any excuse to see you."

But I only saw her briefly. Marsh, the butler, let me in. Ginger was sitting in the living room with her sister, who handed over a packet of papers and then gave me a nod of dismissal. Ginger and I traded private smiles, and I headed back.

It was night now and I was stretched out on my bed, going through the papers Doris provided. They were mostly the type of letters politicos usually receive, kiss-up stuff and mealy-mouthed requests for funding. There was one real interesting missive, though—from Jean Banner's father.

Evidently her daddy and Rogers were close friends. The letter was a sort of contract, headed "Memo of Agreement." It said if anything happened to Jean's father, Mayes Rogers would see after the daughter. He did see after her, all right—to diddle and drop her.

The letters and papers were otherwise of little value. I tossed them aside and swore aloud, only to be interrupted by the ringing of the phone.

The voice on the other end said, "It's Fred."

"You still loafing, flirting with nurses?"

"Naw, they sprung me. Thought I'd give you a ring. Got the word about your visit to the station, and heard something you're gonna be interested in—a guy named Luke Mason confessed to Moore's murder."

"You're kidding!"

"Just a young punk. Came in and copped to it. Claimed it was self-defense."

"Who'd have to defend himself from *that* mousy guy!"

"Kid said Moore invited him over and made a sex play. When the kid said no dice, Moore pulled a gun on him and they struggled and...you know the rest."

"What a load of horseshit."

I heard him laugh. "Yeah, Rod, but it puts you in the clear. I think your buddy Shark sent him. And he sent a top criminal lawyer to represent this nearly indigent kid, who will no doubt walk. Fix seems in. Anyway, Shark must've realized they couldn't pin it on you, so now the heat's off."

"Beautiful."

"Yeah, and something else. Culp said you really were at Moore's house. That right?"

"Yeah, but I didn't tell him that."

"And you, uh...you really are innocent?"

"Of that one I am."

His voice lowered to a whisper. "You get the package I sent you?"

"With that little reminder of old times? Yeah."

"Well, this isn't old times. You aren't a cop anymore, remember. Watch your tail."

Calling from the PD as he was, Fred said he better cut it short, but just before he hung up, he asked, "Say, Bob Bacon's reported missing. Seen him around?"

"Not today," I said.

CHAPTER 5

I gave the chimes on the door a quick ring and stepped back. For a change, I didn't have to wait long. A tall, sharply dressed man opened the door—not a butler, a business associate, maybe a male secretary. He was in his thirties and his expression was pleasant.

I asked, "John Graves available?"

He cleared his throat at my bluntness. "Is Mr. Graves expecting you?"

I shook my head. "Just tell him Rod Dexter."

He studied me momentarily, as if the name maybe meant something, then nodded and disappeared, still leaving me at the ajar door. So I walked in and found a button-tufted black leather chair in a book-lined study off the cavernous entryway. This place made the Rogers house look like a dump.

He didn't take long. I was sprawled out studying the latest *Life* magazine when he came confidently in, his hair still blond, the smile still the same…and it was as though no time had passed between us at all.

"Johnny boy," I said, rising to shake his hand. Our grip was firm, our expressions warm.

"What brings you around, Rod?" His voice was soft and pleasant—he really sounded glad to see me.

"I've put off this visit too long, buddy. Glad to see you finally made the big time."

We both sat, John choosing a nearby matching black leather couch and not putting the desk between us. But the smile had left John's face.

"I'm glad to see you after these years, too, Rod. But don't pretend you made the trip just to congratulate me on my new position." He paused, then added, "Not that I wouldn't relish that."

"You're right. Maybe you heard. Things have been going rough lately."

"I read the papers. I know what that PD job meant to you. I'm sorry."

"Don't be," I put in. "It's not looking like a town I much want to work in anymore. I got bounced while working on the Rogers case. I started poking around and pretty soon I had hold of a toe belonging to pretty damn ugly beast."

He sat back, appearing interested. If he knew what I was talking about, he didn't show it.

I went on. "The Syndicate is moving into this state, Johnny. Gantsville is just the start. Anybody who doesn't join the team gets knocked off—that's what happened to Rogers. I wanted to warn you—a guy in your position could face the same thing."

"You know this to be true?"

I nodded. "I got it from insiders, one of whom was murdered last night. A state rep like you, they're bound to come after. And you know better than to run for help, because you just might find they *are* the help."

"Then where would you suggest I turn?"

"You need protection."

"I have staff."

"Not with my skills. Look, Johnny, maybe you don't think you need help, but *I* need it—by way of a paying job. Hire me on as your bodyguard. That'll get me a gun and a license."

He said nothing, just mulling it. Then he said, "The Syndicate in Gantsville? And in a rural state like ours? That's big city stuff, Rod."

"They pick a starting place. A mid-size town like Gantsville makes a good one."

I filled him in about Shark. He listened intently, then said, "Wouldn't the best way to protect my future be to straighten out Gantsville today?"

"My thinking exactly. When do I start work?"

He laughed, stood up, and said, "Okay. I'll make you legal. But I can't make you smart."

"Understood," I said, and we shook hands again.

I left John's house and gunned my Ford toward home and thought about the old John Graves.

We'd been raised in the same small town, gone to the same schools, shared each other's troubles and laughter. Though great friends, we'd also been rivals, each trying to outdo the other. Johnny was drawn to the world of politics, but I wanted to make a difference in the real world. Or maybe I just wanted to carry a gun.

Maybe you've guessed that what came between us was a girl—a beautiful one, probably the most beautiful I've ever seen. *Jill Raymond.* But she belonged to John. I was his best man and assigned to escort her to the city where the wedding was to be held.

We had stopped on the way for a couple of drinks. Jill seemed to want one last taste of freedom. We drank too much. We got in the car and she climbed all over me, whispering things in my ear. I kept telling myself it was the booze making her say those things, but somehow I knew it wasn't. As the lovely girl flung herself at me, part of me responded while another part told me I could never tell John. He would have to find out about her the hard way.

Maybe it was a blessing that he never did.

All I remember is that it was raining, and even after I started driving again, Jill was all over me, nuzzling at my neck, hands fumbling at my lap. The drink must've dulled me because all I could see were two big headlights and then came the impact. My last conscious thought, seeing the twisted scarlet shapeless lifeless thing next to me, was that Jill Raymond wasn't beautiful anymore.

Took three weeks for me to come around, and then another six to recover. John never blamed me, but our friendship ended there.

We didn't see each other again until three years ago.

I had just made captain when a derelict was brought in for murder. He was babbling about not even knowing the victim, but the odds were stacked against him.

Nobody recognized him. They saw a bum calling himself John Smith. But I saw John Graves, a once-distinguished man in politics. When he saw me, his eyes filled with tears and also with hate and bitterness. Still, putting my new promotion on the line, I made every effort to clear him, and succeeded.

I didn't see him for another year. When he came around to seek me out, he was a different man, a man back on his way to the top, the hate and bitterness gone. We didn't have any long conversation—he just shook my hand and spoke two words: "Thanks, buddy."

But he did say something else before we again parted company. "I was in the worst kind of hell and you pulled me out, Rod. If *you* ever find yourself burning, call me."

That was the marker I'd called in today.

After I got back, I put in a call to Fred at the PD and asked if he could meet me at our regular spot. He said he could but didn't sound thrilled about it.

I'd just dropped a dime in a jukebox when he walked in. He

took a chair at a table in back and waited expressionlessly till I joined him.

"Hope it's important," Fred said. His face wasn't swollen or bandaged anymore, but it had a patchy look. "My new captain might get suspicious."

We both ordered coffees and when they came, I asked, "What's happening on your end?"

"If you mean the Rogers case, what do you think? Big fat nothing. I haven't been pulled off, but my desk has plenty of other stuff piled on to keep me occupied."

"I'm surprised a patsy hasn't walked in and confessed like the kid that copped to the Moore kill."

He smirked. "Everybody from the D.A. on down is satisfied with that one."

"It stinks. Self-defense my ass."

He grunted a laugh. "It would've *been* your ass if they thought they could risk arresting you and keeping a lid on what you know."

"They've got other ways to try to shut me up." I dropped the small talk and got to the point. "John Graves hired me today—as his bodyguard."

He took a long swallow of black coffee and muttered, "What's that going to prove?"

"It proves an ex-cop has to make a living like anybody else."

"So, what? You're moving to the state capitol?"

"Not just yet. I'm looking after Johnny's interests in this part of the state for the time being. In the meantime, he made some calls, and I have a P.I. ticket and a license for that thirty-eight caliber gift you sent me."

Fred tried to look stern but it wasn't taking. "You haven't given up on the Rogers thing."

"Why, you want me to? Last week you got your can trashed

because you tried to help. Did it change your mind about what's worthwhile in life?"

"They'll kill you, Rod."

"They'll try."

He shook his head and downed some more coffee. "You're right about what's worthwhile in life. Like my wife and kids. I can't afford to shoot off my mouth and get fired. And I don't want make a widow and a bunch of orphans out of them. Policing in this town is turning into a lousy way to make a buck, but right now it's all I got."

"You're a family man, Fred. I get it. Me, I'm a loner. I only dream of settling down. And maybe I've finally got a shot at getting something worthwhile out of life myself. But only after I finish with this."

Fred glanced down at his watch and muttered under his breath. He wanted to help and it was killing him he couldn't. He got up, tossed a buck on the table and said, "Be careful, man."

On the wall pay phone in back, I put in a call to Ginger and told her I'd be at her sister's place in an hour.

I made it there in half that. Marsh answered the door, but Ginger was right there to play interference. She escorted me to that little TV room and shut us in, turning a lock to give us extra privacy.

"What do you need?" she asked.

I kissed her, held her.

"Sometimes a guy needs a woman," I said, "and there's just no substitute."

We settled onto the couch and held hands, but my smile wasn't working. She said, "What is it, Rod?"

"Our new state representative, John Graves, hired me. I'll be his personal bodyguard. It makes it legal for me to investigate and carry a gun."

Ginger surprised me by saying, "Good." I went on. "John

and I've been friends since forever. And I did him a king-size favor once. Now it's his turn."

"But if he's involved in politics..."

"John isn't mixed up with this crowd. I know him well enough to know he wouldn't play footsie with the Syndicate."

Her eyes were tense and she was shaking her head slowly. "How can you be sure of that?"

"Oh, they'll try their damnedest to get him on their side. If he cooperates, he's safe. If not, he's dead. But I can pack a gun legally now, and when they come, I'll be ready."

Ginger drew her lips tight. "It'll take you away from me."

"Only briefly. It'll all happen fast."

She squeezed my hand and found a brave smile. "This is what you want, so I'm happy for you. But when this is over, promise me—no more playing with guns. I...I love you, Rod, and I want you alive."

I swallowed those words and let them digest a while. Then I said, "That's what I want, too, honey. But first I've got to kill some people."

Her eyes got wide and her mouth made an "O" that went with them. But she didn't protest.

She only relaxed herself and sank into the couch, her head leaning back, her lips giving me the green go-ahead. I leaned over and kissed her again, hard and long, knowing it wouldn't end there, just like it wouldn't end for us, ever.

She broke away from me long enough to say, "Why can't we leave this lousy place and just—"

"Shut up, baby."

But it sounded like "I love you."

I slept in my own pad that night with the .38 under my pillow, but no one showed. A call from Fred got me up bright and early.

"Got something you'd be interested in, buddy."

"Shoot."

"I'm calling from a booth just off Fourth. Never mind what we talked about yesterday. I give a great big damn today."

"So you've got religion. Preach."

He cleared his throat. "I been snooping. In and around Morgan's, everything on the inside looks on the up and up. But then I stumbled over something in the alley behind the club—an old man, hell beaten out of him. But still breathing."

"Lot of guys get beat up, that part of town."

"Maybe. But guess who he says did it to him—personally?"

"*Shark?*"

"Shark."

I asked where he was, then slammed down the receiver. Without shower or shave or breakfast, I jumped into yesterday's clothes and made tracks to Fourth.

My ex-partner was sitting in a car patiently smoking a cigarette when I pulled over. I hopped out and got a look at the shabbily dressed, stubble-bearded old guy stretched out in the back of Fred's unmarked car, passed out.

I climbed in on the rider's side and said, "You sure he isn't just drunk? And got that blood on his face from a fall?"

Fred shook his head. "There's no smell of liquor on him. Doesn't read like dope, either. He's yours if you want him. Don't say I never gave you anything."

I leaned over and had a careful look at Fred's cargo. Those bum's clothes had cost money in another life, and that face looked like it might have belonged to somebody once.

I asked Fred what he got out of the guy.

"Not much. When he first saw me, he thought I was one of them. The badge finally changed his mind. Then he dropped the name."

"Shark?"

He nodded. "I checked his wallet. No identification. But there was a twenty tucked under the flap, so he wasn't rolled. And who'd roll a guy like that anyway?"

He helped me lug the bum over and into my car, and I headed for the apartment. This time I used the spare pad. Took all my strength to carry him in and when I finally got him onto the bed, my guest started to sit up. He was coming around slowly.

I wiped his forehead with a damp washcloth. Washed the blood off his swollen face. "Take it easy, pal."

He opened his eyes a little, with a start, but I calmed him down with the best smile I could muster.

His voice was sandpaper working on a rusty tin can. "Who… who are you?"

"Rod Dexter. Mean anything to you?"

The eyes flashed wide. "Don't…don't kill me."

"I want to help you. You want some water?"

He nodded. I got him a glass. He guzzled it, then sipped more slowly. He handed it back shakily. By the time I set it down, he was asleep. Or had passed out again.

I slept on the sofa in the front room and was up the next morning before him. I went to rouse him, but he wasn't asleep. He was on his back staring at the ceiling.

I pulled a chair up.

He looked at me with rheumy, suspicious eyes. "Thanks for the bed."

"Forget it."

"But you want something in return."

"Nothing's free in life."

"Yeah, I…I noticed." He shifted his eyes away.

"What's your story, Pop?"

The old man gave me a strange look, like a very wise man

regarding a very slow student. "I don't have a story. I don't count. I'm a just sucker who takes what comes. I'm nothing."

I lit up a cigarette. His eyes tightened with nicotine hunger. I put the cig between his lips and he drew heavily on it, taking the most from the first puff, letting it drift slowly out his nostrils.

"Everybody has a story, Pop. What's yours with Shark?"

He gave me a shivery glare. "I was big once. They liked me when I was big. I ran that place for Morgan himself. But the booze got me and I took the slide down and now they hate my guts." He said something nasty and took another deep drag. "I disappeared on 'em, a long time ago. Until Shark came to town, they didn't bother messing with me."

"You were on the street. Somebody recognized you."

"They came looking. Somebody realized how much I'd seen, how much I knew. And this is what they did to me. They didn't kill me 'cause if my corpse turned up, and somebody honest like you used to be, Captain Dexter, somebody like that ran my prints, they'd make me as one of the local crowd and the heat might come on."

"You mean if the right cop, or the right reporter got hold of you, there would be hell to pay?"

"Hell to pay and more. So they beat me and told me to crawl onto the next freight out of town. And that's just what I'm gonna do."

"No, Pops, first you're gonna talk. Spill everything you know about that bunch."

He shook his head. "Sorry, Captain. I ain't talking. Maybe I don't owe them anything, but I'm not dead and I wanna stay that way. Nice of you helping me out, but you only did it so I'd spill, and comes right down to it, I don't figure I owe you one damn thing."

He'd been tough once, real tough. And some of it was still under there.

I eased the .38 out the hip holster and held it loosely in my hand, like it was a bar of soap, not saying anything, giving him time to let it sink in.

He got a smile going, but it was sick. "You won't use that, Captain."

"I'm not captain of shit anymore. I'm just a guy your former friends screwed over." I cocked the hammer back. His cigarette drooped and sweat beads pearled on his forehead.

"I been through the mill myself, you know," I told him. "You know me. All you hoods know me. I can kill just like you boys do because that's the only way to survive in this jungle."

Tears were trickling down his stubbly face. "You…you won't do it…."

"A bullet makes you a corpse, and like you said, some cop runs your prints, and some reporter follows the leads you represent, and the hunt I'm on gets easier."

"I haven't been on the inside with those guys for over a year!"

My fist tightened around the .38. "Who's number one?"

"…Shark."

"Around here he is. But who does he answer to?"

"He's…the top man."

"I don't think so." I stuck the .38 closer to his wet face and pressed the cold steel gently to his cheek. "Let's back up. Start with *your* name."

"Miller," he gasped. "Bud Miller."

"Bud, you haven't anything to be afraid of. Nothing stands between you and that freight…except me. You want a ride to the train yard, or a trip to the boneyard?"

"Red Duval."

"Who is Red Duval?"

"He's...the Syndicate's man in Capitol City. They've been planning this for years. Gantsville isn't the first town in this state, or the neighboring ones, they've taken over."

I frowned. "Are you saying the capitol is already in their pocket?"

The important man Miller had once been had come out of hiding. His voice was stronger now. "No. But it will be. For now, Duval's just headquartered there. And that's all I know, Captain. I swear to God."

"Get out of bed," I said.

"Huh?"

"You want that ride to the freight yard or not?"

He wanted it, and got it.

CHAPTER 6

I was driving back after dropping the old man off when I finally picked up on the black Ford making each turn I did. If he was tailing me, he was doing a crummy job. I cut right at the next corner on the caution and the red stopped him. I gunned the motor and shot through a back street that took me across town. Alone.

I wound up at Larry's Place where I found a vacant stool and when Larry saw me, he got me a Pabst from the tap and set it in front of me.

"Good to see you alive and well," he said.

"Alive, anyway."

The door opened just as I lifted the mug of beer.

He was a middle-aged guy with a long, thin neck. Black hair was trying to climb itself up from his unbuttoned white shirt and congealed into a pile of greasy black hair on the top of his skull.

The guy walked over to the bar and when no one came to take his order immediately, he banged his fist on the counter.

Larry turned toward his direction and said, "What'll it be, mac?"

"Start with a little service, bud. What kind of joint you runnin', anyway? When I walk into a place, I want to be waited on, and fast."

"So what'll it be?" Larry asked again.

The guy let a twisted, ugly grin come over his lean face. He motioned for Larry to come closer. Larry obeyed.

I saw his hand grab Larry by the collar and shove him back. That was when I slid off my stool.

When he looked up, I was standing over him. The smile had left his face, but if I thought he was scared, I was in for a surprise.

"What's your problem, big boy?" he asked.

"Man said he'd get you a drink. Be nice."

He jumped off his stool and stuck his face next to mine, so close I could smell the sickening odor of cheap hair tonic.

"Some people ought to mind their own business." Then he smiled the same ugly twisted smile, proud of himself.

I grabbed his long hair and slammed his head into the bar, the sound of it like a gunshot. A scream of pain and rage gurgled from his throat as I let go, wiped the grease off my palm on my pants leg, while he straightened and drew a fist back. My right literally beat him to the punch, pulping lips and loosening teeth, the impact sending him pitching back onto the floor like he slipped on a banana peel. He made the mistake of grabbing my ankle, and I plowed my free foot into the side of his skull.

That should have been the limit for any man. But this one was really tough. He made it back to his feet and dug into his coat for something, but I was ahead of him. The left side of my sports jacket was thrown back and my hand was resting easily on the .38. There wasn't a prayer for him and he knew it. So he held his hands up and gave me a big smile through bloody lips. He didn't have much left, and his knees gave way and he hit the floor.

I reached down and peeled back his coat and saw the shoulder holster with a .45.

Like the gun that killed Mayes Rogers. Maybe it was that gun. I removed the clip and tossed it away, then handed the weapon to the shaking fatso called Larry and asked, "Ever see him around before?" He shook his head and I looked back down at the guy. He was still out cold.

Everyone else in the joint was looking in some other direction.

I threw a fin on the table and took the back door out. It would take some work to drag the unconscious man out into the street, but Larry and the other bartender could handle it.

The man in the bar made me think. Not many people in this town carry guns, and if they did, they wouldn't use a shoulder holster with a .45, unless they were nuts.

Or unless they were paid to.

Had that been a set-up to get me embroiled in something fatal?

And I damn near had taken the bait and played guns with the guy, who probably figured he could take me. If I'd taken him, in a public place like that, the PD would quickly put an end to my little crusade.

Anyway, what if he wasn't the trigger man—what if he was just an angry drunk with a short fuse? And even if he did have the contract on me, and I got rid of him, Shark would just send another. At least this one, I knew what he looked like now. And maybe he'd be nice and rattled, if we met again...

I reached John Graves by phone and told him I'd be around in an hour. When I got there, I was politely ushered in by the male secretary.

Johnny greeted me with an easy smile. Without waiting to be invited to sit down, I flung my weight on the couch.

I said, "I think it'll be best if you let me stick with you very closely from now on. I met up with a guy at a bar, big bastard with trouble on his mind. Now that might not sound so unusual, but this particular son of a bitch was packing a .45. He might've been put on my tail, I don't know. But word might be out that we're connected now."

Johnny shifted in his seat. "Sounds like you're ready to go on the clock."

"You got it."

"Fine. Tomorrow at noon, we leave for three days in Capitol City. Can you make it?"

I had things to do in Gantsville, but I just shrugged and nodded.

"Good," he said.

"Nothing good about any of this, John. There's a hired killer, a trigger man, sent to put me out of commission, and maybe you. I think that bastard is who I ran into today. The one with the .45."

I was at the door when I said, "Next time give me a little more notice, pal, or I'll tell you where to go."

"Insubordinate from the start," Johnny said with a grin. "I'm not surprised."

Whatever move I made, you could bet Shark would be on top of it. He had cops on his payroll and an army of hoods. He could have me tailed or sic his trigger man on me, though I was starting to wonder if he was saving me up for himself to have the satisfaction of putting a bullet in me personally. How I'd love to have him try.

But there was no doubt in my mind that he knew I was tied up with Graves, and would be aware of the Capitol City trip.

We landed at the Capitol City airport in John's private plane and checked into the hotel at 3:15 in the afternoon. The lobby was buzzing with men and women, all shapes and sizes, from around the state in for a big political banquet here in the hotel, some talking to others, some trying to check in, others on their way up to their rooms. None of them were quiet about it. But who ever heard of a quiet politician.

As far as I was concerned, I was glad to get to the room and relax. I wasn't interested in walking up to people and having them ask me what district I was from or what representative I worked for.

Graves went to that political banquet at six; it would last until around nine o'clock. With all the reporters and so many others around, he should be safe there. So I went down to the lobby to check out the hotel bar, knowing the politicos would be occupied, and that's when I saw him.

He was standing next to a paperback rack picking up a newspaper. The lobby was empty, everybody at the banquet. There was an elderly man slouched down on a couch across the room, but he was half-asleep.

The guy knew I was staring at him, and he didn't seem to mind. His hair was still greased back and he wore that same smug look, though his lips were still a little puffy the day after our encounter at Larry's Place.

He was the trigger man. Had to be. The man with the .45. *The man who knocked Mayes Rogers off, the man here to try to knock me off, and maybe John Graves, too.*

He found a seat on a long couch and began to read his paper. Every once in a while I'd see him peep over the top of it. But he wasn't jumpy. In fact, he was as calm as could be, which was the exact opposite of me.

Was he alone? It would do no good to get rid of this one only to catch a bullet from a buddy of his. No, I had to let this play out.

So I walked past him, close enough that I could get another good look at his ugly mug, then took the elevator to our room.

I was stretched out on the bed when, an hour and change later, Johnny walked in.

"How was the banquet?" I asked.

"Rubber chicken and boring talk. Where were you to protect me from that?"

I sat up. "Johnny, there's a guy I want you to watch out for. You know the one I told you about, who I bumped into at Larry's bar. Well, I saw him in the lobby about an hour ago. He's the Syndicate killer, all right. He's got long black hair, the greasy stuff. He has a long, pencil-like neck, a lean, ugly face, and he's around forty. If you see him, don't go near him. He might even be staying in this hotel. His boss is the Syndicate's man here in the capitol."

Johnny had been frowning all through that. "Rod, maybe it's best we leave tonight. Cut this short."

"Wouldn't do any good. They'd just be waiting wherever we go next. It'll be best to settle it here."

The fear on Johnny's face was unmistakable.

"If they kill you," I said, "I won't charge you a damn thing."

His grin took the fear away, and he went to bed.

It was a miserable day, filled with all the lifeless things that make up a big city. No one bothered to speak when you passed them on the street—not even my black-haired friend, who kept a close, obvious tail on me all day, just his way of expressing his contempt. But now it was night and you could bet he'd make his move.

The night, the damp night that sings of its misery and misfortune in the faces of the people—everyone who's ever walked the streets after dark has probably felt that same thing. I walked into a drab bar, found a booth, and ordered a beer. When it was thrown in front of me, I tossed the waiter a coin.

The beer went down fast and I ordered another. By this time the place was filling up and the smoke that had already covered the room was making it impossible to discern faces. The music was loud and noisy, hitting a beat that made the people talk louder and drink more. It had no effect on me.

The girls were there. The ones that hadn't found a man for the night were slowly scanning the room in search of one. Maybe they looked my way—I didn't know or care. I wasn't in the mood for women tonight.

I was staring into the mug of beer and brought my head up just in time to see him walk through the front door. He had tailed me here, of course, and just wanted to see where I was sitting. I kept my eyes glued to him until he turned around and disappeared out the door again.

I took the last swallow from the mug and lit up a cigarette. Just as I blew the match out, I saw her gazing down at me. I looked up into the face of a snow-white blonde, a girl who looked more like a college coed than a bar girl. She was young, not more than twenty, with an innocent face and big blue eyes. Even in the dark room, I could see that.

Her body was concealed by an oversized gangster type trench coat, but I could still tell that the stick of female dynamite under it was something that didn't deserve the fate of being hidden. If it was any other girl, I'd have told her where to go. But this one had a look in her eyes, not the dollar-sign kind of look most have, but a look of something I couldn't describe. Not yet.

I motioned for her to sit down, offered to buy her a drink, which she refused, and then kept quiet, waiting.

She bent over, as though she was about to tell me her life's story, and whispered, "I'm not supposed to be here." She giggled and continued, "But I don't care. I'm eighteen and I'm old enough to do as I please."

I shook my head. "It's a big, ugly world with a nasty ending. Don't expect ice cream and roses all your life."

My fatherly advice didn't seem to take. "My name is Becky. What's yours?"

"Rod Dexter."

"Oh, nice to meet you, Rod." She had a funny look in her eyes and I was dying to find out what it meant.

"Your parents don't know you're here?"

She shook her head and frowned. "If they did, I'd be dead. They never let me go out. Not anywhere. They're afraid I'd get attacked or something. Funny, huh?"

"Not really."

"No, they always have to be with me. But tonight I showed them. Tonight I'm going to do what I please." She giggled again.

This girl was in for trouble. She was starved for excitement, something life had failed to give her.

"Think twice, kid. Like I said, it's an ugly world. It's not meant for pretty things like you."

"You think I'm pretty?

That did it.

"Where do you live?"

"About five blocks from here, 1261 Benton Apartments. Why?"

"I'm going to take you home." I grabbed her by the arm, jerked her up from the booth, and went out the door.

I had to get her out of this joint. She was a sex-starved girl who was looking for it tonight. She knew I was serious about taking her home and gave me the directions. Outside the club enough people were around that she should be safe, and her presence might keep me safe a while too.

We walked the short distance to my car in the lot. When I first dug my hand into my pocket, I heard it. The steps were muffled at first, but they gradually became louder. I stuck the key into the lock, but the shot rang out before I could turn it. I dove to the cement, bringing Becky down with me. Another shot rang out and I drew the .38.

I looked at Becky and saw the frightened but excited look on her face. I'd been wrong about us being safe together.

"Rod, I'm scared!"

"Stay down, kid." I cursed under my breath as the guy ran for a different position.

The night was dark and was the only protection besides the parked cars. For a moment it was quiet, then the sound of feet came back and I fired my first shot at its shadow.

At the sound of my shot, he laughed and ran straight for us, and before I could pull off another shot, he was behind another car.

It all happened at once. Becky rose up from the street in panic and ran, and I let out a shout for her to stop just as he fired a round that caught her in the gut and reeled her back to the pavement. She was lying close enough that I could see her big blue eyes staring at the sky just before they filmed over.

The bastard laughed again.

It burned in my gut like a cancer.

I could've taken him out yesterday. If I had, the girl would still be alive.

I could tell by his running around from one position to another that he was an impatient son of a bitch, wanting the kill to be fast. That's why I waited him out. Ten minutes passed before he came out of hiding, running again like a madman. I shot at his back and nipped his hand. The gun flew from it and landed about five feet from where I knelt. The .45.

He started to run and I caught him in the back. He fell against a car, clawing it as he sank slowly to the street, face down. I kicked him over, stared down at his twisted face and watched his eyes film over, too.

A distant siren warned me to let the night swallow me up. I took its advice.

CHAPTER 7

The next day in Capitol City was quiet. No new tail replaced the dead one, and no one connected me to the kill. We left that afternoon and landed in Gantsville by early evening.

The trigger man was dead. So was an innocent fool named Becky. The thought of that poor dumb kid catching a bullet made me sick, but I'd told her about the story's nasty ending, hadn't I? And what did the whole stinking mess prove?

I was back in my own place, sitting on the edge of the bed, thinking those thoughts, when the knock came. I went to answer it, with the .38 in hand, hoping it was Ginger, and when I saw who it was, I was close.

It was her sister.

Doris Rogers had traded her dressing gown in on a fetching red frock, her dark hair brushing her shoulders, her dark eyes flashing.

"You're out and about," I said, opening the door for her. "That's good."

She swished by. "We have to talk."

Not my favorite words from any woman. "Sure."

She sat down on the couch, every bit as lovely as her sister but something gave me a crawly feeling. She wore a strange look and this didn't feel right.

Proving that, she said softly, and bluntly, "I know who killed Mayes."

I was looming over her now. "So do I. And I killed *him*—an out-of-town trigger man."

She shook her head. "No. You won't like this, Rod...but no. My sister did it. *Ginger* is the killer."

I bent down to her. "Explain yourself or get the hell out."

She grabbed my arm and with surprising strength tugged me down onto the couch next to her. Her dark eyes were wild, her nostrils flaring.

"You *must* believe me. Do you think it's *easy* for me to say this? About my own *sister*? But she doesn't love you, Rod. It's all been an act."

My stomach felt all knotted up. "I'm listening."

She moved close to me. "I've overheard her on the phone. She's received calls from that district attorney and that man called Shark. They used her to try to get at Mayes, and it worked at first...you're aware of what a letch he was...but when she tried to get him to play along with that crooked crowd, he bolted."

"You know this from phone calls you overheard?"

"More than overheard!...I listened in. She killed him herself, Rod! She went to him after that party, in the hotel, apologetic, asking for a second chance...and shot him down in cold blood. And you're next."

I couldn't accept it—I couldn't, even though it made a terrible kind of sense.

"I know what it's like, Rod. I loved Mayes, but he used me, manipulated me." She touched my face, her eyes soft now, brimming with tears. "I don't want you to get hurt the way I did."

"If this is true, it's too late."

"It's true. But it's not too late for you to save yourself. Not too late to live." She drew near, licked her lips, and they glistened like her tear-filled eyes. "Maybe...when this is over...."

She wanted me to kiss her, but that was the last thing I

wanted. There was too much of Ginger in her face, and too much turmoil in my belly. I understood the emotions that had to be roiling through this woman, betrayed by her husband and her sister. But love was nowhere in me.

Hate had pushed all of that away.

"If your sister is a threat to you," I said, taking her hand, "you should go into hiding. Find a hotel or motel to camp out in till this is over."

She sighed, shook her head. "I haven't seen Ginger for two days. I don't know where she's gone."

"Do you think she knows that *you* know?"

"Maybe. But I'm not the one who's in danger, Rod. You are."

She rose and walked to the door. From behind, the way she walked, moved, the shape of her, she might have been her sister, if not for the blackness of her hair to say otherwise.

I went into the bedroom and flopped on my back and let darkness envelop me. Then I cursed that darkness, cursed everything, because there was nothing left for me if what Doris had said was true. *Could I believe her?*

Something in me screamed, *No! Ginger is in love with you, you fool. She's been with you from the start, could have killed you any time.*

I did love her. She represented everything good that waited for me after I swept the bad out of my life. And if she *was* the killer, I still loved her. Could never squeeze the trigger on her.

Of course, if Doris was lying or wrong or just plain crazy, and Ginger was innocent of all this, I still had Shark and the rest after me. They knew their boy with the .45 had failed in Cap City. And they knew I was tied in with a powerful, honest politician who could expose them all.

John Graves would start with our crooked D.A. and work his way back to the capitol and Red Duval and his crowd, and the

Syndicate's foothold would be gone. And I'd be at his side, an official investigator for a statehouse committee—a cop again.

But right now I was back on Shark's turf and he and his hoods would deal with me, soon.

Like tonight.

I forced myself to get ready. I showered, got into one of the suits I'd worn to work all those years, the .38 in its holster clipped onto my belt, a box of ammo in my coat pocket. Knowing they'd be waiting, I went down to my car, got behind the wheel, and drove. I chain-smoked and thought about Ginger and how much sense Doris had made, and my gut tightened with dread and rage.

How I felt was at odds with the quiet night, late now, traffic light in town. I headed out into the country, the same direction as Bacon and his pockmarked pal when they took me for a ride. It was really dead out here. Nobody around.

Almost nobody.

Two headlights were coming. The brights were on and drew closer and closer, and the big black Buick came faster and faster, the roar of its engine like a beast ready to leap. *They'd come for me.* And I welcomed it. I eased up on the gas and let them get close.

The nose of the Buick rammed into the tail of my Ford and I bit my lip. As I fought for control of the car with one hand, I fumbled for the .38 with the other, brought it out, and laid it on the rider's seat.

They rammed me again.

I mashed the gas and they did the same, this time slamming me in the side, knocking me off the road. All I saw was a blurry flash and the vehicle shook me like it was trying to put some sense into me. I heard squealing tires and brakes shuddering to a stop and a car door slamming, and another.

Bullets punched through the front window, leaving spider-webs behind, and I got low and somehow got out on the rider's side and crawled into the bushes, found a spot, and waited. The .38 was in my fist but I didn't remember how it got there.

Then they were walking toward me, outlined against the clear night—Shark himself, skeletal and tall in his sharkskin suit, and one of his neckless bully boys from Morgan's. They must have figured riddling that windshield with lead had wounded me bad and I was no threat, because they stalked over making perfect targets. All of a sudden it struck me funny as I opened fire and gave the stooge two in the gut that made him bow to me before he went down in a whimpering, dying pile. At the same time, Shark was running, back to the Buick, to take cover.

I moved down through the bushes as he fired at where I'd been. He had no idea I was coming up behind him when I put the bullet in his gun arm and the automatic he'd been firing went sailing into the night. I was at the rear of the Buick and he was up by the nose and looked back at me with those dead black eyes finally getting some life in them, the fear of a man about to die.

He started to run.

At first he went down the highway, then he cut toward the bushes, where I'd hidden. I had stopped to take good aim and put one in his left calf, laughing as he briefly stood on one leg before going down, pitching forward, skidding through the gravel at the side of the road. Then he was crawling toward the bushes, and somebody was filling the night with crazy laughter. Me, I guess.

Just another snake, I thought, *crawling through the brush.*

He had run out of steam when I got to him. He was on his belly, his good arm out in front of him, between two trees but stopped by a thicket.

He said, "Spare me...and...I'll talk. I'll...I'll give 'em all to you."

"Just give me one name."

He rolled over on his back. He was breathing hard. He'd skinned his face bad on the gravel and it was a grotesque torn thing, streaks of blood, hanging flesh, his black eyes wide in the Halloween mask.

"Ask," he said.

"Who killed Mayes Rogers?"

He swallowed. "Who do you think? That broad."

"Which broad?"

He told me.

And I wasn't surprised by the answer, but he sure seemed surprised when I shot him between his eyes, which suddenly got even deader.

When I walked back to my car, I almost missed a third man who'd been in the Buick. If he was smart, he wouldn't have been anywhere near this tonight. But there he was, a stocky little guy running down the middle of the road, shoes making receding slaps in the night, little echoey things.

I got behind the wheel of the Buick and went after him. Running after the bastard didn't hold much appeal. I pulled up alongside him like I was offering a lift, and he came to a stop and looked at me in wide-eyed horror.

"Mr. Graham," I said, "you surprise me. Crooked D.A.'s don't usually fraternize so openly with the bad guys they're in bed with. But you wanted to see me die, didn't you? I get it."

He started running again.

I let him get a nice head start, and when the nose of the Buick knocked him down, and after the undercarriage ripped him up as the vehicle made its way bumpily over him, I could still hear him whimpering. So I backed over him, and then through the windshield I could see the squashed mess that had been a man.

Maybe five minutes had gone by. Even on a quiet night like this, another car was bound to come along. So I made quick work of it, wiping my prints off the Buick, then getting back into my Ford. The motor had died, but it started up again, even if it drove jerkily now after getting bashed a couple times, and seeing through that windshield wasn't easy with all the bullet holes.

But I had a hunch a mechanic named Moore would fix me up on the sly. And really I was seeing things more clearly than ever.

CHAPTER 8

The real killer would be waiting for me at the big white mansion on the hilltop, but it was the distinguished-looking if hulking butler who answered the door. His eyes barely registered surprise at my appearance—the dirty, rumpled, somewhat torn-up clothing, and the bruises and skinned areas on my face.

He had too much class to say anything but, "Miss Bass is in, sir. Shall I tell her you're calling?"

I didn't have to answer because Ginger was suddenly there, blonde and fresh, in a white blouse and yellow skirt, looking schoolgirl innocent though her lovely face wore distress.

"Thank you, Marsh," she said, and nodded for me to follow her. I did, back to that TV room and the couch where we'd made love. That was where we sat, and she swiveled toward me with concern.

"You look awful," she said.

"You should see the other guys. Well, really, you shouldn't—they're dead as hell."

Her eyes flared much as her sister's had. "What…*what* men are dead? That Shark person?"

"Him and one of his boys, and Gantsville will be needing a new D.A. It's almost over, doll."

She got up and went somewhere, came back with a damp cloth and wiped my face gently with it.

"Where have you been," I asked, "these last few days?"

"I used that apartment the floor up from yours. I only came back here to check on Doris, and pack the rest of my things. I was hoping to talk you into leaving Gantsville and ending all this."

"No need," a female voice said to our left. "The end is almost here."

Doris was in the doorway, a .45 in her grasp, dwarfing the small white hand holding it. She still wore the same red frock, red as blood, red as Satan. Her dark eyes in the lovely face were wild.

Ginger gasped. "*Doris!* What..."

"Shut up! You love this fool so damn much, you can *die* with him."

The .38 was in my hand but out of sight, down between my thigh and Ginger's.

"You're the killer," I said, matter of fact. "No out-of-town trigger man—*you* killed Mayes."

The smile was as triumphant as it was crazed. "*Of course* I killed him. I loved him and I killed him, killed the bastard, who could love so many women but not me. Mr. High and Mighty, who couldn't be bought, but could be had, by any pretty bitch."

Ginger, quietly bitter, said, "He never had me."

"Maybe not. I don't know that I believe you, Sis. And I don't know that I care. Mayes and that hussy he got pregnant, they're both dead now. Just like you two will be in a moment."

She stepped into the room, and came over to stand before us, just a few feet away, the .45's barrel staring at us with its cold black eye.

"I liked you," Doris said to me. "I thought you might like me. I gave you a chance earlier today, but you weren't interested. Like Mayes wasn't interested. I found him in that hotel room with another damn woman. She got away, but I blew his stinking head off...just like I'm going to blow the heads off the two of you."

Maybe three feet away now. Could I lift my gun-in-hand and fire before she did? Doris took one step closer, aimed the gun at me, and her finger gently tightened around the trigger.

The roar shook the room.

But the .45 hadn't made it. A shotgun had. Doris was still standing there, but the top of her was nothing human. A blast from the open door took her head off and splattered it against the far wall, where dripping blood and chunks of bone and gobs of gore and one lonely eyeball stuck there like the work of some cut-rate Picasso. Then a body getting no signals from an obliterated brain toppled on its back with a rattling thud, and the headless body lay limply on the floor.

The man in the doorway for once wasn't standing so straight, nor did he look distinguished at all. Yet he was still the loyal servant, who would have done almost anything for Doris. Who could say exactly what he'd done, in those long nights with the master away?

But there was one thing he couldn't do for her, and couldn't let her do, either.

Not to her sister. Not to Ginger.

Marsh slowly came to the headless form, its ragged neck spilling red like a kicked-over paint can, and, on his knees, covered his face and wept. When his hands lowered, his face wet with tears, he reached for the .45 in the woman's limp fingers and I got there first. He looked up at me pitifully, wanting so much to die, but I shook my head as I stuffed the gun into my waistband.

There had been enough death for one night.

Ginger was in shock, no tears yet, and I walked her out of that room of death and into the living room, and sat her down.

"It's over," I told her. "We're together now, and we have a lifetime ahead of us to make new memories and put this one behind us."

She swallowed and nodded and put her crying face in my chest and her arms tight around me. I knew I should probably leave her to go call the cops.

But what was the hurry?

There was already one here.

The LAST STAND

by **Mickey Spillane**

The day of the dying happens too fast. The sun comes up and it shines in your face and tells you it is time to arise and die the hard death that has been written for you and there is no way you can escape the momentous finale that circumstances have laid on you…

CHAPTER I

He sat there on a rock that was too damn jagged to sit on to start with and wondered what he was doing out in the middle of a desert that was someplace in the United States where nobody would ever look to find him and, so far, not even a vulture was eyeing him for supper.

He knew where he was. He could stick a pin in the map to show him exactly where he had landed and that was great. *He* knew where he was. Trouble was, nobody else knew. He wasn't lost. He was right on course. He had made a great landing, never touching a wingtip to the ground or throwing a pebble into the ailerons or elevators, not doing one single thing to hurt the old relic he was flying except to swerve hard to avoid an outcropping that stuck up out of the arid soil like a dirty middle finger and there he sat, completely whole, entirely unscathed, with an absolutely workable airplane...if he could find whatever part had temporarily ceased to function...and put it right again.

But then, he wasn't much of a mechanic. Oh, hell of a pilot. Six thousand hours in the air, combat time in the wild blue a generation ago, a fistful of bucks to buy and restore an old BT 13A that dated back not to his own time in Vietnam but to his father's era, the plane the flyers in WWII nicknamed the Vultee Vibrator...and stupid enough to get involved in an old timers' cross-country junket when he could have parked his tail on his boat and gone fishing off the Carolina coast.

A nice day, he thought. He had had a good breakfast with the guys, real SOS the way they used to make it, bread toasted on one side in the ovens, curled a little and plastered with creamed hamburger. The young jet pilot tried to insist it was creamed chipped beef, but hell, he was only in Desert Storm, and they'd barely had a chance to eat lunch before the coalition blew Saddam out of the grass. Creamed chipped beef my ass. It was creamed hamburger.

Thirst was no problem. Three beers were jammed into the map case of the old BT over there and three more beside him behind the rock. As a matter of fact, right now he even had to pee and he did. The air was so dry it evaporated without even staining the soil.

He thought about where he might be able to get help. Not from his cell phone, which got no signal out here.

Indians, he said to himself. There's got to be Indians out here in this wilderness. And hell, they weren't hunting the Seventh Cavalry anymore. A lot of them were college graduates, old veterans like himself and guys out to make a living like anybody else. He remembered one from his cadet class, a big, sleek Native American who went into F-4 Phantom IIs and that was the last he had heard of him. His name was T.P. Summers. Naturally, that got changed to *Indian Summers*, after the old song.

The rock got too sharp for his behind and Joe Gillian got up and walked to his airplane. He went around it, looking at the skid marks he'd left in the sand, avoiding up-thrust pinnacles of stone and two windswept mounds of sand that could have made him ground loop. Old 819 sat there as though she was tethered in her parking space back at the home field, both gas tanks three quarters filled, battery at full charge, two sandwiches in a plastic bag under the seat and emergency gear stowed in the proper place.

The only trouble was, the damn engine had suddenly quit.

No warning, no metallic coughing. Just quit. Sudden silence. He had called in his situation and position, but there was no answer. The radio was a little out of date too. But maybe, just maybe, *somebody* had heard his call.

Overhead, the sun turned up the temperature and the dryness of his lips said he'd better either put on some ChapStick or have a beer. He looked around the rocky, sandy, mountainous desert, saw a patch of green and a plant that had a couple of white flowers looking for a bee's kiss, figured that water had to be someplace below and opted for a beer. Those Miller Lites were still cold for now, snuggled in their wetsuit blankets, and no sense letting them get warm.

Joe climbed up on the wing, tugged a beer out of its wrappings and grunted approvingly. Lady Lite was still plenty cold. He popped the top with a quick pull and was about to take that first beautiful swig.

A voice said, "You happen to have another one of those, buddy?"

He turned slowly. There was a man over by the rocks, sitting where Joe had been just a minute before.

"You an Indian?" Joe said. He stepped down off the wing.

"Betcha tail I'm one. Don't I look like one?"

"Not like they have on TV."

"Hell, those guys only show up at the ceremonies. Didn't you ever read Tony Hillerman's yarns about the red men?"

"Sure."

"So how about that beer?"

Joe nodded. "Come on down."

The Indian hadn't been sitting on a rock at all. He was in a squat with his knees up around his neck and when he scrambled down the side of the hill Joe saw a guy as tall as he was.

"You're a big mother," he said.

"I had a white lady for a grandmother. Big job, she was."

He held out his hand and Joe took it. "Sequoia Pete," he said.

"That your real name?"

"Nope. My real name has a lot of vowels in it and has something to do with a running rabbit."

Joe introduced himself and asked, "Don't you speak Indian?"

"Yeah, but you wouldn't know it. I can handle Spanish, do some Portuguese, but hell, you can't make a buck with that talk. Where's that beer?"

Joe made another quick trip on the wing and tossed a Lite down to Sequoia Pete. "Still cold," he said.

"Tastes great, less filling, right?"

"Absolutely."

Pete hoisted the can and didn't put it down until he had finished it, then squashed the empty, glanced around and shook his head. "Now I got to tote this damn can around until I find a garbage bucket."

"What's the matter with right here?" Joe asked him, indicating the primitive landscape.

"Come on, pal, you're talking about my back yard. You toss junk in yours?"

"No, but..."

"You've already parked your old beat-up airplane—you plan to let it sit until it's a heap of trash like those slobs back east?"

"Maybe I should call triple A and get a tow truck." He looked at Sequoia Pete very seriously. "How'd you get here, Pete?"

"I rode part of the way. Walked the rest. Why?"

"From where?"

Pete pointed toward a row of mountains to the west. "Over there."

"Where's your gear?"

"I got it on," Pete said. "I travel light."

"What are you doing out here?"

"Working."

"At what?"

"Right now I'm looking for fossils."

"Find any?"

"Only that old airplane."

Joe swirled the rest of the beer around in his can then hoisted it and finished what was left. He wiped his mouth. "You're lost too, aren't you?"

"Nope. My horse is lost. I'm right here with you."

"Actually, I'm not lost either," Joe stated flatly. "I can show you on the map right where we are."

"Great," Pete told him. He lifted his arm and held out a fore-finger toward the flowering granite peaks to his right. "And I can tell you that right over there, almost on top of us but maybe fifty miles away, are the Superstitions."

"The what?"

"The Superstition Mountains, flyboy. They're on your map too."

Joe frowned and nodded. "I read something about them once…"

"The 'lost mine' and all that jazz?"

"It wasn't a mine."

"Nope, that's just what they called it. It was a cave where the Aztecs or somebody stashed this huge pile of gold to keep it out of the hands of the Spanish devils who were hard on their trail."

"Good story."

"They got prospectors up there still looking for it. Some big brains, too. All kinds of metal detectors."

"Wonder why they couldn't find it with all that technology."

Sequoia Pete looked at the mountain ridge, the tops starting to fall into deep shadow. There was something plaintive about his bland expression. "The earth hid all that stuff, Joe. There are quakes in those hills too, not like they have in L.A. or San Fran, but strange subtle ones like a giant chewing up from below. Nobody's there to see it or hear it and if there are, they don't talk about it."

"Just as well," Joe said. "Can't you see some old weather-beaten prospector finding gold worth billions, all smelted, carved into statues and jewelry and all that good stuff? Man, it would throw his lifestyle right out of joint. He'd have to throw away his shovel, shoot his mule and go buy a Mercedes."

"Not me," Pete said. "Indians don't prospect. They're out here looking for fossils. They get big college educations so they can come back and wear deerskin moccasins again." He let out a little laugh and looked at Joe's feet, then down at his own. "But not this chief, paleface. These boots came right out of the Cabela's catalog and cost me a hundred thirty bucks."

"They stiff?"

"Hell no. They make love to my toes. Now, can I ask you a question, flyboy?"

"Be my guest."

"You going to just stand there or you want to look for help?"

Joe thought a moment, lifting his head to slow scan the sky. Lining the south at about thirty thousand feet were a half dozen contrails with two more crossing them like a giant 'T' in the west. "Maybe we could wave to them." He pointed.

"Sure. Do that."

So Joe waved. He did it twice.

"Look," Pete said, "that's not getting us anywhere. You got a radio on that plane?"

"Yup. It works great around an airport or when you're flying formation with a buddy, but from down here to over there, forget about it. That BT isn't modern equipment."

"Then why're you flying it?"

"We have a club, Pete, one of those old-timers' clubs who do stupid old-timers things like flying cross-country for the fun of it. We dress up in ancient gear and have a ball at county fairs."

"This is no county fair, buddy."

"Damn, and here I was wondering where they were having the chili cookoff."

"So how did you get over here in the red man's back yard?"

"A weather front developed right on my course line. I plotted out an alternate route figuring to go around the thunderheads, and another turned up again and you know where?"

"Right in front of you?"

"On the ball, Chief. So I dodged that. Then I ducked another. Once I found a hole and went under it and almost hit a rock that was some kind of a mountain peak and did some more dodging and ducking and suddenly I was in the bright blue again over John Wayne country. And before I could start to figure out which way was which, that nice big, fat engine of mine suddenly stopped. No warning. Just cold stopped. I was at eight thousand feet, went into emergency procedures, and all I could hear was the wind in my ears."

"And here you are."

"I saw a sign on a hangar once," Joe said. "It said *Flying is the second greatest thrill in the world. The first is landing.*"

"Is that true?"

"Absolutely, Chief. Incidentally, you *are* a chief, aren't you?"

"Of course. All Indians are chiefs. Ask any tourist."

"Okay, Chief, how do we get out of here?"

"We could go find my horse."

"Why?"

"Because he knows the way home, flyboy."

"Pete, if your horse knew the way home he's long gone. You're as lost as I am. I'll bet you were stumbling around till you saw me land and hoped you'd get a free ride back to your wigwam."

"Man, I live in a hogan. That's like a house. Sun-baked bricks. Sod roof two feet thick."

"Warm?"

"Like toast. No electricity. Old-style generator, but it's busted."

"You live fancy."

"Huh. You should see my neighbors."

"Where are they?"

"Nearest is about twelve miles down the trail. Too close for comfort."

"Nice place, I assume?"

"Dirt floors, shutters for windows."

"Well," Joe told him, "being poor can be rough."

"Poor? That guy owns a dozen oil wells in the next state. He's got money coming out his ears. I think he even owns a bank."

"So why does he stay here?"

"What...and go into the big city miseries?" Pete said. "He might be rich, but he isn't dumb."

"Well, let's see how smart *we* are, Chief. How do we find your horse?"

"Beats me. He took off at a full run. Never stopped."

"We got to start someplace."

Pete looked at him seriously. "You like walking?"

"Not too far."

"You got on good shoes," Pete told him.

"So how far do we have to go?"

"We're not going to meet anybody this side of the Superstitions. At least over there we have a chance of running into somebody still scratching for gold, or those tourists who come in to paint pictures of the sun going down behind the mountains. You want to leave a note on your bird in case somebody comes looking?"

Joe thought a moment, walked over to the old Vultee Vibrator, took a pad out of his back pocket, scribbled a note on it and stuck it in a trim tab hinge. When he came back he looked at Pete's face and said, "Told 'em I'd be back in an hour."

"Nobody would believe that."

"I also said the plane was booby-trapped with six sticks of dynamite."

"That they'd believe," Pete said.

Four hours later the Superstitions were still there, not looking a bit closer than when they'd started walking, and the mild breeze had already covered up their footsteps in the sand except for the last hundred yards. The beer was warm now, but still wet. They split the sandwiches Joe had taken from the plane.

By the time it got dark, the Superstitions still didn't look any closer. Pete thought they ought to stop and take a break and Joe was the first to agree with him. Pete went out and found some firewood, laid it on the sandy ground and said, "You got any matches?"

"I don't smoke."

"Didn't ask you that."

"Got a lighter, though."

"What for if you don't smoke?"

"Boy Scout motto. *Be Prepared*."

"Smart, you white guys. Too bad Custer wasn't that sharp."

CHAPTER 2

They spotted Pete's horse in the morning, as the sun came up. It was standing in the vast space between the campfire and the mountain range, the saddle still square on its back and the reins hanging droopily under its chin.

Joe said, "That your horse?"

Pete nodded. "Yeah."

"Then go get him."

"You kidding? It's too late now. That crazy bronc isn't about to let me get near him without a nosebag full of feed."

When they stamped the fire out and kicked sand over the embers, they looked down at the horse. The animal gave a great shake, stared right back at them and waited.

"Now what?" Joe said.

"We go," Pete told him.

"Where?"

"To the mountains. We follow that horse, we'll end up pawing at the ground to get a drink."

"I thought you said he knew the way out of here."

Pete pointed at the mountains. "That's the way out of here."

The green shoots sprouting out of the earth only covered a couple of yards, but Pete zeroed right in on that little patch and, with almost a swimming motion, parted the sand, watching the color change from dampness into wetness until he was able to squeeze out two full cupfuls of water from the little oasis. After a half hour, they had another cupful of beautiful liquid that no flatlander could ever have believed was there at all.

Pete licked his lips and asked, "Good?"

Joe nodded. "I'm glad I met me a real Indian."

"White-eyes, you're crazy. You don't know me at all."

"Sure I do," Joe told him. "You ride a horse you lost. I fly an airplane that conked out on me."

"So we're both losers," Pete said.

The two looked at each other and Joe flipped Pete a candy bar he had in his pocket. "No way," he said. "Another forty miles and we have it locked. Think it'll take us long?"

"You got something else to do?" Pete said.

"Not really."

"So let's move."

Before the sun went down the hunger set in and had it not been for the exquisite tiredness that wanted to melt his body down to nothingness, Joe would have been tempted to dine on the sand and the few ants he had seen scurrying about on the top of the tiny wind-driven dunes.

But Pete had shaken his head. "Come on, Joe. Ants are for chocolate covering and serving at tea parties."

"You ever have them?" Joe asked him.

"No."

"Then don't come to conclusions until you've tried them."

"You ever eat them?"

"No."

"Want to try?"

"No."

"White-eyes, you're going to die of starvation."

"Yeah? I got another candy bar in my pocket."

"Halfsies," Pete said.

Joe broke the Snickers bar in half and handed a hunk to Pete. "Did we do this in the old days?" Joe asked him.

"Nah, we just scalped you suckers and took everything away from you."

To the south, the horse, which had been pacing them all day, whinnied and didn't sound lost at all. It didn't sound thirsty and it didn't sound hungry, but there was something plaintive about the sound it made. Pete said, "Crazy cayuse, trying to smell up a mare."

"You think he'll find one?"

"Sure. He's luckier than you, White-eyes."

"I'm not looking."

"You married, skyman?"

"Nope. Almost was, though. She got teed off and left me."

"Why?"

"I bought an old airplane instead of an engagement ring."

Pete stretched and kicked some sand around. "I guess them white girls are smarter than I figured."

Before the next night fell the Superstitions had gotten larger and darker. The outline of the rocks was clear and the tree line was evident. There was even a different smell in the air, a pine freshness, and twice there was an acrid smell of smoke. Pete sniffed, shook his head in disgust and said, "Tourists. Bagged charcoal. Ever since the government put the highway through they keep coming up looking for the good old days."

"Like when?"

"Come on, White-eyes, you ought to know tourists."

"Where I come from, they're a pain in the butt," Joe said. "They wear shorts and black street socks in loafers and think they're at the beach."

"Hell, man, out here they're buying up store-made blankets and plastic arrowheads and taking pictures of us Injuns with dirty faces to show the folks back home."

"Injuns got dirty faces?"

"Only when we see the tourists coming." For a second Pete

cocked his head into the sun and squinted. Joe tried to follow his gaze and saw nothing, until Pete said, "That cayuse of mine is trying to get back in our good graces."

Joe turned to his left. A couple hundred yards away the still-saddled bronc was standing still, his eyes on the two men, patiently waiting. Joe said, "You going to get him?"

"Hell no. He threw me once already. I'm not going to give him another chance."

"Why'd he throw you?"

"A snake damn near bit him, that's why."

"Oh," Joe said. "Maybe he'd let me ride him."

"No way. He's my horse."

"Mind if I try?"

"Go ahead. You white-eyes are always just looking to be put down."

Joe shrugged and gave a half-hearted whistle and the horse's ears jerked upright. Slowly at first, then a little quicker, the horse cantered over and stopped beside Joe. Very casually, he stepped into the stirrup and swung his leg over the back of the horse.

"You'd better find the steering wheel," Pete said without looking back.

Joe felt for the reins, slowly looping them over the mount's head until he had them in his hands. "Now what?" he asked.

"You figure it out," Pete said. "Do it wrong and that horse will sure let you know it."

Joe patted the horse's neck and its head turned to look at him. "He don't seem dehydrated," Joe said.

"Course not. He's an Indian pony. He dug up a puddle for himself or smelled out a trickle or two in a rock pile."

"Man, this is desert country."

"It used to be the bottom of the ocean," Pete reminded him.

"Comforting thought," Joe said. "How much farther to the Superstitions?"

"A ways. Why?"

"Pal," Joe said, "I would like to see some leafy vegetation. I don't have any toilet paper with me." He frowned at Pete a second and added, "What do you Native Americans use?"

"We air dry, flyboy. What do you guys use in the airplane?"

"Well, for certain emergencies we have a pilot relief tube which is like a funnel on the end of a rubber hose."

"So what about the *other* emergency?"

"We land," Joe told him.

"City critter," Pete said derisively.

Joe let out a snort and climbed down out of the saddle. "Quit being jealous. Here, you can have your horse back."

"Forget it."

"Why?"

Pete didn't answer him.

"Old Indian pal," Joe said, "you're a lousy rider, aren't you?" When Pete still didn't answer, he added, "That's why ole Dobbin here threw you, isn't it?"

A suppressed laugh made Pete's shoulders twitch. Finally, he said, "Man, I drive a Harley, a big hog that really stirs up dust. Horses and me never did get along unless they were inside big, fat cylinders."

"Then why ride him out looking for fossils?"

"Because they don't have gas pumps on sand dunes, White-eyes."

They grinned at each other and Joe said, "Pal, I'm beginning to think more of Custer all the time."

"Don't bother, flyboy. We cleaned his plow. Right now, we're only waiting to do it again. You got no John Wayne to back you up anymore." He paused a second and let out a loud snort.

"Man, how my sister loved John Wayne on the late show."

"You have a sister?"

"Hell, I have six. Why do you think I'm looking for fossils? I have to support the whole family. No brothers. Just me. College-educated and all that and I look for fossils to get a quick buck."

"What do your sisters do?"

"Five go to school. The other one teaches on the rez. She's the one who's been in love with John Wayne since she saw her first Western on TV. Keeps waiting for him to make another."

"That'll be a long wait, Pete. Doesn't she know the Duke's dead and gone?"

"Don't tell her that. She'll lay an axe on your skull."

"I thought you used tomahawks."

"Axes are better."

The shadow of the mountains had moved across the contours of the earth, coming closer to the pair, and before they expected to, they reached a strange outcropping of rock that was wet on the south side. The horse had smelled it first, edging that way, and the two men, after hearing it whinny, held onto the reins and followed the horse's lead.

There was no gushing outpour, but a steady dribble that was like the slow flow from a household tap.

They let the horse drink first. It tried lapping at the face of the rock, then pawed at the ground and opened up a hole that filled with water. It satiated itself before giving a mighty shake of its head and drawing back, well-filled.

Joe said, "You first."

"You 'fraid to drink after a horse?"

"Just being polite."

Pete shrugged, cupped his hand and drank from his palms. When he was finished, Joe took his turn. It took another hour, but they cooled off and bathed down before the night came on them. Pete took the saddle off the horse, used the blanket to cover them, and they squirmed down into the sand.

Joe asked, "Any ants around here?"

"Just scorpions," Pete told him. "Go to sleep."

A rim of light barely touched the horizon when Pete shook Joe awake. They each had half a Snickers bar and filled themselves with water before heading toward the mountain again. Both men licked the remnants of chocolate from the candy wrapper, knowing this was the last edible they had.

Joe peered through the dim light and asked, "How far away are we?"

"Could be four days' walk. Maybe one."

"You're real encouraging. If it's four, what do we eat?"

"Ever try snake?"

"Never."

"Let me ask you a question, flyboy. *Would* you?"

Joe said, "Let me ask you a question, redskin. Would *you*?"

Pete shook his head. "I'm college-educated, flyboy. I eat out of cereal boxes and cans. Sometimes a TV dinner."

"We're in real trouble, aren't we," Joe said.

"You'd better believe it," Pete told him. "That is, unless it *isn't* a four-day walk."

Pete gathered the reins of his horse in his hand and they started out.

CHAPTER 3

They were a strange trio, two men and a horse. The only thing that tied them together was the survival instinct. None were worn out, no desperation in their movements, but they knew that there could be no faltering, either.

It was a full day later before Joe looked over at Pete, suddenly feeling a new source of encouragement. They'd walked through the night, and as the sun rose he saw that the mountain range they called the Superstitions was large enough and near enough that for the first time he felt sure they could make it.

Bluntly, Joe asked, "How far now?"

"Tomorrow," Pete grunted. He pointed to the track of a sidewinder rattler in the sand and added hoarsely, "Can you go that long without eating, paleface?"

"Absolutely."

Then the horse let out a soft whinny, ears pointed straight up and nostrils flared. Pete said, "Water."

The horse trotted off at an angle. Twice he halted and looked back, and when the pair started to follow him, he edged forward. Twenty yards ahead he stopped.

What looked like a small rise in the desert floor was deceiving. Seasonal winds had hidden another rock outcropping, and on the north side, the sands were wet. Where droplets of water shimmered, small animals had been drinking until the horse's feet, pawing at the area to bring up the water, had scattered them.

Neither Joe nor Pete minded the horse's nose nudging them while they drank. Nor was there competition between them, just the sheer pleasure of knowing they could stay alive for the final stretch to the mountains. The morning was wearing on, but they lingered by the water source, resting up, taking that final sip, then angling back toward the mountain range again.

The sun had started on its downward trend when a small cloud cover moved in, giving them shade, and the trio paused, still breathing the heat but not being subjected to its full force. The clouds moved slowly and during the break Joe squatted near a patch of scrub, noting some small animals watching him from several feet away. Apparently humans were new to them, but represented no threat at all. The horse stood comfortably spraddle-legged with Pete squatting in its shadow. He seemed to be chewing and Joe wondered if he had decided to eat a lizard after all. There were enough of them around.

Idly, he kicked at the sand and that small movement uncovered three whitened forms, nearly identical in shape and size. Joe had seen rib bones before and with the toe of his shoe he pried up half a skeleton of some long dead animal he didn't recognize. He was about to cover it up with sand again when he saw something that wasn't bone, reached down and dislodged it from its position. He knew what it was immediately: an arrowhead. The tip of it was still embedded in a rib a good half inch until he pulled it out.

Even arrowheads weren't unfamiliar to him, but this one *was* unusual. It was delicately formed from some clear material, about two inches long, serrated beautifully along its sides and balanced almost to perfection. The deadly point was still needle sharp and when Joe ran his finger across the edges, it had a sharpness like a razor blade. There was no spur of a shaft at all, but that would have been of a wooden material long since disintegrated by the desert weather.

Joe dropped his find in his breast pocket and walked back to where Pete and the horse waited. Overhead, the edge of the cloud cover was about to let the afternoon light through and it was time to start walking again.

Ahead were the Superstitions. Now they were within reach. Each hour made the central mountain loom larger and before they reached its base the foothills were there and the plants that Pete knew, so that they had something to eat again, and the horse had green, if limited, fodder. And when they had all settled down that night there was no talk of their trek, no talk at all of their ridiculous, unsupervised, unplanned walk across a forbidding stretch of land, no talk at all about their extraordinary find of watering places. The desert is filled with such things if you only look for them.

The three nestled down in the slope of the mountainside; quiet now because safety didn't need much discussion. The horse was still nibbling at an outcropping of bushes and Pete and Joe were laid back in comfortable hollows watching the sun set.

Pete said, "We made it."

"Yeah."

"What do you do now?"

"Look for a telephone," Joe told him. He reached into the pocket of his shirt. He fingered out the arrowhead and handed it to Pete. "Okay, college boy, let's see what you know about this."

Idly, Pete took it in his hand. His fingertips felt the surface of it and when he ran his finger along its edge blood welled up and he sat up straight. For the first time, he looked at it closely, examining the clear form of the arrowhead, and when he was finished, he sat back and was silent for a long time.

"Damn," he said.

"What?" Joe asked.

"I'm the fossil hunter," Pete told him, "and you're the one who comes up with the big find. Damn. This arrowhead is priceless, man!"

"That's ridiculous."

"You know what it's made of?"

"Nope."

"Neither does anyone else. Look at it…clear as glass."

"So?"

"Flyboy, here is a college-certified Indian, a respected and well-thought-of fossil hunter who has come up with some museum-quality artifacts in his short career, and you, a flyboy white-eyes who dropped down into the desert, hands him the greatest find of all."

"Hell, Pete, don't come unglued. It's only an arrowhead. It hit an animal and the animal ran with the thing still in it until it died. What's the big deal?"

Gingerly, Pete fingered the artifact, turning it over in his hand, inspecting every detail of it, then said, "Joe, no exaggeration, this is the find of the century."

Joe grimaced. "You can have that damn arrowhead. It's yours. I don't want it."

Very seriously, Pete said, "My friend, you don't know what you're giving away."

"Pal," Joe told him, "I don't care. If you like it so much, you can have it."

"You sure?"

"Absolutely. Why, what's it really worth?"

"Collectors have offered a couple million bucks if anyone found one."

"Why? It's only an arrowhead."

Pete said quietly, "That little piece of a native mineral is an absolute rarity. Only traces of it have been found. Do you know who the Anasazi were?

"Sure. Ancient Indian tribe, weren't they?"

"Very ancient."

"They make that arrowhead?

"No. It's a thousand years older than the Anasazi."

"Who says?"

"The scientific geniuses the government employs. Ever since they've been looking for something like this. A round ball of it was found in a temple in South America. Another one was uncovered in a dig for some Egyptian Pharaoh. It was the clubbing end of a weapon only the king used."

"What makes it so important?"

"For one thing, it drives a Geiger counter crazy."

Involuntarily, Joe took a step backward. "Man, you mean that thing is radioactive?"

"No," Pete said. "It seems it has a power far greater than mere atomic energy."

"Like what?"

"They wouldn't tell us. We're just stupid Native Americans." He paused and stared at Joe. "You want to take a close look at this thing?" He held out the arrowhead in his hand. Joe picked it up between his thumb and forefinger and felt the fine point draw a droplet of blood from his flesh.

"See those semi-circular designs along the edges?"

Joe nodded. Each one seemed perfectly formed, coming to the end to taper into a pinpoint.

Pete told him, "With flint, the arrowhead makers heated the stone, touched it with a drop of water and a chip flaked off. It took a long time to make a proper head, carved drop by drop to fit onto a shaft. That's why those guys were big wheels in the village. Whoever did that one was a real master. Here, let me have that back."

Joe handed him the arrowhead, Pete laid it on the ground, took a fist-sized rock from the sand and brought it crashing down on the crystal. Nothing happened. He did it twice more, then handed the arrowhead back to Joe.

Not even scratched.

"It looks like glass. But the ancients didn't make glass." Pete looked at him. "There is an old song in the village. The old men remember it. They sing about the clear rock all the tribes danced around, the one that sang and danced with them and threw many sparks into the sky. When they got near it, the old ones could have babies once again and the young ones would get twice as strong."

"What happened to this rock?"

"They say…one day the sun disappeared behind the moon. When the sun came back again the rock was gone."

"That sounds like a fable, pal."

"It's what the old men tell."

"And you can speak the language?"

"So can my sister. She's college-educated too." After a few seconds he asked, "You kidding me about giving me that arrowhead?"

Joe said, "Nope, it's yours."

"Suppose I sell it for a million dollars?"

"Good for you."

Very carefully Pete took out a worn red handkerchief and wrapped the arrowhead in it, then just as carefully, put it in a shirt pocket and buttoned the flap.

Joe said, "If that thing *is* radiating at all, you're a dead man, pal."

Pete scowled a moment, then said, "How come you don't care none about all that money?"

"Nothing I need, Geronimo."

"You need to get your airplane fixed."

"That'll come," Joe said. He grinned broadly and added, "If nobody steals it."

"Steal it? Hell, man, those bozos from our village would probably think it was a pterodactyl and have bad dreams for a year."

"Suppose they had college educations too?"

"Flyboy, you're on the poor edge of society here. Alcohol addiction is at an all-time high, malnutrition is common, more people are dying than are being born…hell, who can qualify for college anyway?"

"You did, buddy."

"And the whole tribe thinks I'm some kind of nut."

"I don't believe that."

"Why not?" He let out a short laugh. "My horse ran away from me and I picked up a white-eyes flyboy in the middle of the desert."

"And you found a priceless artifact."

"Not me…you."

"Man, you were the guide. You knew what it was. That thing is your baby."

Pete turned and looked at Joe, his eyes boring into him. He finally said, "You're speaking straight, aren't you?"

Joe nodded.

"You know, Joe…right now, if I had a knife and you had one, too, and these were the old days, we'd slash our hands, draw blood and shake."

"The old Indian blood brother oath?" Pete nodded. "Can't we just shake hands without all the gore?"

Pete held out his right hand and Joe took it.

Nobody was there, but a great audience was watching. It was a solemn group that made no noise, whose appreciation was silent acknowledgement and for a moment Joe's face had a strange look.

Joe stared down at his hand, then half-hid it behind his back.

"You and me, flyboy," Pete said. "We're brothers now."

"Suppose I don't like that?"

"Too bad," Pete said. "Now, let's get ourselves some dinner while there's still light."

Joe ate his first snake when Pete caught and killed a rattler. Stretched out it was six feet long and thick around as a man's calf. Pete skinned it, offered the scaly pelt to Joe who refused it. The meat was almost snow white and the carcass could have fed a half dozen, but Pete selected the finest portions, cooked them slowly away from the flames and, when they were finished, held out a good-sized chunk of rattlesnake meat on a stick. Joe fingered the meat off the wooden rod, bit into it without any reluctance at all.

"You like that?"

Joe shrugged. "Hell, man, I never even had a bad meal in the Air Force."

"Damn," Pete told him. "You might make a good Indian after all."

CHAPTER 4

Joe saw the contrails, long streaks of artificial clouds generated by the airliners crossing the country at thirty-some thousand feet. The almost invisible dot ahead of them was winged tonnage tearing through the sky at six hundred miles an hour, the distance too far even to hear the rumble of the great jet engines.

After squinting at the sky a few seconds, Pete said, "How do they breathe up there?"

"It's pressurized. Air gets fed to them like we get it down here."

"Yeah, I figured that, but suppose it stops."

"Then the oxygen masks drop down from the overhead and you do like the instructions told you to. That is, if you were listening before takeoff."

But Pete was insistent. "Suppose something happens then?"

"Pal, hold your tongue."

The glance that Pete threw at him made Joe say, "You go on oxygen above ten thousand feet. That's FAA rules. Some people can fly all day at twenty thousand without getting anoxia and passing out, but that's only a few."

"Where do you stand, flyboy?"

Joe let out a little grin. "I hate to tell you this, but the first time I went through the altitude chamber back in the old AAF days, I stayed at thirty thousand for a full four minutes before the instructor slapped the mask on my face. I was talking like a drunk, and my handwriting kind of went off the page, but I was still operating."

"So why the mask then?"

"Because real fast I could go blooie and he didn't want me to have to be carried out of that chamber."

"You think I could do that?"

"Don't try it. Stay on your horse."

"Hell, he won't let me ride him. I must be a lousy Indian."

"Nah…you're just a lousy rider, Pete."

"You didn't do so hot with your ride."

"I got it down, didn't I?"

"You know what's wrong with it?"

"Not yet, but I'll think about it."

"Maybe you'd better ask my sister. Her degree's in engineering."

A low whistle came from Joe's lips. "Aeronautical?"

Pete shook his head. "Automotive. She can fix tractors and that kind of stuff. Saw her take a generator apart and fix it for Uncle Sho-Sho once. He woulda froze that winter without it."

Overhead another set of contrails left their imprint on the big blue, this time going in the other direction. Pete checked his wristwatch and said, "Those are the Las Vegas flights. Right on time."

"How do you know that?"

"They go by every day at this time. See the direction? Right out of Vegas, those. Just like arrows. We turn here."

Joe looked at the side path Pete was steering him to. "Why? I thought we were going toward the Superstitions."

"Right. We *were*. We turn here and head for my hogan. My sister will be real glad to see you."

When they made the turn Pete's horse let out a whinny and his ears pricked up. The horse took a couple of jumpy steps, stared at the two walkers to make sure they weren't going to change their minds, then took up a place beside them. Up ahead there was a small rise on the horizon that was either a big rock or a small hill and they made that their aiming point. Once, Joe glanced behind them and their tracks in the sand formed a perfectly straight line. Halfway to their marker Joe remarked, "If we weren't going there, why'd you give me all that bull about the Superstitions?"

Without turning his head, Pete answered, "To keep your mind cooking, White-eyes. You city types need to have points of destination or you fall apart. Me good guide. Me show you mountain to look at. White-eyes stay happy. Eat snake."

The object on the horizon Joe thought to be a rock or a hill turned out to be the weathered remnants of an old, broken wagon. Sand had covered most of it, leaving the front end and part of the seat projecting upward.

"Prospectors," Pete muttered. "They probably ate their horse and walked the rest of the way. Lot of them did that."

"You never saw it before? I thought you knew this area."

Pete informed him, "One big wind will uncover one thing and blanket something else. Nothing stays the same out here."

"So how do you navigate, pal?"

This time Pete gave him a big grin. "By airplanes, brother. We watch the tracks they leave in the sky. Always the same. Always on time. At least, most of the time."

Joe noticed the drone of the twin-engine plane before his buddy became aware of it. When it got closer he said, "Twin-engine Aztec. A private job."

With a quick look upward, Pete nodded. "It's going into my territory. They make a trip twice a month. Last time they stayed a full week before they pulled out."

"You have an airstrip?"

Pete gave a small shrug. "Just a runway the tribal police

scraped out the time the Governor flew in. The state even bought us one of those wind socks and found a metal shed so they could paint the name of the field on it."

"Man, I never saw any field mentioned on my charts."

Once more, Pete squinted at him and nodded. "Not a name, really. Just a number, a big, white 21. You can hardly see it now. The state even had a radio installed there. And don't ask me why. Nobody except Cholly Blue Sky knows how to use it. He used to have one like it in his truck that he took out of a wrecked B-25 that had to land out near the mountains. Ran out of gas, that one did." He paused and his eyes met Joe's. "You know what a B-25 is?"

"Sure," Joe answered him. "I got about ten hours in one of those." For a moment he paused, his mind ranging over the past few days. Finally he said, "Tonto...what are those guys doing out here?"

"The ones in the plane, Lone Ranger?"

Joe nodded.

"They buy our fossils."

"Bull. The only fossils you have out here will be bleached-out horse bones. Maybe an ox." He knew Pete was going to throw it in, so he added, "...and an old cowboy or two."

"Come on, Joe, you even found one yourself. That arrow-head—"

"Made a great story," Joe finished for him. "You even bashed it with a rock that probably was a piece of sandstone that wouldn't rip toilet paper."

The hurt look on Pete's face didn't last long and Joe could see him trying to formulate an answer. Then Pete said, "I just figured you white-eyes liked to hear wild stories from us native types."

"We do, pal, so tell me what kind of fossils you were really looking for in the desolate sands of your state."

Sequoia Pete ran his fingers through his hair and made another eloquent shrug. "The income-generating kind, flyboy."

A small smile started at the corners of Joe's mouth. "Damn. You already hinted at it, didn't you? It's all tied up with that story about the gold reserves in the Superstitions, right?"

Pete didn't answer him.

"A lot of guys have scrabbled around in those hills for generations, haven't they? And now it's starting all over again. Well, pal, if it attracts money to your encampment I can't blame you a bit for encouraging it, but you sure are going far out to advertise it, aren't you?"

"Flyboy, our economy is floundering. Y'know what I mean? The Native American is only something on the History Channel. You see the memorial at Wounded Knee. Sometimes one of us shows up in a battered pickup truck or doing a ceremonial dance for tourists, but you never see what alcohol has done. You never see one of us in a Cadillac convertible. You hardly ever hear of an Indian sports figure except Jim Thorpe, or one of us up there in Congress. Hell, man, you even give us a name from a place none of us have ever been to. India. Man, I had curried rice once and didn't like it at all."

"So?"

"We figured we had it made for a time. The government thought we had a uranium deposit on our land. Turned out to be a trace of something not worth fooling with." Pete paused reflectively. Then mused, "Probably the best thing for us. The government would have run us off our land again."

Joe disagreed. "They couldn't do that, pal. Those days are gone."

"Who do you think you're kidding? The government can do anything it wants to."

"Tell me about the gold."

"It wasn't bullion."

"Dust?"

"Not even nuggets."

"Then what's it all about?"

"Feet. Little feet."

Joe looked at him in bewilderment.

"One of the kids found them out in the desert—about two inches long and had broken off the legs. The boy thought they had come from a doll and gave them to his sister. When papa bear heard the story, he took them down to the trading post and sure enough, it was gold all right."

Joe asked, "Where are the feet now?"

"Come on, buddy, old papa bear was a whiskey Indian. He traded them in for a few quarts of rotgut and didn't come home for a week. The old man at the trading post showed 'em to a tourist one time and sold them on the spot. A month later a guy showed up who said he was from some state college and wanted to know where they were found."

"Somebody tell him?" Joe asked.

"Nah. Nobody knew. The kid had even forgotten. He just waved at the desert and said it was someplace out there."

Deliberately, Joe let a full minute go by before he said, "Then somebody found something else, didn't they?"

Pete nodded. "It was another kid. He found a shiny gold head with feathers on it. Maybe the size of a quarter. Broken off the rest of the upper body."

"I hope it didn't get turned in for some booze."

Pete said, "This one smart Indian boy, this one. He took it to the right places. He had the top guys at the university examine it and they all finally agreed on what it was."

Joe just waited. He knew Pete was holding back the punch line to irritate him, but he played the game.

After a long silence, Pete said, "It was Aztec gold, flyboy."

"Their campgrounds were pretty far south, Man-Who-Can't-Ride-Horse," Joe said. "What would they be doing up here?"

"They were being chased."

"Posse?"

"Army, White-eyes. Spaniards in metal armor. Carrying old funnel-nosed guns loaded with black powder and projectiles. Made big noise. Killed people far off. You know?"

"Yeah, I know."

"The story is, those Aztecs knew the Spaniards were after their images, gathered them up and took off northward. By the time the Spaniards got wise to what happened, the Aztecs had a good lead on them." He shook his head. "Hell, those statues didn't have a monetary value to them. They were part of their religion. They signified something else, something more important. Not money."

It was a story Joe had heard before but never paid much attention to. Gold was a great metal to play with—soft and could be carved into articles of jewelry, or melted and cast into larger shapes. Freely available in some locations, and rare in others and, where the Aztecs lived, must have been plentiful enough to use in slingshots.

"They probably transported it in leather bags," Pete said. "No traces of wagons or travois poles ever showed up. No bones of pack animals, though between scavengers and sand erosion, bones wouldn't have lasted this long."

"So the feet and that head probably just broke off and fell through a hole in one of those bags."

Pete nodded. "Something like that."

"Where were they going then?"

Pete turned his head and looked at the mountainous ridge in the distance. "There," he said.

"How do you know?"

"Because there are other stories nobody paid attention to. Stuff like chunks of weathered gold being picked up out there. A long time ago a tribal elder had a gold plate with a feathered bird carved on it. I saw that. Don't ask me where it is now."

"There's a story you haven't talked about so far, isn't there?"

"Man," Pete exclaimed, "you got a mind like a cop."

"So tell me the story."

"Sure. Whenever there was a find, it always came from a place in a straight line from south of here right up to the Superstitions. Hell, flyboy, there was no place to hide anything between their home grounds and the mountains anyway."

"Nice story."

"Brings tourists around."

"Where do you come in?"

"Me native guide."

"Ever find anything?"

Pete bobbed his head. "Tourists believe anything. We salt the sand with arrowheads, carve wooden heads and let them weather out, throw in a clay pot or two and you can satisfy any city dweller."

"Pete…what were you doing up on that rise where I met you?"

"Heck, man, I told you…"

"Your horse was way ahead of you. Where were you coming from?"

"Come on, Joe, I was fossil hunting. I already said…"

"No tools, no sacks to carry anything in?"

"What tools do you need out there? The wind does all the work. If there is anything at all it sticks up like, like…well, the toe on your foot. And fossils don't come very big, pal. This isn't like dinosaur valley where Tyrannosaurus Rex roamed around."

"Pete…"

"I was looking for Miner Moe. He's a prospector."

"Miner Moe," Joe repeated. "Great moniker."

"He's about eighty-five and lives on the desert. Someplace he has a dugout, though I've never seen it. He finds fossils, I trade for them and that's all there is to it."

"Indians are lousy liars," Joe said.

"I'm not from India," Pete reminded him.

"I thought we were blood brothers."

"…Old Miner Moe has picked up some pretty odd-looking fossils, if you want to call them that. He had a golden feather that had been broken off from something else and the handle of a vase. Solid gold, that was, weighed maybe three pounds."

A small whistle came from Joe's pursed lips. "You trade him for that stuff?"

"He just showed it to me. We're kinda good old friends, y'know?"

"You ever tell anybody about it?"

"Just you. I don't have any other blood brothers."

"Think he did?"

A furrow highlighted Pete's forehead. "No. Moe has been on the sand too long. He knows who he can trust."

"He trusts you then?"

"Sure."

"Why?"

"While back, I found him unconscious out near a water hole. Somebody had tried to kill him. They tore open his bag, ripped up his clothes, but they didn't get anything at all. Stole his tobacco pouch, is all. I carried him on my back to my hogan where my sister took care of him for two weeks until he was well enough to get back on the sand by himself."

"You still haven't answered my first question."

Very patiently, Sequoia Pete said, "I was on that hill because my damn cayuse threw me and wouldn't let me get near him. Now, you know that."

"What about Miner Moe?"

"Twenty miles east I found where he had camped out. I couldn't tell how long ago it had been. It was on a rock outcropping. Moe's a moccasin wearer and hardly leaves tracks. There were none that I could follow."

"You knew where to look for him."

"Sure. He knew there were people from the south running away from something and they would take a hard ground path if they could. Stretches of that trail still show up when the desert wind comes in from the right angle."

"Does it do that often?"

"No." He thought for a moment, then added, "Maybe every ten years or so."

"Maybe?"

"Moe said the last one he remembered was when he was still young."

"Pete…do you remember any times like that?"

Another pause for thought, then: "When I was in college. Uncle Fast Turkey said it had happened. It didn't mean much to me then."

"So what did you want from Miner Moe?"

"To tell him to keep away from the rez, man. Those bozos who fly in here are after more than old clay pots and arrowheads. I've seen white-eyes with gold fever before and they sure had it when they saw what little trinkets the tribal elders had."

"Like the little feet?"

"Right on, flyboy."

"That's not much to get excited about."

"Remember Sutter's Mill? It brought half the population of the east out here."

Joe nodded. "This isn't about digging up natural gold. All you have are some little bitty artifacts that originate in some foreign country and aren't in heavy supply to start with. So what are you sweating about?"

"The last time those white guys flew in here they had a new face with them. An older guy, like mid-fifties maybe. About your age."

Joe grimaced.

"Well-dressed. Big education. He had to think hard to use little words. He was all smiles and asked a lot of strange questions hardly anybody could answer."

"Pete, old buddy, could *you* have answered them?"

"Sure, but he never asked me. Hell, I wouldn't have given him the right time of day, either. The slob was a professor who specialized in 'ancient cultures of the Americas.'"

"How'd you know that?"

"Because he lectured twice at State University when I was a senior. A real Aztec lover, that guy. On his watch chain he dangled a tooth from some warrior who had been dead for centuries."

"Nice guy," Joe said.

"He was a tony civilian, that one. Didn't have much to do with anybody who wasn't a top dog. Never hung around with any of the other instructors and was completely turned off by the undergrads. How the hell he got mixed up with the tourist trade guys I'll never know."

"But he knew about those little artifacts somehow, didn't he?"

"So could anybody else. Hell, they were on display at the tourist trade store for a month. A reporter from some Arizona weekly did a piece on them."

"Who has them now, Pete?

"The Whistler. He owns the trade store."

"He whistles?"

"No. He just has a lousy set of false teeth and when he talks it whistles. No tunes."

For a full minute the two men sat quietly, saying nothing. Joe was staring at the horizon and nodding to himself. Finally, Pete said, "You're thinking pretty heavy, White-eyes. Want to talk about it?"

Joe's head bobbed slightly. "Everything's happening at once, isn't it? I come in on a power-off landing; you lose a horse in the desert, and all this after little gold feet get found in the sand. You get a creepy old professor out here parleying with tourist trade runners and Miner Moe flitting around like a ghost."

"You left out the best part."

"What, finding your magic arrowhead?"

"No," Joe told him. "Watching you eat snake."

"Wish I'd had a beer to go with it."

"You white-eyes are all nuts." Joe got up from his crouch and stretched. "Let's go to my hogan. Sis should have my Harley fixed by now."

After two hours of steady plodding in loose sand, Pete held up his hand, checked his watch and slow scanned the skies for a good two minutes. He finally saw what he was looking for and pointed it out to Joe. It was a faint contrail coming out of the west toward them, a finger-like man-made cloud that followed the dot of a commercial airliner ahead of it.

"He's ten minutes overdue," Pete growled.

"So?"

"Right now we make a forty-five degree turn to the left. I have to compensate for the delay in that plane's schedule. Damn, I wish the FAA would get on their controllers' necks.

Screwing up the timetables can get a lot of us natives lost out here."

"You're kidding."

"The hell I am," Pete told him. "You see me with a compass?"

"Then how do you figure out a forty-five degree left turn?"

"Native intuition, that's how." Pete waved his finger toward the rise of sand in the distance. "We go thataway."

Up ahead the horse was on a straight-line course as though he had heard every word. Joe let a small grin twist at the corners of his mouth. "You're just following that daggone cayuse, partner. He's got no compass either."

"White-eyes, he's got a nose. There's a mess of bagged oats behind my hogan."

"And your sister will have supper on the table too, I suppose."

"Certainly. She sees us on the horizon and she'll slip a couple more TV dinners in the microwave."

CHAPTER 5

She was waiting for them. She stood there motionless, doused in sunlight, little flashes of brilliance sparkling from beadwork in her leather vest. Her hair was a scintillating black that framed skin coloring that was a beautiful, distinctive hue, a natural glow no temporary suntan could possibly imitate. Her fringed dress was short so that the soft musculature of her thighs and calves made Joe catch his breath in admiration.

"Go ahead and whistle," Pete suggested quietly.

Joe just breathed hard. She slowly turned her head toward the sun and in profile Joe saw a perfect shape he could imagine seeing on an ancient coin. Then she turned back to watch them approach.

"Damn," Joe said.

"She does that to all the guys," Pete said. "Works them up at a distance then drops them dead when they get close. Look what's in her hand."

It was hard for Joe to focus on the object, but he saw what it was. She was holding a foot long open-end wrench. She had on a tool belt that had a couple other tools snapped on it.

"Good woman," Pete said. "Work hard. Fix brother's Harley. Got pot on stove cooking grub. Company no problem."

Fifty feet away Joe knew that no movie actress could come near her for sheer beauty. There was no makeup, but those quietly flashing eyes didn't need any. Her lips were full with a natural dampness, startling red against her darker flesh. He didn't let his eyes roam over her. He didn't have to. He knew that whatever he saw would be the fullness of womanhood.

Pete said, "This is my sister, Running Fox." He waved in Joe's direction. "This my friend…no, my—" and he said something in his native tongue that made his sister's eyes jump to his with a new expression "—whose name is Joe Gillian. I found him in the desert. He landed his airplane way out there."

Running Fox simply said, "Why?"

"It broke," Joe muttered, not able to think of anything else to tell her.

"Oh," Running Fox smiled. Her whole face lit up.

"I couldn't fix it," Joe added. "Hell, I don't even know what broke."

"You look?"

"No. Your brother found me first."

"He was drinking a beer," Pete told her.

"In the desert?"

"Best place in the world to have a cold beer, Sis." He added, "He split a can with me."

Running Fox's glance said that gave him an extra brownie point at the most.

"I nailed a rattler and cooked it," Pete mentioned casually. "He ate half."

"Big rattler?"

"Six, eight pounds maybe. We ate about a pound and a half apiece."

This time Running Fox looked directly at Joe, a new light in her eyes. "Mr. Joe Gillian, did you like that snake?"

"Not bad, but it coulda used a little seasoning."

"Well, come on in and get some real seasoned grub. We have beans, very hot. Squash, very hot. Animal stew, very hot."

"What kind of animal?" Pete demanded.

"Don't ask," she said. "And we have some very, very hot sauce."

She smiled, then turned with a swirl that made the hem of

her skirt whip up the sides of her legs and when she walked toward the open door of the hogan, Joe forced himself to keep his eyes on the ground. All he could think of was that here he was, a bachelor, head of his own business, plenty of unspent cash even after buying the plane, not so young anymore maybe but in damn good condition for a man his age, and a target for every enterprising unwed—and sometimes wed—doll who laid eyes on him.

And here he was out on the sand of nowhere with not even a change of socks or a toothbrush, dirtied up like a citified street urchin who played in a garbage dump, and suddenly feeling his sap rising because of an Indian princess-type with a *Playboy*-style shape, a college education, and a toolbelt she wore around her waist.

All Joe could say was, "Damn."

The sun had set by the time Joe felt the fire in his stomach lessening. He could handle the very hot beans and the very hot squash, the very hot animal stew, but it was the very, *very* hot sauce that took the starch out of him. The fire was diminishing, but something was happening with his insides and when he had finally figured out where the outhouse was and carefully plotted a course to that sanctuary, he squirmed in the seat of the visitor's Lazyboy, keeping the back upright and the footstool down so when the time came for him to bail out, he could hit the deck in record time. If Pete had been the only one there, he wouldn't have had to be so meticulous, but having the princess watching every move he made with some kind of a knowing smile on her lips, he had to be very, very careful. Like with very, very hot sauce.

He had a dry sweat on his forehead, hot like the summer sun, but with no cooling moisture. Dry sweat. It was a paradox.

He couldn't even pay attention to what Pete was talking about as he embellished every minute of their meeting. The blood brother routine made Running Fox look at him with strange eyes, then Pete showed his ace card. He reached into his pocket and palmed the clear crystal arrowhead, holding it out for his sister to see.

She didn't have to be told what it was. Arrowheads were like pebbles in the sand to her. But this wasn't an ordinary arrowhead and her rapt attention to the object in her brother's hand made the muscles in her face go tight and her eyes took on an odd expression. She didn't touch it. For a full minute, she simply looked at it. Then she said to Pete, "You found it?"

"No." He nodded toward Joe. "He did."

"Then it's his."

Her brother shook his head. "He gave it to me."

"Did he know what it was?"

"Sure. I told him. He didn't want it and said it was all mine."

She turned to Joe for confirmation. "This is all true?"

"Absolutely."

"You know what it's worth?"

"Pete told me. I don't want it."

"You could sell it and buy anything you want."

"I got everything I want," Joe told her, then his expression went soft and he added, "I think."

Pete said, "He wants his airplane fixed."

With a quizzical expression, Running Fox asked, "Is that all?"

Joe's stomach was talking to him now. That was a very loaded question and when he took in the face of the beautiful Indian princess, he wanted to say a million things to her, but nothing proper would come out of his mouth. He let his mind jump to old 819 stranded up there in the hills, squatting like a tired old bird, knowing that one day he'd come back and take care of matters.

He said, "I'll take care of the plane. No trouble. You guys just keep your arrowhead."

"You wouldn't miss a few million dollars, Mr. Gillian?"

"No."

"You very rich, Mr. Gillian?"

"All my bills are paid. I own a business. I don't have any wants." When he looked into Running Fox's eyes, he knew that last was a lie.

And so did she, because she smiled back with a smile that was hers alone.

Running Fox folded the arrowhead in a small cloth, and tucked it away in a pocket. "We can get an expert opinion on that tomorrow."

The monster rolling around Joe's insides suddenly said it was time to go and he pulled the chocks out from under his wheels with a quick yank and somehow or other he made a proper-type exit to the grand throne of pleasuresome relief and gave up the very, *very* hot sauce that spiced the just plain very hot meal, and when all naturalness returned to him, he washed his hands and went back to the main room in Joe's hogan.

The night sky was blistered with stars that beamed with such intensity that they didn't seem real. There was no artificial glow from any nearby city to diminish their brilliance and if you watched carefully you could even see them move against the clothes-drying poles in the yard. They were almost like live things, yet so absolutely exact in their movements that the best chronographs ever made used them as timing ideals, but never could reach their perfection.

Pete came out of the hogan and handed Joe his freshly laundered clothes. "My sister said you'd better hit the trade store tomorrow. My duds won't fit you and you haven't got the right configuration for buckskin."

"I got four full changes up in my airplane," Joe said. "When do you think we'll get back there?"

"Well, there's only one part I need for the Harley and I can get that on the rez when we go in. Maybe the day after tomorrow?"

Joe turned and looked at his friend. The starlight made his expression stand out very plainly.

Pete let out a short chuckle. "Boy, she really got to you in a hurry, didn't she?"

"What?"

"Old White-eyes is suddenly in love. Right?" Sequoia Pete's teeth shone in the moonlight.

"You know," Joe muttered, "you Indians certainly have a very sophisticated attitude."

"We college graduates, flyboy. Not rez schooled…State College with real professors and a chemistry lab. We even had a Bunsen burner."

"What, no Petri dishes?"

"Sure, we had two of them. One broke and we had to use the plastic fruit cup container from somebody's lunch."

"If I was in love with your sister, you'd be carrying an axe."

"You check my belt in the back?"

Joe looked at his watch, the numerals a faint green in the darkness. "We going to sleep on the ground again tonight, pal?"

"Hey, you're company, man. Sis hung you a hammock out back right next to mine. I can't stay in my own room 'cause I have to guard you."

Indignantly, Joe demanded, "From what? You got mosquitoes?"

"Not this time of the year, but a lot of curious animals prowl around looking for strange white-eyes to chew on."

"Knock it off, Pete, I'm no schoolboy."

"So let your foot hang over the side tonight. You'll find out."

"And the natives are out of the loop, right? They get a free ride?"

"For sure, man."

Joe muttered something, got up from his rock and climbed into his shorts. When he tossed Pete his old blanket, he said, "Your sister's very, very hot sauce is doing things to me again. Where is it?"

With a forefinger, Pete pointed to the north where the corner of the hogan blanked out the stars.

They took the Ford pickup out of the barn at dawn. It was six years old but the engine hummed to a tune that only a top mechanic could play. It had a big eight-cylinder power plant that drove a four-by-four train with all the goodies the dealership could put on it. Some were expensive extras like the GPS system that could plot your present position in the world right down to the inches of space your feet occupied. Discreetly built in under the dash was a VHF radio. Joe nudged Pete who sat in the middle and said, "That VHF is illegal, pal."

"Tell me about it."

"It's for marine use."

"I told you, all this used to be part of an inland ocean."

"Who owns the truck?"

Without taking her eyes off the road, Joe's sister said, "It's mine. I paid for it in cash. All the taxes have been tendered."

"This baby must have cost twenty-five grand!" Joe said.

"More," she told him calmly, "and if you're wondering about illegalities, there's an AK-47 rifle under the seat with five hundred rounds of ammo and two G.I. boxes of old-fashioned hand grenades from WWII beneath the tarp in the truck."

Joe felt a damp sweat come over him.

The beautiful Indian princess added, "And to keep you from running to the authorities to turn us in, remember that now you are a co-conspirator or an accessory. Take your pick."

Only Joe's eyes moved to take in his companions. Neither one was smiling at all. Softly, he said, "You're just kidding, aren't you?"

Ten seconds passed before Pete let the grin show. "As the British say, just pulling your leg, old man."

Even Running Fox let out a chuckle and the tip of her tongue flashed wetly across her lips.

Joe felt better now. "Who's on the other end of the VHF?"

"About a dozen others. All good guys, y'know? They all also got regular CB so we can stay in touch if the hills don't get in the way."

"They have Global Positioning, too?"

Running Fox swerved around a rattler sunning in a dirt tire track and said, "Just us, city boy. All our red brothers think it's stupid having an instrument to tell you where you are."

"Stupid?"

"Of course. Everybody has to be someplace and everybody is right where they are wherever it is. Like us. We don't have to look at the GPS to know where we are."

"Why not?" Joe quizzed.

"Because we're right here, even when we're moving."

Joe wasn't about to argue with that bit of Indian wisdom. "Where's your antenna?"

"Topside. It's got a little tribal flag attached to it. Looks like an ornament."

"So we're riding in a 'Q' ship right?"

"Right you are, Man-From-The-Clouds. A real 'Q' ship, a plain old freighter plowing along the ocean swells and when the enemy sub sees her, he doesn't want to waste an expensive torpedo on her so he surfaces to blow her away with the deck gun. And when all the crew is out of the sub to watch the fun, *BAM!* The 'Q' ship drops the phony disguise around *her* big gun and that baby lets the first round go and tears the sub apart. Just to make sure, she fires a couple more eight-inch armor-piercing explosives at the waterline, then closes up shop and goes looking for another sucker."

Joe poked his forefinger into Pete's arm. "She a real girl?"

"You'd better believe it, bluecoat. Incidentally, she's a history buff."

"I suppose she studied karate, too," Joe whispered.

"Black belt," Pete whispered back.

Ahead, the tire tracks made a long sweeping turn to the south, avoiding a wide area of rock outcroppings that came up out of the sand like teeth, rows of them forming nasty-looking semicircles, like a family of sharks looking at survivors in a leaky lifeboat.

Before he could ask, Pete said, "Monster Teeth Hills. Beneath all those vicious incisors is the silent monster. He is quiet. He never moves."

"What does he do?"

"He just kills, paleface."

"How do you know?"

"Because nobody who ever went in there ever came back."

"Who do you know who went in?"

"We can't mention their names or we get it too."

"Like it's taboo."

"Joe, you're getting more Indian every day."

Leaning over, Joe hissed in Pete's ear, "Your sister taboo?"

Pete's eyes widened and out of the corner of his mouth he mumbled, "Taboo? Taboo is sissy stuff. That female is deadly!"

"One more question." This time Joe brought his voice up. "This here pickup runs into big bucks. Where do you get the money for all of this?"

"Fossils," Pete said seriously. "Artifacts. Some are even legal.

For eight years this area has come up with some prime pieces of history."

"History isn't a big money-maker, Pete. I fly a piece of ancient history and it costs me a bundle to get it off the ground."

"Too bad yours isn't made of yellow metal." He smiled gently. "Like those little feet."

Joe's smile was just as gentle and he said, "Old buddy, don't try to give me any snow job. If there were any gold deposits under this sand, news of the find would hit the computers in the same hour and you'd have the prospectors pouring in the way they did at Sutter's Mill. This time they'd come with all the new technology, dump your sorry cans out of the rez so fast your eyes would click together."

"You're the one who told me the government couldn't run us off our land again!"

"Who said anything about the government? I'm talking about private enterprise. And those guys can do anything they want."

For a second Pete's eyes clouded.

Joe said, "You still got gold thoughts in your head, haven't you?"

Behind the wheel of the truck Joe saw a small twitch at the corner of Running Fox's mouth. Even a sidewise glance at her made his stomach feel as if someone had punched him there.

In front of the truck the terrain turned into soft rolling hills. Seemingly buried into one was another hogan built of red clay bricks and strengthened with poles that stuck out a good two feet. Off each one hung strings of edibles and beside the door, drying in the sunlight, were two hides of animals foreign to Joe. Past the hogan was a corral where a pair of horses were tethered with a half dozen goats lying in the shade of the planking that made up the corral.

Joe pointed at the chimney. "No smoke coming out. Nobody home?"

Pete nodded. "Sure. He's got a generator in back. Runs an electric stove and refrigerator."

"You know him?"

"Uh-huh. He's my cousin, like sixth or seventh. Same tribe."

The dirt road had been rising steadily for a good five minutes. Then, when they had suddenly reached the apex, it was as though the whole world had been exposed. From horizon to horizon the hills had flattened out and in one glance you could see a panoramic view of a totally different way of life.

Ahead in the distance the buildings of the reservation complex stood out in the clear air, distant, yet wholly visible. Some were of cinder block, others of adobe, and here and there were old log structures standing firm in their midst, remnants of another age, still sturdy, vibrant tradition flaunting itself in the face of modern civilization.

On the near side of the area Joe could see the activity that was enclosed by a wire fence. A small oval encompassed a raked-out four-acre area and modest stands of boxes and barrels made a seating place for spectators. Some refreshment stands were half erected and smoke had already started to curl up from slow-burning fires at the perimeter of the grounds.

"What's happening?" Joe asked.

Running Fox jerked the wheel, missed a rut in the road and said, "Big feast day. Everybody shows up."

Joe pointed out the window. A mile away the small dot of a building sat alongside a carefully graded runway that seemed to be about a hundred feet wide and half a mile long. He squinted, and saw the outline of a windsock dangling from a pole on the south side of the small building.

Before he could ask, Pete told him, "That's our airport, the one I told you about."

"A sand runway?"

"Nope," he said. "No sand. That's packed hard stuff. Once an old C-47 came in there. Some government plane. No problem. Today a few more will be in."

"Indians?"

"Come on, Joe, we don't own airplanes."

"Then who?"

"Guys looking for more little feet," Pete said.

"Come on."

Very seriously, Pete said, "They'll be looking for Miner Moe."

"Why?"

"Word got around old Moe has latched onto something new."

"Damn."

"Maybe I'd better tell you something else, too," Pete said.

"Oh?"

"Somebody may have spotted you here last night. If so, word's gone around—talk travels fast in these parts. Some on the rez may already know where you spent the night. That includes a young man known around here as Big Arms…who has big eyes for my sister."

Behind the wheel, Running Fox looked grim.

"He's willing to fight for her," Pete said.

A cold sweat seemed to form on Joe's chest. He felt it run down into his beltline, then the sweat started under his arms and he knew the sun wasn't up that far or shining that hot. "Fight who?"

"*You*, man from the skies," Running Fox said. She was looking straight ahead, very serious. "He's going to think he's got a rival now."

"Word goes 'round about your staying with us," Pete said, "people will draw their own conclusions."

Joe leaned back and let out a laugh. "Like I'm a threat to

him. I'm probably twice his age. Anyway, nobody knows me. Nobody knows anything about me. Hell, I haven't even met anybody except you two."

"They call him Big Arms for a reason," Running Fox said softly. "He picks up train wheels. He plays with tree trunks. Sometimes he lifts cars right off the ground."

"A whole car?" Joe asked.

"Only from the front or back bumper," Pete explained. "He can't get his arms around the whole thing."

"Good for him," Joe said. "He must be some bruiser."

Running Fox and Pete nodded together.

"And how am I supposed to fight him?" Joe asked.

Something in Pete's tone of voice made Joe's blood run cold. "You better find a way, White-eyes."

The sweat around Joe's waist got even colder.

CHAPTER 6

With some shopping for essentials out of the way, along with plenty of curious looks cast in Joe's direction, they headed to the one place Running Fox said they could get the parts they needed. A blacksmith shop and horse stalls were on one side of the building and on the other a very carefully disguised machine shop. The walls were lined with shelves stacked with parts and four stripped trail bikes leaned up against a workbench waiting to be repaired.

Willie Joe was a grizzled old guy with a full head of coal black hair and eyes to match. When Pete introduced him, the handshake said that Willie still had a lot of years in him.

"What do I call you?" Willie Joe said. "Can't have two Joes around here."

Pete said, "Call him White-eyes, Willie. He's in our playground now. You know he ate a snake?"

Willie Joe let a little laugh rumble out of his chest. "Damn," he said, "you're not one of Custer's boys after all, are you?"

"You guys sure hold a grudge," Joe said.

Willie asked, "How do you like my works, Joe?"

"Neat, but why hide it?"

"We don't want the tourists to get wise. They come in here looking for old range culture...tom-toms, war whoops, big feather headdresses, all that kind of stuff. They don't like to see us modernize."

"I hope you're modernized enough to have a phone in here." He'd left his cell back on the plane.

"Sure. In the office. This got to be a long-distance call, so I hope you got a credit card."

"No sweat."

Willie indicated the plywood-sided office in the back corner. Joe told him thanks and walked toward it, tugging at his wallet in his pants pocket. He got his telephone charge card out, dialed the number of his home base, and got old Davie on the phone.

The dispatcher was gruffly pleased to know that Joe was alive and 819 was intact and soon to be repaired. Joe had called just in time to scrub search parties that were scheduled to leave from four different airports to look for his sorry remains somewhere along the prescribed cross-country flight course.

"When you coming back?" the old dispatcher demanded.

"As fast as I can get out of this sand trap," Joe told him and hung up. Going back to the front of the garage, Joe spotted some framed black-and-white eight-by-ten photographs featuring a good-looking young guy in near-hippie clothes, his arms full of books, and a large brick building in the background. Another was of the same guy, arms outstretched to pick a football out of the air, surrounded by the concrete structure of a stadium.

"You a college man too, Willie?" Joe asked cautiously.

Willie snorted. "Of course, White-eyes. Got a degree in geology, then took a year at Colorado School of Mines, and don't ask what I'm doing here. This place is a cash cow. Any of the red brethren, they come here from miles around. Heck, I get trade from five hundred miles away."

"Motorcycles?"

"Sure. They're great things in this open country. If a guy owns one, then he's got the wherewithal to fix it."

"'Wherewithal'?"

"I took courses in English, too. The Prof was a German. We finally made a melting pot out of this country."

Running Fox came in from a back room, her arms heavy with parts boxes. She looked at Willie and raised her eyebrows. "He giving you the local history, Joe?"

Joe just grinned back.

"The times they're a-changin'," Pete cut in. He glanced at Willie and asked, "You going to the big powwow, Willie boy?"

"Sure," Willie told him. "Gonna be more fun than usual." Then his eyes shifted toward Joe and he said, "Gotta see the white-eyes fight old Big Arms. Man, everybody's waiting for that."

"When did you hear this?" Joe blurted. They'd been on the rez only, what, an hour by now? Word *did* travel fast around here.

"Everyone's talking about it, pal. When you drove down with Foxie here…"

"Willie Joe!"

Her tone put Willie in his place quickly.

He said, "Anybody who even looks twice at Running Fox here, old Big Arms takes on." He paused briefly, then added, "Whether that 'anybody' wants to fight or not."

"Look, I'm a tourist. I got lost. Pete found me and took me in. All I want is to get my plane fixed and get out of here."

Very softly, Pete half-whispered, "You want that Big Arms slob to nail my sister?"

Nobody heard what Joe muttered under his breath.

Running Fox broke the sudden silence. "Let's clear the air here, citizens. I don't care what you think and I certainly don't care what Big Arms thinks. I don't have anything to do with that anthropoid type and he'd better stay the hell away from me."

Sequoia Pete paid the bill for the Harley parts and the so-longs were silent. Almost funereal. Outside, a small group had collected and stared at the visitor as if it would be the last time they would look at him alive.

Joe shook his head. “Man, I should have stayed with my plane until they sent a search party out.”

“You afraid of Big Arms, Joe?”

“Come on, I never even met the guy.”

Pete nodded at a figure across the street. “Well, there he is, White-eyes. He’s watching you and if you so much as blink, he’ll have your head.”

“Don’t you have any police around here?”

“Both of them are chasing a bootlegger up in the hills.”

“Just two cops?”

“It’s Federal land, Joe. The FBI come out here sometimes. Gotta be a big deal, though.”

Joe stopped and turned, looking straight at Big Arms, and the air went quiet. No bird chirped, no kid yelled and even the wind died down.

Big Arms was weight-lifting huge. He stood well over six feet, his bare waist rippling with musculature. His legs filled out his dungarees and his boot-clad feet were placed straddle-legged on the pavement.

He could have been handsome, but his expression made a cruel mask of his face. He looked like he wanted to spit when Joe’s eyes met his.

To one side, Running Fox was watching Joe. Very softly, she said, “Let him alone, Joe.”

Just as softly Joe whispered back, “I can’t.”

“You see why they call him Big Arms,” Fox said.

“Of course.”

“Aren’t you afraid of him?”

"He forgot something, doll."

"What's that?" she asked him.

Joe didn't answer. He started across the street and a muted gasp from the onlookers hovered in the air. Big Arms didn't budge. His mouth twisted in a quiet sneer as Joe got closer. He was waiting for a groveling-style apology, a sniveling plea of remorse begging to be let off the hook and not be punished by this huge animal of a man who gloried in his brute strength.

Then Joe stepped up on the sidewalk, that final push of his foot giving greater impetus to the power behind the fist that cracked against the side of Big Arm's jaw and the guy dropped like a poleaxed steer into a crumpled heap on the packed clay earth.

This time the gasp wasn't muted. It was if the whole town had let its breath out all at once. They had just witnessed the impossible.

Only Running Fox, suddenly at his side, had stayed placid. "How'd you do it?" she asked.

"Pretty hard to grow muscles in your jaw."

"Oh," she said.

"I guess that fight is still on."

"Only way it won't happen now is if you run."

"Why should I run?"

"He'll never let you do that to him again."

"Then I'll have to think of something new, won't I?" He walked casually over to the pickup, Running Fox beside him.

For a few seconds she didn't say anything, but thoughts were running through her mind. "Joe...please don't play him down. He's a dangerous man. Many Thunders—that's his real name—was the star football player at state school until he went to the tryouts for a pro team where everybody else was as big as he was and he didn't make the grade. He quit school, got all wrapped up in that attitude of his. And now he's going to be worse than ever."

"And he wants you," Joe said quietly. Before she could answer he added, "Can't blame him for that, though." He reached out and took her hand in his and squeezed it gently before letting it go.

"There's more to it than that, Joe."

"Like what?"

"This is Indian country. It has its own culture. Certain rules are bred into us. You may just see poverty, but there's pride, too. This is a defeated nation, Joe. It's been trampled into the ground, cast aside, made fun of in the movies, totally ignored in the scheme of things..."

"Hey, I'm in your back yard. Hell, your brother even taught me to eat a snake. There's nothing I could teach him about survival out here."

"You sure taught him something, White-eyes."

"Like what?"

"Like how you could take Big Arms down with one shot."

Joe said, "He won't be easy to sucker punch again, will he?"

Running Fox shook her head sadly.

"Better think of something else, huh?"

"Won't do much good. Many Thunders will be ready."

"How's this fight going to come off?"

Solemnly she said, "There will be a circle of watchers. There will be no place to run. You will have to face the enemy and fight."

"For how many rounds?"

"There are no rounds. When one is dead or disabled, the other will be the winner."

"And Big Arms is pretty good at this, right?"

Fox's nod was sad. "There were three before that he challenged. A visiting tribal chief from the Elko reservation. Big man. About three hundred pounds. Very fat, but strong too. They had to take him to the hospital near Jenkins City."

"So what was that fight about?"

"The visitor wanted to sit with me at a feast."

"And the others?"

"One was a local cowboy. Did the rodeos, won a lot of medals, made the motorcycle circuits and won there too. He was fast and Big Arms had to run him down, but he smashed him just once in the chest, broke his ribs, then dislocated his jaw, and for good measure picked him up and slammed him into the ground."

"Lived through it?"

"Barely. He sold his motorcycle and hasn't even ridden a horse since. Keeps some sheep up at his ranch. If he had the nerve he'd shoot Many Thunders down like a dog."

"You say 'Many Thunders' with a sneer, Fox."

"How do I say 'Big Arms,' Joe?"

"Like you enjoyed seeing me punch him out. As a matter of fact, I think I saw signs of pleasure on a few other faces too."

"Can I offer you a sincere piece of advice?"

For a few seconds, he studied her expression. It revealed nothing, but there was a serious note in her voice. He said, "Certainly."

Slowly, she turned her head and looked at him and for the first time he saw that her eyes were not exactly black at all. There were blue flashes there and a tinge of green.

Running Fox said, "Our people still have the old ways. If you were to have a bad dream, or feel the wrong medicine in your mind, you could run to a safe place until you know it is time to return. No one will think bad of you at all."

"How would Big Arms react to that?"

"He would say nothing. He would know that he was the winner

even without a fight. The people would all know that too and would understand."

"What about you, Pretty Fox?"

"It's Running Fox."

"Sorry."

"I would understand too," she told him.

"What would you *like* me to do?" Joe asked her softly.

Something new had happened to her face. A sudden and quick expression she tried to hide, couldn't, then disguised with a gentle smile. "I would like you to do exactly what you are going to do," she said to him.

Across the street, Sequoia Pete was coming toward them, several boxes of parts for his Harley under his arms. He tossed everything in the back of the Ford pickup, got in beside Joe and Running Fox and turned the key in the engine.

As they drove out, heads turned toward them, expressions on the faces curious, but with no animosity at all. Joe said nothing, but thought that they would have made great spectators in the Roman Coliseum when the gladiators chopped each other to pieces. Or one did all the chopping on his little opponent.

One plane sat at an angle off the dirt runway. The pilot had shut it down where he had pulled up. To start it would blow dirt everywhere and since there were no chocks under the wheels, that little Cessna could take the corner right off the building with its prop.

"Who's the junior birdman flying that machine?" Joe asked Sequoia Pete.

"Probably Maxie Angelo," Pete told him. "He acts like he owns the state. He owns the plane, but he doesn't fly it. The Baxter kid is usually at the wheel." He turned his head and spat. "Lousy flier, that one. Can't make a cross-wind landing at all."

"What does he do?"

"Comes in head-on into the wind no matter there's no other runway. Twice he almost what do you call it…?"

"Ground looped?"

Pete nodded. "Yeah, that's it. Luckily for him, he was alone. Old Maxie is one of those nervous types who'll crack you open if you shake him up."

"Mean, huh?"

The expression on Pete's face told Joe he agreed with the remark, but he said nothing.

"He wears a gun," Running Fox said quietly. "A flat automatic, probably a .38."

"How would you know that?" Pete demanded.

Without taking her eyes off the road she said, "Out here that's the smallest size that would do any good. He's a city type. He's the kind we can do without."

"Running Fox," Pete said, "you never should have taken that psychology class in college."

Joe gave him a gentle nudge. "You have a better opinion, pal?"

"Nope. She's probably right. Hell, she's always right. I don't like the guy either. Nobody does."

"Then why's he here?"

"He's got money, paleface. He buys artifacts. He pays the drunks to find pottery shards and arrowheads. Once Charlie Fourlegs brought in something he had wrapped in a worn-out gunnysack and Maxie Angelo gave him four fifties for it. Charlie went on a drunk that lasted two weeks, almost killed himself. When he was over his hangover he had the shakes for another two weeks."

"No family to share the wealth with?"

"Sure, but Charlie's an alky. I told you, the Indian culture is going down the tubes."

"Where's Geronimo when you need him, right?"

"Right," Pete agreed.

*

Outside the hogan the sun had almost settled to the horizon, the small hills sending out long, mighty shadows, the faces of the mountains in the distance painted a grimacing black. Even the shimmering lights from the packed sand changed colors second to second and the air had cooled to a pleasant temperature. Joe breathed it in deeply.

It was too nice an evening to spoil with small talk, so Joe and Pete just sat there in the canvas camp chairs sipping at a cool beer and inside Running Fox cleaned up the eating area. Pete had warned him about trying to help out with the housework. That was woman's work, he told his friend. Maybe the liberals wouldn't like it, but out here they could keep their mouths shut up or land headfirst in a slit trench.

"I like those rules," Joe told him.

Pete just Indian-grunted his assent, then turned and grinned. "You think we're only partly civilized?"

"Hell no," Joe said. "Anybody who can catch a snake, skin it, eat it and burp to boot is fortunately very *un*civilized."

"You'd better believe it," Pete replied.

Behind them Running Fox's feet shuffled almost soundlessly in the sand and she eased herself into the other camp chair with a motion like pouring milk into a pitcher. She had changed into a soft golden leather outfit that was beautifully beaded with symbolic native designs, her black hair spilling down her shoulders in soft, lusty waves, the ebbing light making it glint as it swirled.

Joe had to hold his breath. She was gorgeous before, even in her working clothes. Now there was no description that came to his mind except a strange wonderment, a feeling of *how could this be?*

Damn, he thought. She was one amazing beauty. She was completely out of place in the desert. She was the original

All-American Girl. Miss America! Hell, she could make any of those stage queens shrink next to her.

Pete stopped looking at the horizon and turned to Joe. "Pal, you should see your face."

Running Fox smiled a little herself. "Squaw make you uneasy, Joe?"

He started to say something, but Pete interrupted with, "She knows what she did to you. I told you, she does that to all the guys."

"Man, I'd hate to turn her loose in the big city," Joe told him.

"Why's that?" she asked softly.

"Because you'd hear cars crash and people bump into each other and whistles blowing…"

"What would you do, Joe?"

"I wouldn't want to tell you." This time he took a deep breath and let it out slowly. "I'm just glad there's nobody else here to share you with."

Running Fox shifted her position and crossed her legs. It was a very deliberate move. The last of the evening sun glistened off her skin and for a brief moment she was a magazine cover model, something absolutely incredible, a rare gem sparkling in an inaccessible area, a grand delight that made a man's body ache and his mind pulse with wild thoughts.

It was totally dark before Pete flicked a match to a kerosene lamp and the yellow glow brought a soft light to the area. Breaking the silence, Pete said, "You want to get your plane fixed tomorrow, Joe?"

"Sure, but I haven't explained…"

"Come on, Sis already figured out what's wrong with it."

"How could she?"

"You told her."

"What?"

"Sure," Pete said, "you told her it stopped running. Bang. Just like that. No noise. No warning. Just sudden quiet. Plenty of gas, plenty of battery. Just no-go. Right?"

Joe bobbed his head. "Right."

"Means it's electrical," Running Fox explained softly. "No big deal. I'll fix it in the morning."

All Joe could do was shrug. The world was upside down. His instruments had stopped working, his maps had blown out of the cockpit, he was going down deeper and deeper and he didn't even have a cold beer left.

CHAPTER 7

Running Fox's expression was that of an amateur, but dedicated, artist looking at a Da Vinci painting in the Louvre. There was a glow in her eyes and the pleased pursing of her lips made Joe's mouth water. Her heavy breathing was noticeable as she ran her hands over the metallic skin of the BT 13A. Her fingers made little petting motions on the plastic cockpit hood and when she opened it and slid it back, it was as if she was undressing her lover.

Joe asked, "Like my baby?"

After a moment Running Fox said, "She's beautiful. Absolutely beautiful."

Sequoia Pete gave Joe a gentle nudge and whispered, "Up till now it's been nothing but Harleys and old cars."

"Can I sit in her?" Running Fox asked without turning her head.

"Slide on in," Joe told her.

"This cushion…"

"That's my parachute. Flip the metal clasps out of the way and sit on it."

For a moment she studied the situation, then threw her leg over the fuselage, got her hands in the right places and slithered down into the seat. Her eyes roamed lustily across the instrument panel, her tongue touching her lips in a sensual gesture.

Pete remarked, "You may never get your plane back, Joe."

With a grin Joe told him, "She's a two-seater, pal. I may never want to."

*

For a brief second their eyes met, their minds on the same thought. Somehow, mighty Big Arms had to be taken out of the action.

And old 819 was just an antique training plane, the buffer between a primary Stearman biplane and the advanced AT6. The Vultee Vibrator was far from being a P-51, the great piston-engined fighter of those years long ago.

They both saw the comparison. The outlook was plain. One punch did not a victory make and the next time there was a head-on approach Big Arms would smash the old trainer to the ground and make a victory pass right over him.

Running Fox didn't take long with the flight manual before she nodded and began unfastening the nuts on the cowling. Joe followed her every move and in twenty minutes she put her wrench down and tapped an innocuous-looking connection with a greasy fingertip. "Your trouble, White-eyes. Something fried the vibration snubber that used to be here and the connection just shook loose. No noise, no sparking, just a sudden quieting of an athletic, but granddaddy, engine."

"Can you fix it?"

"Sure. It's a standard part we use on Harleys. I have a couple in the tool box."

Thirty minutes later the cowling was back on, grease wiped off hands and the paper towels stuffed in the garbage collector in the back of the pickup.

Pete and his sister stood back soundlessly, their eyes on Joe.

He gave them an Air Force salute, legged it into the cockpit, made sure the controls were unlocked, then set the prop and gas controls in the proper positions and pumped the choke. He yelled "Clear," watched until they nodded back, then moved the ignition switch to the left, waited while the starter turned over to speed and flipped the switch to start.

And start it did, with a blast of smoke from the exhaust, then settled down to the pleasant throaty roar of that great radial engine. When he was thoroughly satisfied, Joe cut the power, locked the controls and climbed out of the cockpit.

"Beautiful," he told the two standing beside the wing.

Pete said, "You can't wheel that plane off on this ground, old buddy. You need some kind of runway."

"Got any ideas?"

"Just one. I have two tires in the back of the pickup. If we tie one on the other we can drag them along and smooth out some kind of roadway. It'll be rough but should get you off."

"And if it doesn't?"

"You crack up and die and we bury you out here with the lizards."

"Thanks a bunch."

"My pleasure. Want to give it a try?"

Joe nodded. He turned and stared at the worried expression on Running Fox's face. "Maybe you have a better idea?"

Fox shook her head after a moment and walked to the pickup. The three of them dragged the tires out, fastened them one atop the other, then snagged the chain hook into the spoke of the lower one. Pete got out a rake and with the handle pulled a furrow along the sand, checking back constantly to make sure it held a straight line, etching a guide to make sure they had a straight path. What loose rocks marred the line they tossed aside, along with some half-buried scraps of colorful butsun-bleached wood that Pete explained were bits of branches from long-dead trees. After an hour of steady dragging, the tires had laid down a respectable runway, carving into fairly stable hard-surface dirt. When they finished they topped off the fuel tanks in the wings from the containers they'd brought with them in the truck.

"Instant airfield," Pete said.

Joe walked the length of the takeoff area twice until he was certain that the tires of the plane would be well-supported and when he finished he got back to his friends. "I'm going to make one go-around, land, and if the ground holds, we can get out of here."

"To where?" Pete asked him.

"To your home airport, pal."

"Think you can listen to a clever Indian brave, buddy?" There was a serious look on Pete's face and Joe felt invisible fingers go up his back. "Those other big city guys with their plane aren't the kind I'd want on my side in combat duty, friend. If I were in your shoes I don't think I'd want them to know I had a plane and could fly it."

"Why not?"

Pete tapped the side of his head. "Native intuition."

Joe nodded. "You got it, Pete. Old George Custer should have been smarter than to even get near the Little Big Horn."

"Him slow learner," Pete said.

"Him deader than hell, too," Joe answered.

Running Fox kicked some sand at Joe's legs. Before she could ask, Joe said, "Don't get your feathers riled, pretty girl. I'll give you a ride right now."

She went over and delicately brushed the sand from Joe's pant legs with the toe of her boot. "Me happy squaw, White-eyes."

"Get in that back seat, college girl. And no more native talk."

"Right on, buster," she said as she scrambled into the plane.

When Joe checked her seat belt and shoulder harness out,

adjusting it to fit securely, he told her not to touch the stick and to keep her feet off the rudder pedals. The throttle and prop controls were his to adjust and all she had to do was look and enjoy. There would be no violent maneuvers to make her sick, but, he said, if she did feel a little nauseous, she should pick up the mike, thumb the button and let him know.

She gave him a long slow look with those lovely dark eyes. "I ride Harleys, city boy. Desert riding. Big bumps, long jumps. Sick I don't get."

Joe grunted. Harleys touched the ground. They rode over bumps. They never had the sky fall out from under them or got tossed almost upside down by a freakish windblast. He just said, "It's different at altitude." Then he climbed in the front cockpit, buckled down, set up for takeoff and when Pete was clear, he started the engine.

The trim was set, the mags checked out okay, and he eased the throttle forward, revving up faster than usual. Until the wings took on lift he could feel the softness of the sand under the wheels, then, with a gentle touch of the stick, there was air under all of old 819 and she was back in the blue where she belonged, alone in the sky with not even a contrail from the great airliners to scar the perfect day.

To check on his passenger, Joe tilted the mirror over the cowling. Running Fox wasn't looking back. Her eyes were on the ground, reveling at the sight of miles of land, totally enjoying the expanse set before her. Her head went from side to side, looking in admiration at the place where she lived, the stark beauty of what so many others thought of as barren and uninhabitable.

Banking into a slow turn, Joe let her see the world suddenly tilt, then rolled the plane into a tight one-eighty, pulling a couple of G's. In the mirror, her expression was that of a kid on a roller coaster. No fear, no anticipation of sudden disaster, just wonderful fun that she never wanted to stop.

Before he could take his eyes away, he saw her suddenly jerk her head, stare down a moment, then try to see behind her. Joe picked up the mike and touched the button. "You spot something?"

Without speaking she pointed abruptly downward and Joe wheeled the plane around. He cut the speed, gradually retracing their route. Below, clumps of foliage cropped up like an unruly haircut and hillocks of sand made lumpy mounds that cast small shadows, but nothing was recognizable until Running Fox started to bang on the instrument cowling in front of her and pointed downward.

Then Joe saw it. Legs. Arms. It looked as if it were a body cut in half. On the second, lower pass over the area he saw it was a body, all right, but blowing sand had covered the middle part of it. An even closer run over it showed an empty whiskey bottle in one protruding hand and when 819 thundered by, the hand jerked.

Running Fox had the mike in her hand and was trying to talk, but Joe had to indicate to her to hold the *speak* button down. When she got the message, she blurted, "*That's Miner Moe down there! We have to get to him!*"

With a flick of his wrist, Joe put his mike back on the hook. Talking to her now would be useless. He wasn't going to land in that sand. The only alternative was going back to the handmade runway and putting down there. He pulled up to a thousand feet, spotted his touchdown area, made an old-fashioned approach and set the BT 13 down in a perfect three-point landing.

Running Fox unbuckled and jumped to the ground before Joe did. Her words, half English, half her native tongue, were unintelligible to him, but he got their significance. Both men tried to get her slowed down, then Pete held her by the shoulders, and said, "Hush!" His sister looked at him, startled a moment, then said, "Damn, I'm sorry."

"Okay, Sis, okay. Just quiet down and spell it out straight."

She took a deep breath and told him. "Miner Moe's out there in the desert. He's alive, we both saw him move, but he has a whiskey bottle with him, he's out in the sun, and if he stays out there like that, he'll be dead by sundown."

"How far?" Pete asked.

"We can make it by truck in a half hour," Joe said. "He's at a heading of thirty degrees from here. From the air, it looked like it was all sand and the truck tires should handle it with no trouble."

"How about the plane?"

"It stays right here. Who's going to steal it anyway?"

Miner Moe was alive. Drunk and incoherent, but alive. His fingers had to be pried from the empty bottle and he could only mumble through sun-dried lips. He was limp when they lifted him into the bed of the pickup, wetted him down under the shade of an old tarp they had rigged up, ChapSticked his parched lips, and gave him a gentle massage while they tried to make sense of the fragmented words he was mouthing.

Finally Pete said, "Hell, he's swearing. Listen close. He's cursing somebody out."

For a few seconds, Pete stopped wiping the sweat from the old man's face. "Something's wrong here." He looked up at his sister. "I thought he was off this stuff."

"He was. He hadn't had a drink for two years. When the doctor told him another binge could kill him, he went cold turkey. Nobody ever saw him take another drink after that."

"Somebody did," Joe said.

Pete's eyebrows drew together in a frown. "Why?"

"He have anything of value?" Joe asked him.

"Nothing worth killing him for," Pete said. His frown deepened. "But this is a heck of a way of doing it, isn't it? Moe wouldn't wander around the desert all alone. Hell, he always had his horse with him."

Joe said, "I remember an Indian feller whose horse left him alone out here. Young guy, too."

Pete let out a grunt, then said, "Moe's horse never would have left *him*. Those two were practically married."

"So what do you think?"

"If they got Moe really plastered they could have dumped him way out here to die. You'd find an empty bottle and that would be all. Miner Moe just went out the way he used to live."

Running Fox reached out and felt Miner Moe's pulse and gave a nod of satisfaction. "Which brings us back to the original question." She glanced up at the two men. "Why?"

"Could he have found some more of those gold artifacts?" her brother asked.

"The penalty for murder is still pretty steep for a few chunks of metal."

"Didn't he seem to have a line on how that stuff got here?" Joe asked. "He wasn't a newcomer to the desert scene and he'd know enough to keep his mouth shut if he found anything valuable enough to get killed for."

Running Fox suddenly held up her hand. "That's the answer, White-eyes," she said quietly.

Both men looked at her and she ran her fingers over Miner Moe's mouth, separating his fiercely chapped lips. They were both bruised and cut, but the wounds had dried. Blood still stained his teeth and the gums around his lower incisors were torn and one tooth was loose in its socket.

"Moe didn't drink that rotgut," she told them. "Somebody forced a bottle in his mouth and made him swallow it. It didn't take much to work his body up to a total alcoholic stage and he was absolutely helpless." She paused, flipped an eyelid up and felt his pulse again. "We got him just in time."

"How long you think he has been out here?" Joe asked her.

"Hours," Running Fox said. "It wouldn't be the sun that would kill him. He was pretty well suntanned up. It was the booze that would do it. He'd lie there and choke on his own vomit. Nobody would ever call it murder."

"There's got to be tracks where they left him," Joe said.

"Not the way this sand blows around," Pete said. "See any tracks from our truck?"

Both of them looked out the way they had come. Only the faintest tire marks were visible.

"They got a good start on us," Pete said.

"Uh-huh," Joe agreed. "But they don't know they dropped him right in our laps. You suppose we ought to keep him hidden?"

Running Fox cut in. "We need to get him to a doctor. Let's get Moe over to Mama White Bird's house where he stays, get someone to look at him."

"Harry Hamilton always comes in for the big shebang," Pete said.

"He'll do," Running Fox said.

For two hours Sequoia Pete kept the pickup's speed as high as the terrain would permit. They came on a well-tracked area then and followed the old worn path of other vehicles and pack animals; they even spotted the bootmarks of the lone hunters who were always scouring the desert, hunters looking for anything that could be turned into a souvenir.

In the bed of the pickup Miner Moe twitched, made some gurgling sounds and Running Fox wetted his lips again. His hands, crossed over his stomach, knotted and came free, then drooped uselessly. Joe's eyes met hers and he said, "He's in a bad way."

She nodded, her face taut with worry. "Somebody tried to murder him. Somebody knew how he was and deliberately tried to kill him."

"Who knew about his condition, Fox?"

She shrugged. "Everybody." She lowered her head for a moment, then looked up at Joe again. "Alcoholism is one hell of a sickness on the rez. Civilization took away everything we own and gave little back."

"You and Pete are doing okay," Joe reminded her.

"There are always exceptions," she said. "Not everybody gets caught in the booze trap. Some of us wise up and walk a straight path. We own property and have bank accounts. We have educations and can drive the slickers who try to beat us out of our property right up the wall."

Joe gave her shoulder a gentle squeeze. "What's really going on here, Fox?"

She gave him a half-shrug and said, "I don't know. I can feel it, that's all."

"You feel something but you won't talk about it?"

Her tongue wet her lips and a slight scowl touched her brows. "I could be wrong."

"There's a nearly dead man in the truck here, Running Fox. He's an old man who can use all the help he can get. What about him?"

Very slowly, her eyes drifted up to his. They were clear and determined, not misty but stark with thought, and she said, "Something's definitely going on."

"I figured that," Joe told her, "but what?"

"What makes the world go 'round?"

Joe didn't have to think about that.

"Money," he said.

Mama White Bird was one big Indian. She stood about five ten, was built like a wrestler and weighed close to two hundred pounds, but had a face that belied the fierceness you might expect. She picked Miner Moe from Joe's arms like he was a baby and nodded for the others to follow her into the house. Unlike the other buildings on the rez, Mama White Bird's home was as orderly and clean as a *Good Housekeeping* advertisement. The only odd part was that it had an astringent odor and one bedroom painted creamy white with a pair of hospital beds at either end.

Joe had a quizzical expression. Running Fox said, "Mama White Bird is a registered nurse."

"And Miner Moe stays here with her?"

Running Fox nodded. "Eight years ago Moe kept her from being robbed by a couple of punks from outside. One had a gun."

"What happened?"

"Moe jumped in front of Mama and took the shot. Damn near killed him. But Moe had a snake-gun in his boot, pulled it and hit the punk. The rez police came in and nailed them. Mama took Moe home and wouldn't let him leave until he was well and sobered up. He came back whenever the booze got too much for him."

Pete used the phone in the house to put a call in to Harry Hamilton, and just a few minutes later Hamilton's car skidded to a stop outside the house, sending up a cloud of dust that made Mama White Bird shake her head. The doctor was a weather-beaten desert type in a big sombrero and well-worn boots and if he weren't carrying an old, worn medical bag, he would have looked like some beat-up cowhand.

With a nod of her head, Mama White Bird indicated the sole hospital room and they went in together and closed the door.

It took an hour before Harry Hamilton came out of the room. Through the open door Joe saw Mama White Bird bending over the bed, tenderly covering up Miner Moe with a woven blanket.

Before being asked, the doctor said, "He'll come out of this one all right, but one more battle with the bottle and Moe's going to be looking for a six-foot fall. His insides are real shaky."

"Is it okay for him to stay here?" Running Fox asked him.

"Mama won't let him out of her sight for at least two days. Let him sober up and he'll be back on the sand again."

"Think he'll ever sober up?"

"You see his mouth?"

Running Fox gave Joe a glance before she nodded.

"He didn't get drunk because he wanted to," the doctor told her.

"We noticed it," she told him.

"Who'd want him dead?" the doctor asked them. "Hell, he hasn't got any money." Neither spoke and the doctor's eye narrowed. "So he knows something," he mused, then added, "or somebody *thinks* he knows something, and around here that can only be one big piss pot of loot."

"They *think*," Joe said.

"You know anything about this?" the doctor asked sharply.

"I just got in," Joe replied.

"Staying around long, sonny?"

Joe's eyes barely flicked toward Running Fox, but she saw it and heard him when he said, "That all depends."

When Mama White Bird closed the door behind the doctor, she said, "Moe is under sedation and he'll be sleeping for a good ten hours or so. I'll make sure nobody comes near him. Now, can you tell me what the hell is happening on this rez?"

After a quiet moment, Running Fox said softly, "Trouble, Mama."

"It's got to be about gold," Mama said. Neither of the pair said a word. "It's about those damned gold feet, right?"

"Sort of," Running Fox said.

Nobody had to go any further. The unspoken word was as loud as a lion's roar. Mama White Bird simply nodded knowingly, then looked at Joe Gillian and asked very matter-of-factly, "You the one Big Arms is going to kill at the powwow?"

Joe didn't know why he smiled but he did and very stoically said, "No way, ma'am."

"What makes you think so?"

"Pussycats don't kill tigers," he told her.

On the way to the pickup Sequoia Pete nudged Joe and said sarcastically, "Tiger!" He shook his head. "You'd better act like a greyhound."

"Why?"

"When word gets out you called him a pussycat you'll need to run fast."

"Who's going to tell him?"

"There were two heads outside the open window in there, pal."

Joe said quietly, "Great."

"What are you thinking about?"

"A horse," Joe said.

Pete gave him an exasperated side glance and shook his head. "Man, you planning to ride off this rez? You think..."

"I'm thinking about Miner Moe's horse, pal. There weren't any tracks around where we found him."

"The wind would have covered..."

"Bullshit," Joe said. "That was Moe's horse. He had him a long time, didn't he?"

"Maybe ten years," Pete replied.

"You think that horse would have just left him there in the desert?"

After a moment's thought Pete shook his head. "Hell no," he said. "That old nag was like a dog, always at Moe's heels. When Moe walked, the horse would nudge him along if he stopped at all. One time..."

"Where would the horse be, Pete?"

"Only one place he could be, if he's not with Moe: out at Long Weed's place on the other side of town. Old Long Weed and Moe are two of a kind, borrow from each other, share a hogan, grubstake each other. A couple of loners enjoying this earth."

"Let's take a look."

"Man, you don't want to go through town, flyboy. Old Big Arms will get the word and won't be waiting for the powwow to nail you, and believe me, you won't be pulling any smart stuff on him again."

"I got you to back me up, haven't I?"

"Man, I'm an Indian. You White-eyes. You scalpable. You think I want to get squashed on your account?"

A new trailer park had sprung up on the east side of town. Only one old sedan stuck out among the collection of pickup trucks. All seemed to be the same color—desert dust. Festivities hadn't started formally yet, but a few groups were having a happy time around a big tub that shimmered and sparkled in the sunlight.

"Beer party," Pete muttered.

"Where'd they get the ice?"

"Boy, you big city types think we're *really* uncivilized out here, don't you?"

"So where'd they get the ice?"

"Billy Sheepherder's got an icemaker in the back of his store. Now don't be a wise guy and ask where the utility poles are... Billy has a gasoline engine that operates a generator."

A pair of almost-teenagers saw the two of them and although their expressions said nothing, the curiosity in their eyes was plain enough. There was neither surprise nor derision there, but interest in the courage that would enable an outsider to come so calmly to his gravesite. Big Arms' reputation had been well established and though the outcome of a clash between this white-eyes and their champion was a forgone conclusion, silent applause had to be given for the courage that was being displayed.

Pete said, "You're a cooked goose now, partner."

"He's got to kill me before he cooks me buddy."

Pete turned his head and stared at his friend. "You know, you're nuts."

"Thanks for the confidence."

"No, I mean that. You are plain, stinking nuts, flyboy. You are walking straight into a bear trap, you know it's there, you don't pay any attention to it at all and you're not even scared."

"The hell I'm not."

"Yeah? What are you scared of?"

"Of Big Arms *not* showing up."

A couple of teenagers rode by, their horses churning up a

cloud of dust, and Joe let the cloud settle before continuing down the street. The crowd was still coming in, no shouting or jostling, simply small groups, men in one, women in another. Children herded by their mothers and the older ones forming teenage cliques, boys acting out their roles in front of girls.

Sitting on a box outside the general store was an old crone swathed in multi-colored clothing, a high feathered hat on her head and a lit pipe in her hand. The adults all made some gesture of respect toward her as they passed, but they didn't stay to speak. Twice, she said something to a pair of boys who had played too close to her and whatever she said scared them into instant submission before she waved her hand and they both broke and ran.

"Who's that, Pete?"

"That's our resident witch, buddy. She casts a spell on you, you're done."

"She just park out on the road like that?"

"White-eyes, she's like the six-hundred-pound gorilla. She sits wherever she wants. The whole rez is scared of her. They say she pointed her finger at Old Paulie's wagon and the wheels came right off."

"Why?"

"Old Paulie called her something ugly, that's why."

"Hell, she's just an old lady, Pete."

"Yeah, well even Big Arms is scared to death of her. Somebody told him she would turn him inside out if she laid eyes on him again."

"I thought Big Arms wasn't afraid of anybody."

"Our resident witch isn't just anybody."

Joe stopped. "I think I'll go meet her." Then, before Pete could grab him, Joe walked over to the old lady, smiled, held out his hand. When she took it, she looked directly at him and her eyes widened and widened some more until they were momentarily huge, then she smiled too and squeezed his hand.

"I'm Joe Gillian," he said.

The old lady nodded. "You White-eyes," she said. Her voice was soft and unexpectedly clear.

Joe could think of nothing to say at all. He just nodded back and kept smiling.

"Poor Big Arms," she said in a near whisper as her eyes grew huge again for a second.

The crowd on the street had come to a standstill. It was as though they were all holding their breath.

"Friend," Pete told him when he was back in the truck again, "you sure like to tempt fate, don't you?"

"I don't believe in that witch crap," Joe said.

"She's not some nice old lady, buddy. They say she's put some pretty heavy spells on a lot of people who offended her."

"I didn't offend her. I said hello."

"She said something to you, didn't she?"

Joe nodded. "She called me White-eyes."

"Man, I don't think I should be near you any longer. You're probably on her list now. I could be killed by a lightning bolt or something."

"I thought you were college-educated, brother."

"I'm culture-conscious, flyboy. I still have a lot of Indian in me. I've seen too much of this supposed superstition stuff turn into reality."

They reached the edge of town, got off the roadway and turned toward the sun, walking quietly until Pete pointed out the cramped building seemingly built into the rise of a low hill. There was a rickety corral to one side built of old, weathered two-by-fours with a watering trough and a half-full feed box inside and a pair of placid brown mares nibbling at a pile of straw.

Both horses looked up a moment when they approached, and satisfied, went back to eating. Pete identified the nearest one as old Miner Moe's horse, then went and knocked on Long Weed's door.

After a few seconds, Moe's pal pushed the door open and squinted at the two men. "Man," he said hoarsely, "that powwow's not till tomorrow. What you come get me for now?" He looked at Joe and narrowed his eyes. "Who you, pardner? I ain't seen you around before."

"This is Joe Gillian, Long Weed. Good buddy of mine."

"Come in for the killing?" Long Weed grinned. "Old Big Arms got him another sucker."

"I'm the sucker," Joe told him.

"You?" Long Weed said disbelievingly.

"Somebody has to be," Joe said.

"Damn. How'd you put old Big Arms down right out in front of the town?"

"I sucker-punched him," Joe said.

"You guys want to come in?" The smell of stale smoke and something unpleasant cooking came out the open door and Pete shook his head. "We just came to see if Miner Moe's horse was here."

"Yup. Came in by himself. Moe must be scavenging somewhere and let the critter run loose. He always comes back. Had some blood on his flank this time. Moe okay?"

"He's resting," Pete said. "Had a little trouble."

"He hurt?"

"Pretty bad."

"I told him he shouldn't go anywhere alone anymore."

"He didn't, Long Weed. Somebody held him down and poured a bottle of booze into him."

"Why?"

"They wanted to get something from him."

"Damn," Long Weed said. "What were they after?"

"You think Miner Moe had anything valuable, something really worth stealing? Not by anybody around here, but by outsiders?"

Long Weed frowned, stepped out of the doorway and sat down on the old board sill, indicating for his visitors to do the same on the dirt. When they were all readjusted, Long Weed said, "Moe was always talking about his secret stuff, but hell, everybody has secret stuff. Not worth anything, but it's still secret stuff. You got to have something to talk about out here if you ain't got TV."

"So what did Moe have?"

"Oh, he was always picking up something in the desert. He'd tell some damn big stories about funny people from way down south, how they come up this way carting *their* secret stuff, then getting killed off or something, and he found a lot of their goods. You believe that?"

Pete and Joe looked at each other briefly.

"Never said where he hid the stuff, or what exactly it was. I'd guess it was all in his mind."

"You really think so?" Joe said.

Long Weed shrugged and spit between his feet. "He showed me a few things, but other guys got stuff like that too." He spat another dribble, hitting the heel of one worn-down boot this time. "Said he had a cache in a box where the moon went down."

Joe watched Pete go tense.

Pete said, "Where would that be, Long Weed?"

"Who the hell knows? He was drunk when he said it. Anyway, that's what I thought he said. Couldn't have been much anyhow because old Moe never had nothing to spend. You gonna leave his horse here?"

"Moe'll come pick him up."

"Okay then. You tell my partner to get sober and come the hell home."

CHAPTER 8

The Federal Agents had made no attempt to be inconspicuous about their arrival on the reservation. Long-body pickups hauled their trailers to a camping spot on the edge of town and four government sedans parked nose-out for a quick exit right beside them. The small group of men were in casual clothes, looking very much out of place, but as if they were deliberately doing so. And they were. They wanted everyone to know they were there and who they were.

The tall slim man in the pressed jeans and dark blue Polo shirt was obviously the team leader and although none wore holsters or insignias, you automatically knew there was a badge in their pockets and a government-issue firearm strapped to an ankle or discreetly hidden under their untucked loose shirts.

Nobody paid any attention to them. Four times a year they made routine stops at the reservation, held closed meetings with the elders of the tribe, took typed notes of Indian requests back to Washington where they were promptly filed, and after spending a week of leisure away from the city, they would leave and nobody would miss them at all.

But this was not a routine visit. One had been made just a month before and never had the schedule been interrupted since the reservation had been established. There were two new men in the group who didn't wear the same garb as the others. One had a nearly military bearing and wore starched khakis, a loose-fitting jacket of the same material around his shoulders. The other was older and had an expression like the professors that came from the state school to study Indian culture, make inspections for hidden relics the people would unearth on government property, and confiscate them.

Pete nudged Joe with his elbow and nodded toward the new encampment. "The troops are here."

"Somebody in trouble?"

"Somebody will be," Pete answered. "This isn't a regular stop, that's for sure. A pair of new guys are with them. They've never been on this run before."

"Maybe they came for the powwow."

"Not these jokers. When they change their routine something big is going on."

"How about that other bunch that flew in?"

"You tell me," Pete said.

"Well, they'd probably file a flight plan. They'd be on record someplace. They're on government land, so any business they do would have to be scrutinized by a regulated authority."

"Flyboy," Pete told him, "you don't know souvenir hunters like we do. The residents on this protected land are dead broke and have no qualms about doing business with shady characters as long as cash money changes hands. And where is the regulated authority to scrutinize their business tactics?"

"Okay then," Joe said, "just how much worthwhile stuff can be found in this area?"

"Enough to attract guys like Maxie Angelo. And we're not the only group that feeds his business. A lot of people from other tribes come and go. They deal in clay pots and old jewelry that brings a small fortune from museums and private collectors."

"You *know* these people?"

"Sure. We're probably cousins." He paused a moment and shook his head. "Like they say, Indians are just Indians."

"Like Big Arms is just an Indian?"

Pete said softly, "Brother Joe, you scare me. Do you know that? You make my insides go all flaky. You come down out of the sky with a six-pack of cold beer and some candy bars like it's picnic time and everything gets turned upside down. Do you know my sister is starting to flip over you?"

"She's flipped over my airplane, that's all."

"The hell she is. Right now, she's worried sick about what Big Arms is going to do to you."

"So?"

"And that's what scares me, brother. You can fly the hell out of here any time you want and instead you got to pull that big ape's chain. And there's no way you can keep him from tearing you apart. You think he doesn't know how Fox feels about you? Man, Big Arms is chewing nails until he can get to fight you again. That sucker punch you laid on him was just a teaser. An insult. Something that can never happen again." Pete paused and took a deep breath. He turned his head slowly and stared at Joe. "I'm going to miss you, my friend."

"Why, you going somewhere?"

"You're scaring me again."

"Maybe I'll scare Big Arms."

Almost sadly, Pete shook his head. "Not this time, Joseph, not this time. Big Arms doesn't know fear. He choked and killed an adult bear one time when it went for his dog."

He turned his head and looked at Joe and his eyes narrowed.

Joe's eyes were bright. "We ever going to get something to eat?"

Pete shook his head, then grinned. "Sure. We'll stop at Little Eagle's place right up the road. He's got good hamburgers, only he serves them on bread, not buns. Got snake, too, if you're interested."

They cut around a couple of teenagers on old motorcycles,

kids out eyeing the squaws who dutifully gave them sidelong glances. One boy gave a half-hearted wave and got a half-hearted wave back.

Ten ramshackle cars were parked outside Little Eagle's building. One side had been made from an old Coca-Cola bill-board and the rest of scrap lumber, with a roof of a half-dozen layers of black tarpaper. Pete didn't see the last car until he pulled in next to it. This was a Ford Explorer covered with desert dust, the side windows blacked out by whatever was on the inside. The plates were from California and some kid had written in the dust on the rear cargo gate, "*WASH ME*."

"That's Maxie Angelo's rig," Pete told his friend. "His low-profile stuff. On the outside he rides in a chauffeured Mercedes."

"Who told you that?"

"He did business at the State U, one time. Donated some ancient artifacts like a reputable citizen. We saw him. Couldn't miss the slob."

"He know you?"

"Sure. Come on in. I'll give you an introduction."

"You don't like him."

"Like I enjoy cobras in my back yard."

"No cobras in these parts, old buddy."

"There's one now," Pete replied.

Maxie Angelo could have been typecast by any movie studio. You'd start with a face like Capone's, work in a little Luciano, touch it up with some John Gotti, add a splash of egotistical stupidity, and you'd have Maxie Angelo. It would make you wonder how such obvious creeps could even exist in an orderly world. But this was far from an orderly world. It was a world where a scorpion could live in a city and a rat could dwell in a penthouse.

The guy sitting beside him was in his late twenties and wore a built-in snarl that said he hated everybody, knew everything, and only worshipped at the throne of money. There was a sharpness there too, the animal astuteness of some feral beast.

Pete seemed to feel Joe's scrutiny and said quietly, "The kid is Maxie's pilot. He's ferried his box in here four or five times. He's a mean one. Got a knife in his boot and carries a chrome-plated .25 automatic in his back pocket."

"Tough?"

"Stupid. That chrome reflects light like a mirror. Someday he'll pull it out and wonder why he got killed."

Maxie saw them come in and nodded. The gesture wasn't friendly recognition at all. It was wary, like one dog sniffing another. He said, "Hello, Pete."

"Hello, Mr. Angelo." He waved his thumb at Joe and said, "Here's Joe Gillian from white man's country."

Maxie shot a thumb at his pilot. "Meet Ted Condon. He flies my plane." The pilot sipped his coffee, not even bothering to nod. "You taking a vacation out here, Mr. Gillian?"

"A short one," Joe told him.

"Long drive from the east," Maxie said.

"Worth it."

"Not much to do in these parts." His statement posed a question.

Joe said, "Came out for the big powwow tomorrow."

"Yeah," Ted Condon chipped in. "Heard something special was happening then."

"Heard that too," Joe told him with a tight grin, then sat down on the upended box at the plank counter.

Little Eagle walked over, his eyes going over Joe as if he were peering through a microscope. The whole town had been talking about the white-eyes Big Arms would kill and here he had this amazing curiosity right in front of him. He didn't try to disguise his inspection at all. This white-eyes had already taken down the monstrous Big Arms with a single blow so great that everyone who saw it happen described it differently.

When he finished, he said, "You want hamburger?"

And everyone heard Joe when he said, "Your sign tells me you got snake."

Little Eagle remarked, "Five-footer. Fresh killed this morning. You want fried…got it in pan now."

"Fried it is."

Little Eagle forked out two big white ovals of rattlesnake and served it up on a paper plate with a side dish of tortillas. The silence in the room was total when Joe bit into his first forkful. He mixed in some tortilla, washed it with coffee and had another bite. Pete ordered the same delicacy and halfway through Maxie Angelo and his pilot had enough, paid their bill and left.

Pete waited until they both had finished and went outside into the hot desert sun again. "Joe," he said, "you are a pisser. You are one hundred percent off your rocker. Tell me, do you want to be buried or cremated?"

"I thought you Indians put the dead out in the sun to mummify."

Pete didn't have time to answer. Maxie Angelo's Ford Explorer had left and in its place was a clean black Ford Taurus with only a patina of local dust on its surface. The two men who came out of it didn't have to wear an FBI insignia on their shirts to identify them. They were athletically trim, purposely composed, with expressions that told you they were experts in the game they were playing. They were used to others being intimidated by their peculiar behavior and when it didn't happen here, a noticeable squint came to their eyes.

Sequoia Pete said, "Hello, Mr. Walker. Good to see you again."

"Pete." He nodded. "This is my assistant, George Chello."

"And this is my brother…blood brother…Joe Gillian."

They all shook hands and suddenly Mr. Walker threw a sharp glance at Joe and said, "Gillian? Joe Gillian?"

"That's me," Joe agreed.

"You a pilot?"

Joe nodded. "Why?"

"We had a notice the other day about some old-timers' club of guys flying antique planes. One never showed up. They assumed he went down in the mountains someplace. Could that be you?"

Joe let out a short laugh. "Most likely. I put down in the desert and would have ended up a skeleton if I hadn't been saved by my Native American buddy here."

"No radio?"

"Our planes have original equipment. That long-range stuff hadn't even been invented then. For a BT 13A anyway."

George Chello's eyes suddenly went wide. "Damn, that's early 1940s stuff!"

"Fun to fly."

"You guys are crazy," Chello said.

"That's what I've been telling him," Pete added. Then, "What's happening, Mr. Walker? You come out here to eat snake?"

"We came out here to see you two."

"Why?"

"Can we sit in my car and talk?"

"Sure," Pete said. "Just get the air-conditioning going."

Walker got behind the wheel, Pete sat beside him, and Joe and Chello got in the back. When they were comfortable, the A/C going full blast, Walker said, "We have heard some information about an arrowhead you brought back from the desert. Is that true?"

"Man, I have boxes of arrowheads…"

"This wasn't an ordinary arrowhead, Pete. I think you know what I'm talking about."

"I found it," Joe said simply.

Eyes darted toward him.

"It was imbedded in a bone of a small animal," Joe said. "The animal was hit, but ran off with the arrow still in him. I gave it to Pete here."

"Did you know what it was?"

"Not until Pete told me. Why?"

"That's classified information," Walker said. "Where did you find it?"

"That's classified information," Joe said.

"You know what we could—?"

"You could do nothing, Mr. Walker. Now, let's stop the garbage and tell us what this is all about. I have a small idea based on rumors, but I'd like to hear it firsthand from you."

"What have you heard?" Walker said.

"It drives Geiger counters off the wall, right?"

The two FBI agents glanced at each other, then, with silent agreement, both nodded.

Pete said, "Mr. Walker, everybody on this rez knows about that mineral. The Anasazi medicine men used it in their rituals and passed down stories about it that still come up when the old ones sit around the campfire and tell wild tales. Hell, man, Chief Johnny Elk gave two samples to the State U before he died. The lab was going to do a big study on them."

"Those samples have been missing for over ten years," Walker said.

"Missing?" Pete said, "The way a Geiger counter was supposed to react to that stuff there's no way you couldn't track it."

Walker didn't answer.

Pete said, "It was stolen, wasn't it?"

Walker still didn't answer.

"Big government secret, Mr. Walker?"

"We're going to confiscate that arrowhead, Pete."

"Oh, boy," Pete said. "Do I take it that we're into some international chicanery?"

"Not really."

"Mr. Walker, let's get down and dirty. None of that stuff has ever been found outside this reservation, and we covered one heck of a lot of square miles. It's scarce, but it's here and, so far, it's only been a toy, something the old men played with when they couldn't hunt anymore. Maybe at one time it wasn't a toy, and now it looks like it *isn't* a toy anymore at all." He paused, and stared at Walker, his eyes hard and bright. "So what is it, government man?"

At first Walker didn't answer.

Joe said, "Do we need clearance from Washington?"

The two FBI men looked at each other and when Walker spoke his voice was hoarse and low. "I have to watch my words."

"Why?" Pete asked him.

"Because national security is at risk."

"Don't give me that," Joe said.

For a few seconds, time seemed to stand still. Walker frowned in thought, then asked, "Well, what do you know about it so far?"

"It pushes the needle on the Geiger counter to the limit. At least that's what I hear."

"And it sure isn't radioactive," Pete added. "At least so far nobody's died from being exposed to it." He gave the FBI man a look. "Or have they?"

"No."

"You try crushing the samples, Mr. Walker?" Pete asked.

Ten seconds went by before Walker said, "Only extreme pressure could make it flake."

"Yet somebody made that arrowhead," Joe said.

"They never had equipment that could exert that kind of pressure in those days," Walker replied.

"But they did it."

"Yes. We don't know how."

Walker's expression said they might be discussing the atomic bomb.

"It's all about power, isn't it? Something you're looking for because if you find it it'll give you control." Joe pointed toward the horizon. "It's like the stories of the lost mine over there in the Superstition Mountains. A hole in the ground filled with billions of dollars worth of gold. Enough to buy an air force or a hundred nuclear submarines. Find it and you can upset governments or install own your own. This mineral you're looking for must be even more powerful."

The rest of Walker's face was unreadable, but his eyes weren't. They were trying to see inside Joe's words to where the secret truth was, to discern what information he had and what Walker could use to pry it loose. He said, "Don't screw around with me, pal."

"No way, friend. You're FBI, we're just citizens. Trouble is, we're inside a vest pocket like a hidden ace in a card game. We know about that arrowhead I found out there in the desert, but can't quite remember where we found it. Now, if you're nice, you'll buzz off and let us roll all this wild information around in our heads. I have more to do than worry about stuff some ancient Indians made."

"What have you got to do?" Walker demanded.

"I've got to fight a gorilla tomorrow."

Walker gave Joe a long stare. "Good luck," he said, and spit out the window.

When they got back in the truck, they watched Walker drive off and Pete said, "He's a good actor, isn't he?"

"You think he's acting?"

"I've seen him pull some pretty rough stuff."

"He wasn't acting, Petey Boy. He doesn't know a damn thing about that arrowhead or any other samples they've located. He only knows what he's been told, that it's damned important they get hold of more of it. The big question is who told FBI about that arrowhead?"

"The FBI has an in with some of the big mouths around here and somebody got to a telephone and passed the word."

"That somebody acted awfully quickly."

"A buck's a buck."

"You know where the arrowhead is right now?"

Pete nodded. "Running Fox has it, remember?"

"She on the ball about keeping these things quiet?"

"Joe…are you kidding? She's beautiful and smart, but secrets aren't anything she can keep. By now half the women on the rez will have the story about your great generosity and will probably embellish it with you coming down out of the blue and getting ready to knock out Big Arms again just for her and—"

"Buddy, hold it, hold it," Joe cut in. "Your sister and I—"

"At ease, brother. I know my sister. I know the ways she tossed guys over her shoulder. Even the big chief types from the other tribes who came this way to make their points went home holding their heads in their hands. The Profs from the State U tried hitting on her along with the jocks and she out black-belted them all."

"Hell, Pete. I'm not climbing her frame. All I am to her is a white-eyes who owns an old crate."

"Man," Pete said, "you're the joker in the deck. Whether you like it or not, you have to be the winner in this damn game. You don't even have a choice."

"Why?"

"You know what they used to tell the Roman soldiers who were going off to war?"

"What?"

"*Either come home with your shield or on it.*"

"Now what's that supposed to mean?"

"Think about it."

"Sure. Big Arms is supposed to kill me."

"That's what he's planning."

"He's planning murder?"

Pete shook his head. "No, it'll be a fair fight. Just you two, and this time you won't be able to sucker him. He'll be ready for anything you try and while you're trying, he'll break your neck."

"And what will you do, blood brother?"

"I'll have to watch."

"Not help?"

"It's supposed to be a fair fight. The audience will all agree. Even the FBI will be watching and when you're dead they'll bury you wherever you want to lie."

"And I got no chance at all, right?"

"Right. I don't like it, but right it is."

"I thought I was the wild card," Joe said calmly.

Pete took a step back and stared long and hard at him. Finally, he said, "That's what *really* scares me, flyboy."

Miner Moe lay still and stretched out, the sheet rolled down to his waist and his hands folded across his stomach, his chest barely moving with his shallow breathing. They came into his room softly, almost soundlessly, and stood by his bed. Moe either heard them or sensed that they were there and his eyes opened enough to show his pupils, large and black. They moved slightly, taking in Joe and Pete at the foot of the bed. Joe said, "He looks like a cat."

"Sort of," Pete said. "He's got four more lives to go, I think."

Joe put his hand over Miner Moe's and asked, "Can you hear us, buddy?"

Moe's answer was a slow blink. After a long moment, he took a deeper breath and made a small nod.

"Don't talk if it bothers you, Moe."

Moe's tongue licked over his dry lips. Joe picked up the ChapStick from the bed table and ran it over Moe's mouth.

Moe nodded his thanks and whispered, "The bastards made me drink the whole…damn bottle."

"Who, Moe?"

Moe's eyes opened a little wider while he searched his memory. "That kid. The one…who…"

"Maxie Angelo's pilot?"

Moe's head made another nod.

Joe said, "Where'd he find you?"

"I was…at Long Weed's place."

"Alone?"

"Long Weed was up…on the range. I was waiting…for him."

Moe closed his eyes for a few seconds and Joe asked, "You okay?"

"Yeah."

"What did he want, Moe?"

"He…got talking about finding things in the desert. He even…showed me a couple of pieces."

"Gold?"

Moe made a barely perceptible nod. "One was…a feather. Pure gold."

"You sure?"

"I…have one just…like it."

"You tell him that?"

"Maybe. I remember he…took out the pint bottle. I guess I had a drink."

"How many, Moe?"

"We finished the pint. He went out to his…car and got another one. Then…" His eyes slid shut.

"They took you out to the desert and dropped you there, Moe. Do you remember any of that?"

A crease deepened on his forehead. He said, "The bastards…they got my map!" He half rose into a sitting position then fell back, exhausted.

"Map of what, Moe?" Pete asked

"My treasure. Damn, they got my treasure. All them years…"

"How much was there, Moe?"

Moe was staring at the ceiling now, answering absently. Pete bent over and said, "How many horses would it take to carry it, Moe?"

Softly, Moe answered with, "That you Sequoia Pete?"

"Yeah, Moe, it's me."

"Four horses, Pete."

Joe said, "That's a lot of weight."

"Think their plane could take it?" Pete asked.

"Not in a single trip."

"They'd never get back in here to make a second one." Then he thought for a few seconds and added, "But one haul out ought to set them up for life. Hell, the weight of the gold is nominal. It's the historic value of the pieces. The price would be a thousand times the value of the metal."

"All gone," Moe said weakly.

"You can't remember where you hid it?" Pete pressed.

Moe's blank expression said it all. He had stashed it in a

place that could only be found with latitude and longitude markers. And these he had not committed to memory. Joe raised his eyes to meet Pete's and the conclusion was plain to both.

The silence that followed was like thunder. Then Pete reflected quietly, "A long time ago I saw surveying equipment at Long Weed's place. It was real old stuff."

Joe leaned over. "Were you ever a surveyor, Moe?"

A full half minute went by and Joe said, "He's falling asleep again."

But Miner Moe struggled through the lapse and forced his lids open to stare up at the two men. "Once…I studied…" A small smile crinkled the corner of Miner Moe's mouth. "Correspondence," he half-whispered.

"That's what happens on the rez in wintertime," Pete said. "Nothing to do. They try correspondence schools. Try anything."

"You don't pick up surveying that easily, pal."

Pete said, "He wasn't surveying. All he wanted was a location to stash his treasure."

"You've been reading my mind," Joe said.

"What have I left out?"

"The coordinates, blood brother."

Pete looked at him blankly.

"The big 'X' that marks the spot," Joe said.

On the bed Miner Moe had laid his head back on the pillow and a few little bubbles came from the corner of his mouth. His lips worked and some muscles moved in his cheek.

"He's trying to say something," Pete said.

Joe put his head down, his ear close to Moe's mouth. The words were almost inaudible, but Joe heard them clearly enough. When he stood up again he told Pete. "Old Standard Oil map, he said. Top corner. Top corner."

"That's what he said?"

"That's what he said. At least that's what it sounded like."

"He didn't have anything on him when we found him," Pete reminded him.

"So where would he hide anything?"

"I'd say we ought to shake down Long Weed's hogan again. Whatever he wrote it on had to be kept out of the weather and Long Weed's place was about as permanent a spot as Moe ever had."

"The odd couple, right?"

"You'd better believe it."

The two of them took a long look at Moe before they turned to leave. When they did, Mr. Walker and another FBI man stood there silently.

"Outside," Walker said.

It wasn't an invitation.

CHAPTER 9

The big Ford van the government men operated out of was packed with modern technology and staffed by experts with all the earmarks of long service. Pete and Joe sat side by side facing four interrogators. There was a water carafe in the center of the table with six glasses around it, a fresh box of Kleenex, a clean ashtray with no cigarettes nor matches. In one corner was a small icebox. An empty metal wastebasket sat beside it. No empty beer cans. No Coke bottles. No smell of smoke.

"Nice," Pete said. "What do we talk about?"

"A crystal arrowhead," Walker said.

"My buddy here found it."

"Yes. And he gave it to you."

"Right."

"And we want to know everything you know about it."

Pete leaned forward, resting his chin on his fists. "Come on, Mr. FBI man, what could poor ignorant Native Americans know about it?"

"Quit being a smartass," Walker told him.

"Then say something sensible," Pete snapped. "I not only graduated from the State U, I have a master's degree in geology, too."

This was news to Joe, and apparently to Walker as well.

The silence only lasted a few seconds, but it seemed like an hour. Finally, Walker nodded. "I'm going to assume you know a little more than I supposed about this mineral."

"You assume correctly. It's a power source, isn't it?"

The sudden shifting of eyes from one interrogator to another was a giveaway. Walker leaned back in his chair and folded his arms across his chest. He made a motion with his finger to the man on his right, who put his hand under the table and touched something that made a small *snick*.

"We are not being recorded now," he said.

Joe said, "Why?"

Walker said, "Whatever that material is, one ounce of it has more potential than ten tons of pure uranium. It represents a source of energy never before known to man."

"Not to white man, maybe," Pete said. "The ancient ones shaped it, Mr. Walker. We can't even dent it, but they made it into trinkets."

Walker didn't argue. "In time we'll do the same."

"But not into trinkets," Joe said.

Walker's eyes were cold agates when he looked at him. "No," he said. "Not into trinkets."

"Weaponry?" Joe said.

"If necessary," Walker said flatly.

"But first you have to find more of it."

"We have the means to do that."

"Then what do you need us for?"

Once again the eyes around the table all looked for each other and somehow they came to an agreement.

Walker said, "We need that arrowhead. It'll be the largest piece we've got at this time, the only thing that we can use to locate the mother lode, so to speak. And if we can't locate more, it's that much more important that we have this piece. Other specimens seem to cut off the innate power before we can control it. Picture an electric bulb where the filament burns briefly but doesn't throw off any light."

"Damn," Pete mused. "You guys have a problem, don't you?"

"Not if we have that arrowhead," Walker said.

"And you want me to give it to you?"

"Correct."

"Let's put some figures on the table," Pete said. "What's the offer?"

Without hesitating, Mr. Walker said, "Millions if it comes to that."

Pete just bobbed his head slowly, "What could I buy with that?"

"You can buy anything you want," Walker said.

"But I don't want anything," he said. "Me pretty dumb Indian."

A voice said, "You can be a pretty dead Indian." The man across from Joe had abject patriotic hatred in his expression.

Very slowly, Pete got to his feet and Joe followed him. Nobody else moved. This time Pete's eyes were as cold as theirs and he said, "I'll think all this over. Very carefully. I'll try to remember what I did with that ridiculously expensive piece of nature and get back to you. Okay?"

There was no answer.

Pete went on, "Suppose I don't want it to change hands?"

"Something could happen to you."

When they were outside and well out of earshot, Joe shook his head and wiped the sweat from his forehead. "Man, you sure pull into tight turns, kiddo. Those guys were big FBI types and you play games with them."

"White-eyes," Pete said, "most people never even see a Fed Op, but they're here all the time. This is government-owned land. They took it away from us and now they try to tell us how to use it. The old redskin gets kicked around, boozed to death, wiped out of the marketplace, yet when the big chips are down and they need us for something, suddenly we become essential heroes. We even get big medals. Plenty of purple hearts. Pretty graves."

"You got any medals, Pete?"

"Not yet," he said.

"Where's the arrowhead?"

"Wherever Running Fox put it."

"Then I'll assume it's safe," Joe said. "Let's go shake down Long Weed's hogan."

The door was unlocked and the two mongrel dogs on the south side of the hogan didn't even let out a warning howl. Either Weed was satisfied that he'd done a good job of hiding his valuables or he didn't have anything to steal.

Joe took the north side and Pete scoured the other areas. In five minutes, they had completed a close scrutiny of all the possessions in sight, Long Weed's and Miner Moe's. They found nothing at all. They laid the small handful of items they wanted to look at in greater detail on top of the upside-down crate Long Weed used as a table.

The paperwork was mostly receipts for feed, seed and oil supplies. Long Weed had four letters from a county agent about re-nourishing a garden and one letter from a tribal dentist notifying him to come in for a checkup.

Miner Moe had two small catalogs for mining tools with a penciled checkmark beside a set of small handheld hammers of the sort fossil hunters and geologists hang on their belts.

Joe showed them to Pete who nodded immediately. "A lot of people here have them. They go out bone digging when the weather is right."

"Where?"

"Over in the foothills. Since they found those mastodon bones in that area a few years back, the major universities have been sending in student teams to see what they can find."

"Don't they need experts for that, Pete?"

"Why? Ninety-nine percent of the finds are accidental and most are discovered by rank amateurs."

Joe eyed three Polaroid snapshots he'd found in a trunk in the back. All three were of Big Arms and on the ground in front of him were twisted things that used to be human.

Cold sweat oozed out of his forehead and when he muttered something under his breath, Pete came over and looked at what he held.

"They dead?" Joe asked.

"No, but I bet they wished they were."

"This guy is pretty bad," Joe mused.

"Quit thinking about it."

"What were these fights about?" Joe pressed.

Pete let a few seconds go by, then he let out a little cough and said, "Same thing. They made passes at my sister."

Joe laid the photos down and blew the dust from a few dozen small sheets of paper held together by a rubber band that broke as soon as Joe tried to open it. The pages were nothing more than three- and four-year-old receipts.

The last item turned out to be a well-worn map that had been folded and refolded so many times it almost fell apart at the tattered seams.

Carefully, Joe laid it on the crate top and both studied it. The front and back surfaces had been used as a notation board for buying household supplies and meeting people with names like Cut Face, Owl Hand, and Leaping Deer. Using an old-fashioned indelible ink pencil, Miner Moe had made strange little circles with crosses in them in about fifty areas of the wide-open spaces that took up most of the map.

Joe turned one corner of the map down and said, "Look. Standard Oil."

Pete ran his finger along the lines that were noted with the circled *X* marks. "What do you think these indicate?"

"Places where Moe found treasure?" Joe said.

"No." Pete shook his head slowly. "He'd never put that down on a map and leave it lying around."

"What is it then?"

"You note the date on this map, White-eyes?"

"Sure, 1932." He paused and frowned, thinking. "How many cars did they have around this way then?"

"Not many," Pete answered. "So we're not looking at roads."

After a few long seconds' study, Joe nodded and asked, "Trails?"

"Keep looking."

"They weave from left to right, straighten up some and start weaving some more."

"That's all desert in that area." Pete said. "Think about it."

"I'm a city boy, Pete. Why don't you just say what you're trying so hard to tell me?"

"When there are big rainstorms, water channels right down those paths."

"That's an old riverbed?"

"Where those 'X' marks are could be waterholes."

Joe said, "Spell it out, will you? I can read maps, but this is beyond me."

Pete sucked on his lower lip, his eyes running up and down the old Standard Oil map. He tapped the marked locations. "There's nothing there now, but it's possible a few shoots of greenery would show up at those locations and an old sand hound like Miner Moe might have noticed it."

"Something like that would make an impression on him?"

"Damn right. In a barren area like that you'd better believe it."

"Why, Pete? He'd be carrying his own water supply out there."

Pete stared at him like the tenderfoot he was. "Go back a few centuries, White-eyes."

"So?"

"So those damp spots could have been life-saving waterholes fed by an ancient riverbed running under the surface. There's a rock bed under all this sand. That old river still runs through it, but every so often there's a crack in the pipe-like system and the water seeps to the surface under pressure."

"What are you getting at, Pete?"

"City boy, think about Miner Moe's hypothesis. A group of Aztecs are fleeing north with all the golden treasure, statues, idols, ornaments the Spanish Inquisitors are after."

Joe was frowning now, trying to put all this information into perspective. Then he finally saw what Pete was getting at. "They camped out by those waterholes?"

"Man, you got it. They were worn down to skin and bones. They had to stop and get their strength back. Most likely they spent a day at each layover."

"What about food?"

"You like snake?"

"Wasn't too bad."

"These guys probably were used to whatever moved."

Pete paused, and for a while was quiet.

Finally, Joe asked, "What's on your mind, Pete?"

"It doesn't rain much in this area," Pete said.

Joe looked slantwise at his friend.

"But there are sandstorms," Pete said. "They come up real fast. One almost covered up my truck in fifteen minutes." He looked long and hard at Joe. "Imagine that bunch trying to get their belongings together in the middle of a gale like that? They've come a long way, their coverings are tattered, they are pretty well worn down and when the storm passes a lot of artifacts are buried in the sand."

"This doesn't happen at every stop, does it?" Joe asked.

"Hell no, probably not, but whatever they carried their wealth in was getting ready to fall apart. And if it was getting heavy it might gradually be discarded so they could keep on going."

"Where were they heading?"

This time Pete's finger moved up six inches and tapped the mountainous area on the map. "The Superstitions. They would have had runners out ahead of them scouting the land. They knew where the mountains were."

Joe said, "And from this legend comes the tales of the great treasure hoard in the hills up north."

"Legend my foot," Pete snapped back. "Old miners have found those artifacts in those rocks."

"Why haven't those finds been documented?"

"You crazy, flyboy? They were traded in for money. Greenbacks. Heavy cash from collectors. Those pieces wind up in some millionaire's mansion and if the public is lucky, they're donated to a museum years later as a tax deduction."

"Now make your point, Sequoia Pete. It must be a beauty."

Pete nodded. "Miner Moe had it all figured out. Someplace he must have one hell of a big stash."

Joe turned his head and indicated the abject poverty of the room. "Pete...look where he lives."

"Don't you get it? Money has no value to these guys. They'd trade a priceless artifact for a tin of tobacco and think nothing of it. The big deal is getting it. Beat some other slob to the punch. Hide it and yell ha-ha at the world, then forget where you hid it. That's Miner Moe and that's Long Weed. In one way they're lucky. Nobody would believe they ever found anything at all. Oh, I'm not forgetting the way the little golden feet showed up or some of the other trinkets that got heisted by the city boys who got wind of these things. But the big find? No one would believe it."

"What about the arrowhead, Pete? We have another priceless trinket here."

"Joe…it's a dream."

"What?"

"You heard me. For twenty years, they've had teams out here with all sorts of instrumentation trying to locate more of that crystal. You think the scientific minds of this country are going to let something like that go past their noses?"

"What have they come up with?"

"Nothing. They have the bits Mr. FBI mentioned, but bits are all they have. Five years ago, they came out here in a big semi hauling a few million bucks worth of scientific equipment. You know what they found?"

Joe shook his head.

"Nothing, that's what. Now they're all stirred up over that arrowhead."

Overhead, the drone of a twin-engine plane whined by, then changed its tone as the power was cut back.

Pete said, "Maxie Angelo's crate. This is his big weekend."

"How come?"

"The locals will have all their carefully secreted valuables up for sale."

"Like little gold feet?"

"Maybe," Pete said. "Maybe."

Miner Moe's eyes were red with tiny blood-gorged veins. His fingers clutched the top of the sheet so tightly his hands looked death white. His expression seemed permanently fixed and his breathing was fast and shallow. His right pinky and the finger next to it were raw and bruised, the nail on his little finger partially torn off.

Mama White Bird motioned with a forefinger for them to come to the other side of the bed. She raised the steel gate that kept the occupant from rolling out and pointed to the nasty indentation in the metal framework. "Rifle bullet," she said. "Somebody shot at him right through the open window."

Pete ran the tip of his finger in the little hollow. "Whoever took the shot used a lead-tipped job. The railing stopped that round, but a steel slug would have gone right through into Moe's head." He paused, and glanced up at Mama White Bird. "Anyone hear the shot?"

"Little Dewey heard it," she told them. "He said it came from the other side of the road."

"He had a telescopic sight then," Pete said. "He probably figured he nailed old Moe and just took off. Anybody hear any cars leave?"

"Plenty of cars around here all the time," Mama White Bird said.

Joe tapped Pete on his shoulder. "Think he could have had a silencer on that rifle?"

"Could be, but hell, everybody has some kind of homemade muffler. Nobody wants to get nailed taking down a deer out of season."

Mama White Bird held up her hand to quiet them and stared down at Miner Moe. His tongue worked at his lips again and his eyelids flickered. Pete bent over the bed and kept his voice soft. "What is it, Moe?"

"They got my goods, didn't they?"

"Moe…we don't know. We don't know where your stash is."

"They got it. All them years of working…"

"Moe…tell us where it is and we'll check it out. If we can nail those lousy…"

"Too late. The kid made me tell," he muttered. "He took my map, the one I made. It had...compass coordinates on it."

Joe pushed Pete aside and looked down into Moe's eyes. They were rheumy and watery and Moe blinked twice to clear them. "Lats and longes, like on the boat."

"What's he talking about?" Pete demanded.

"He's talking about latitude and longitude coordinates, buddy."

"Come on, how would he get them?"

"You have global positioning instruments in your truck, haven't you?"

"Sure, but—"

"Before those gadgets came on the market there were earlier devices. They were bulky and crude, but they worked. You want me to describe them?"

"Never mind."

Joe nodded. "And you said he had a smattering of surveying in his background..." He looked down at the old man in the bed. Moe's mouth was working as if he wanted to say something. When Joe leaned over he heard Miner Moe say, "*Big bird tree*," then Moe closed his eyes and fell back into his troubled sleep.

Joe stood up and Pete asked, "What?"

"He said 'big bird tree.' "

"Hell, there are no trees out here!"

"That's what he said, Pete."

"You sure?"

"Positive."

"He's hallucinating."

Pete walked in closer and stared hard at Miner Moe. The old man's face was placid now, almost contented, but a little tic pulling at the corner of his mouth reflected some inner turmoil going on in his mind.

"What were his exact words, Joe?"

"Like I said... *big bird tree*."

Their eyes met and Pete raised an eyebrow. "You remember when we were clearing a runway to get your plane out of the soft sand."

"Yeah." Joe thought back, mentally reviewing dragging the tires until a runway was etched into the loose ground surface.

"You asked what those colored scraps were that were broken up all over the place."

"You said they were pieces of tree branches."

"This wasn't always a desert, Joe."

Joe waved his hands impatiently. "So what's on your mind? Those were hunks of branches miles away from here. What's that got to do with a *big bird tree*?"

Pete tilted his head and looked through the window, up at the sky. "Not even many vultures these days. Hardly any eagles, either."

There was no use doing anything but waiting Pete out. Joe took a deep breath and composed his expression and let Pete ramble on about just how big a vulture or an eagle can get and how they would search for food from a high place like a cliff face or while soaring on a thermal high above the earth.

Joe said, "Or a big tree, right?"

Pete simply smiled and answered, "Right."

"Those were only pieces of branches we saw on that home-made runway."

"You're getting there. And on bigger branches grow smaller branches, but bigger branches grow on…"

"Big trees," Joe agreed. "But, like you said, there are no trees out here." When Pete just looked smug and didn't answer him, Joe said, "But there were at one time?"

"For that you get one feather in your crew cut, white boy."

Joe turned his head from one side to the other, mentally seeing the rise and fall of the gentle mounds of white sand that made up the desert.

*

They left Moe to Mama White Bird's tender ministrations and walked outside. They went around the buildings opposite Mama's house and finally found the spot where a shooter could have stood to home in on Miner Moe. While the light was on in the room they could see Mama tending to her patient and it was easy to see that this could have been a deadly shot if only the rifleman had elevated his rifle barrel a fraction of a degree upward.

There were no prints in the soil, no sign of an ejected shell casing, and several ways to exit. What should have been a clean kill had opened the door to a full investigation.

Joe asked, "You going to bring the tribal police in on this?"

"With the FBI squatting on our doorsteps?"

"There'll be another try on Miner Moe, you know," Joe told him.

"Yeah, but hopefully there'll be a breather in between." Pete pounded one fist into the other. Then, "Mama White Bird knows the tricks. She'll have Moe covered nicely. She's got storm shutters on all her windows and she'll have a half dozen young bucks covering the yard area."

"Suppose they threw a firebomb?"

"I don't think they could get that close," Pete said.

"Okay, then we're the outside troops. Where do we go from here?"

"I guess we find the big tree Moe was talking about. First we go pick up Running Fox."

"Why? Can't the two of us..."

"White-eyes, the only way we're going to scout for a tree that isn't there anymore is in your airplane, and that is one place I won't go. I'll stay in the truck and you can lead the way in the sky."

Joe nudged him with an elbow. "Geronimo would have fired you, buddy."

"Geronimo was another tribe." Pete grinned. "But first things first. Let's make sure that arrowhead is in a secure place. Fox is just liable to leave it out on top of her dresser."

Running Fox was sitting on a homemade bench outside their hogan sipping a hot brew from a coffee mug. She watched them drive up in the truck and when they walked up she said, "The government men are really after that arrowhead, aren't they?"

Pete nodded and sat down beside her. "This is only the first contingent. They'll be bringing in the heavyweights next."

"When?" Running Fox asked. She looked up at Joe, her face serious.

"This ol' world is in one hell of a mess," he told her. "You'd never think that out here where there's nothing but sand and mountains, you'd be sitting on a little hunk of power that could change the future."

Her eyes flashed to her brother and he simply looked back at her and dropped his head.

"Change the...? That *arrowhead*?" she asked.

"Where is it?" Joe asked.

With the kind of a smile only a beautiful woman could give to a man, Running Fox dipped her hand into a pocket of her jeans and held it out to them. In her palm was the arrowhead.

"You know," Joe said, "the Trade Towers in New York City went down, the United States Congress is at each other's throats whether or not we should be fighting a war, the stock market is going wild like a runaway roller coaster, the millionaires who stole everyone's money are facing jail terms, and here we are out in the desert holding all the cards."

"What's that supposed to mean?" Running Fox asked.

"The powers that be have all the guns," Joe told her.

"Oh?"

"We have the cartridges."

It took a few moments for it to sink in.

Pete took a step forward and said, "We're in the asshole of the United States and yakking about a lousy arrowhead and somehow it's going to affect world affairs. Are we crazy or something? Damn..."

"World War One started with an archduke and his wife getting killed in a remote part of Europe. That one washed itself out, then Hitler came along and the world came apart again."

Running Fox said, her voice deadly soft, "You want the arrowhead?"

"No," Joe replied, "but if we knew where you were going to put it..."

"It'll be in the outhouse," she said, "behind the west hole."

CHAPTER 10

The day of the dying happens too fast. The sun comes up and it shines in your face and tells you it is time to arise and die the hard death that has been written for you and there is no way you can escape the momentous finale that circumstances have laid on you, and all you can say is, "Oh, shit."

A nasty expletive but warranted.

Out in the sand is old 819, sitting there idle, waiting for her flyboy to take her back into the blue, wondering if it will ever happen or not, a metallic thing that never breathed life but had a life that others could breathe into her, and there she sits, waiting.

"I'll be back," Joe said silently.

819 said, "I'm waiting."

The day of the powwow began long before dawn. The cookfires burned, but not on the ground or in handcrafted brick structures. Sears had supplied the metal cookout charcoal trays and while it was still dark, the glowing embers were like fireflies. Then, as the sun rose, the encampment came to life, a quiet sort of medley, and what you first noticed was the lack of noisy, running kids. Everyone was busy. Everyone had a job to do.

Joe turned his head and glanced at Pete. His native friend stood there, arms crossed against his chest, his buckskin pants a pale gold in the early light. He wore moccasins and his chest was bare. Stuck in his hair was a single white feather. Pointing to it, Joe asked, "That come from an eagle?"

Without turning, Pete replied, "Hell no, White-eyes. That's a duck feather. Took it off a kid last year."

"I thought only big brave bucks could wear a feather like that."

"I'm big," Pete said.

"So how's the bravery thing?"

"I'm entitled. I support a mess of sisters." He paused, then added, "How's *your* bravery thing?"

"Why?"

"Look over there, blood brother." He nodded toward the outlying fires.

A small circle of people gathered around a motionless living statue of pure muscle. In the early light the oil on his skin glistened wetly, giving off a prism-like glow when he moved. There was a reverence in the way the onlookers watched him. The Egyptians did it when their Pharaoh rode past them in his chariot. The Aztecs did it when Cortez came into town. Reverence mixed with fear.

"What are you thinking about, flyboy?"

"Y'know, pal," Joe said, "Belshazzar once felt just like that slob."

"Who?"

"He was the king of Babylon," Joe told him.

Puzzled, Pete asked, "Big man?"

"The biggest. He was king of the entire area."

"So what happened?"

"A hand wrote something on the wall of his big, beautiful teepee."

"What did it say?"

"It told him to get out of town."

Pete thought about it, then shook his head. "Flyboy, you got a screw loose."

Joe just asked, without expecting an answer, "You got any chalk, buddy?"

Across the field Big Arms had shifted his position ever so slightly so that he was looking directly at Joe. There were a couple hundred feet between them, but Joe could see the hunger in the man's eyes. Not a challenge, just a hunger to kill, then savor the blood flowing from a broken body. You just had to look at him to know what his body language was saying. Everyone knew. It was something they didn't want to witness, but they were going to have to watch it anyway and any who opposed the action would have to face the same kind of destruction themselves.

"Where's the FBI when you need them?" Joe asked.

Pete told him, "They'll be here."

"Won't they try to break up the fracas?"

"They won't disrupt any tribal customs, pal." He paused and shifted his eyes away. "Besides…they won't be able to."

"Why not?"

"Big Arms does it so quickly. It'll be over before you even feel it."

"Thanks."

"It's better like that."

"Balls. What are *you* going to do?"

"Nobody can carry weapons at the powwow, Joe."

"What about the FBI?"

"They'll all be on the east side by the cars. It'll be over by the time they see what's happening. No way they can get to you."

"So explain the program. Hell, I'm an out-of-towner here. You guys want me served up on a platter like a chicken and I don't even know the rules of the barbeque."

"You scared, Joe?"

"Curious," he told Pete.

"Damn," Pete said. "You're just like Crazy Horse. Nothing bothers you. Down you come into our desert, take apart the native champion with a sneak punch and you haven't even got goose pimples when he's about to turn you inside out."

"I thought Indians were supposed to be taciturn," Joe said.

"Your civilizing ruined us."

The crowd had grown noticeably by now, although the sound of its conversation was subdued. Every so often heads would turn toward where Joe and Pete stood and Joe knew they were talking about him. Suddenly he asked, "They hate me, Pete?"

His friend's face drew taut, worry lines plain by the corners of his eyes. He shook his head, the feather in his hair wagging like a parent's finger. "Buddy, they *like* you. What they couldn't do, you did with ease. You know what you did? Big Arms was the black knight around here. He took what he wanted, did anything that pleased him, and nobody could complain at all. Then you walked right up to him and blammo."

"It was a sucker punch."

"Yeah, but you did it. You put him on his back and *O-U-T* for the first time in his life and everybody in the village saw it."

"Big deal."

"It was," Pete said softly.

The sun was well up now. The groups around the campfires had eaten and had merged into other groups, men with men, women with women, and the kids scrambling about in quiet play. A crowd of young bucks stood circling Big Arms, admiring their champion.

Nobody bothered to look at Joe at all, except with sorrow, real or feigned.

Behind them Running Fox said, "Big dust clouds over the highway. Must be a hundred cars on the road." There was no smile on her face at all.

"I thought this was a private party," Joe remarked.

"We have telephones," Fox said.

"Hell," Pete said. "Nothing exciting ever happens in this place and if it does the news goes out like a rooster after a hen. You'd think Evander Holyfield was fighting Mike Tyson in the middle of the town."

"Which one am I?" Joe asked.

"According to the odds, you're the hero, but you're dead meat, flyboy."

"Then why isn't everybody crying?"

"Like you said, we're taciturn."

Far away, somebody laughed. The sound carried on the breeze.

"How is this going to happen?" Joe asked.

Pete held his finger out, pointing to the center of the field. "See that stick? When the sun is directly overhead it will throw no shadow. You will walk out there and Big Arms will be waiting. All the crowd of men will close in behind you, the women behind them so they won't see you die."

Joe turned slightly and looked at Running Fox. There was a very odd expression in her eyes. "Where will you be, doll?"

"Right here waiting for you."

Joe winked at her.

Consternation showed on Pete's face. His eyes flicked between his sister and his friend.

Quietly, Joe said, "I'm going into the village. I won't be long. You suppose they'll think I'm running away?" He nodded toward the collecting throng.

"Not if I go with you," Running Fox said and held out her hand. Across the field Big Arms was watching them. Joe pointed his forefinger and thumb at him in a pistol gesture and walked off holding the gorgeous Indian maiden's hand as if he'd already won her.

A gasp came from the onlookers. Big Arms had fire in his face.

They took the truck to the center of town and, going up the main street, stopped outside the garage. Joe told Running Fox to stay in the cab and he went inside. He stayed for twenty minutes, then came out wearing a new set of cotton gloves. Fox stared at them wonderingly, but said nothing. Joe told her where to go and she pulled away from the curb.

The streets were empty. Even the raggedy-looking mongrels had followed the crowd out to the battlefield where they could lick up the blood and howl their appreciation of the stupid pageantry into the dry, still air.

"Turn here," Joe said and Running Fox took the long street that intersected with the highway a half-mile away. The expression in her face betrayed a moment of doubt: was he going to make a break for it after all?

Then Joe held up his hand for her to stop and she stepped on the brake. The truck eased to a halt opposite the chair the old lady was seated on and he got out, walked over and kissed her on the top of her head. She raised her eyes and Joe saw the dampness in them.

He said, "You're all alone here in the village."

"I have my little people. Only I can see them."

"I have my little people too," Joe said. "They tell me when I can get in trouble up in the sky. Like when a storm is closing in around me."

Her voice had a cracked softness to it. "They didn't tell you this time, did they?" Something deep and dark was in the way she said the words, as if she had seen it all earlier, all the events of the past few days.

Joe shook his head. "I got down okay."

"You had to," the old lady said.

"Why?"

"Because somebody had to save Running Fox. Because somebody had to do the big thing."

Joe asked, "And what is that?"

"You will know," she told him.

"Not if Big Arms kills me."

"Big Arms can't kill you, Man-From-The-Sky."

"Why not?"

"Because Big Arms can't kill big White-eyes."

Joe nodded.

"You know that?" the old one asked.

"That's why I came to town," he told her.

When he got back in the truck, a scowl pinched between Running Fox's eyes.

She said, "The shadow of the stick will be getting very short now," and her foot leaned heavier on the gas pedal.

The circle of people opened to let Joe through. The ground had been cleared of any tiny obstacles and the grass had been trampled into a green flatness that gave off a pleasant sweet odor. The stillness was like a storm that had already broken but hadn't touched the earth yet.

In the exact center Big Arms stood, naked to the waist. His huge pants had been cut off at the knees and his calves were like giant hams. Even his slow, steady breathing made the unseen forces beneath his skin ripple and flow like a mighty dynamo.

Joe looked at the stick. There was no shadow now. The sun was directly overhead. Big Arms reached down and pulled the stick out of the ground between his thumb and forefinger, throwing it into the crowd. He didn't smile. He grimaced. He was death let loose for its moment of triumph.

Joe took his gloves off and dropped them in the dust.

Slowly, very deliberately, he walked up to the huge bulk in front of him and heard the man say with a sneering tone, "White-eyes, you die now."

But Joe had assumed a loose prizefighter's stance, fingers curled into loose fists, hands held protectively in front of his face. It had no effect on Big Arms at all. From the muted hum the spectators knew what was coming and it was going to be primitive savagery that everyone might not enjoy but would remember for a lifetime.

The sinews tightened in Big Arms' forearms as he lifted them. There was only a second between life and death now.

Only Big Arms heard it when Joe said in a low whisper, "*Old lady say Big White-eyes win.*"

And his hands flashed open and the big white eyes painted on Joe's palms were staring at Big Arms with a grisly humor only he could see, and before he could move at all, Joe's right hand closed tight and went hard into his throat where there was hardly any mass to protect him. The brute's breathing came to a sudden, wounded standstill. Spit ran out of the prairie giant's mouth in a long dribble and while his hands clawed at his neck his knees gave way and he collapsed into a twitching piece of tortured human that could only jerk and drool on the dirt of the arena.

There was no sound from the crowd. They hadn't seen what they had expected to see, but the results were satisfying enough.

It was over.

Silently, Running Fox had come up beside Joe and her hand slipped into his. "Will he die?" she asked. There was no emotion in her tone at all.

Joe shook his head. "He'll survive. He'll recover slowly, but he'll live. If he learned anything, he'll behave."

"What if he doesn't?"

"The old lady will tell you what to do."

"Were you frightened?"

"I've made dead stick landings before."

"What's that supposed to mean?"

"You'll know when I teach you to fly."

Running Fox held onto Joe's hand as they walked back to the truck. When they went by the small knot of FBI personnel, Joe winked, got a wave back.

Pete was holding the door of the pickup open for them and a strange expression pulled at his eyes.

With the sun at their backs, Joe and Running Fox paused at the open door, stood still for several seconds, then Joe's hands went to her shoulders and turned her around slowly.

Her lips were red and full, more exotic than ever, inflamed with excitement. There was the barest tremble to her bottom lip and her eyelids half-shrouded her pupils. Then her arms went around Joe's back as he brought his mouth down to meet hers and someplace across the sand of the plains thunder rumbled in applause while Pete simply shook his head in amazement. Because Indian maidens didn't do things like that. Especially with a white-eyes flyboy.

Others had seen them too. They had been peeking from the protection of their vehicles forty yards away. They had children now, but they too had been young once, as she was. They smiled and nodded at one another. They knew what had happened and did not disapprove.

On the way out the steady stream of traffic was like a march of army ants, coming in from all directions and then funneling into a single long parade of pickups, gaudily painted heaps packed with young people, occasional campers and dozens of small trailers hooked on to older sedans. Joe glanced at his watch. "They're starting the powwow kind of late, aren't they?"

Pete shook his head. "It's a three-day affair, buddy."

"I thought the big fight was to be the main event."

"It was," Pete said. "The big story comes in the telling, White-eyes." He shot a sidewise glance at Joe's hands where some of the paint still showed. "It will get bigger and bigger with every telling. From now on you will be like Sitting Bull."

There was a sudden break in the traffic and four new sedans and a pair of SUVs rode into view, one behind the other. Joe didn't catch the license plates, but Pete nodded toward them and said, "There are some of the money shoppers. Cash and carry. They'll park, the ones with antique valuables will offer their merchandise and gladly take a fraction of what they're really worth and everyone will go home happy."

"No sales tax?"

"Ha."

"Just cash deals?"

"Right," Pete said. "No booze or cigarettes. They can trade for that stuff later. Out of sight of the Feds, of course."

"Damn."

"Won't last long," Pete remarked.

"Why not?"

For the first time Running Fox spoke up. "The red man is getting wise to the white civilization's ways. They're opening casinos, most on their own reservation property, and there's little the government can do to stop them. It's all legal, bankable and taxable. The public feels so badly about the poor Native Americans they flock to the tables."

"But the money men are coming in for the powwow, aren't they?"

"Not for the ceremonial stuff," Pete told him. "They don't even give a damn about the artifacts that got dug up in the hills or snatched from old gravesites. These guys aren't dumb. They're after the heavy stuff. Gold. Statues, ingots...anything of that sort that comes their way. Laws forbid them from peddling artwork, but melted down it can still come to a hell of a lot of money."

"All you got are some little feet and trinkets."

Pete wagged his head and frowned. "Those were accidental discoveries, flyboy."

"Oh?"

"Miner Moe had the right answer. He took the time to do some research. He used to go to the State U library and write away to agencies in Madrid, Spain, and he put things together that sounded crazy, like the Aztecs or somebody fleeing northward with armed Spaniards behind them."

Joe said, "I suppose nobody believed him."

"Who would?" Pete demanded. "The native red man here hardly believes anything you white-eyes tell him. You take away his land and feed him booze. Why should they listen to old Miner Moe?"

"But you did," Joe said.

For a full minute, Sequoia Pete sat quietly until his sister nudged him with her elbow. "Tell him."

Another minute passed and Pete said, "One day Moe showed up at our hogan half starved to death. We fed him, made him stay two nights, filled up his grub sack and hung two big canteens of water off his horse's saddle and told him so long. Before he left he reached into his goodie bag and brought out an old engraved metal helmet that was a duplicate of the ones the Spanish officers wore on their rampage into Mexico."

"Where is it?" Joe asked.

Running Fox said, "I cleaned it up, painted it red and yellow, decorated it with tribal markings and hung it up in the living room."

"Joe, she planted flowers in the thing. You can't even tell what it was anymore."

"There a value on it?"

"Guy at the university said one that was authenticated could be worth a few thousand bucks."

"So why didn't you sell it?"

"Because it was a gift from a friend," Pete said. "But it proved that Miner Moe's theory had turned to reality. Out there in the sand is the grand wealth of a defeated nation."

"Only nobody knows where it is," Joe said.

"Miner Moe does," Pete said. "That's why they tried to kill him. If they got him drunk enough he could have told them. Then they tried to kill him to keep him from talking about it. Twice, they tried."

"He still told us, didn't he?"

"The big bird tree?"

Joe nodded.

Finally, Pete took a deep breath and exhaled slowly. "Miner Moe was right. Someplace he's piled up a huge stash. He's just a shaggy old man who lived on the sand and hardly had anything to show for it. To him gold would be just a thing to chuckle over, not to gloat over."

They rode in silence a few minutes, watching the color of the terrain change as the sunlight bounced off the gentle, winding slopes of the sand. When Running Fox squeezed his hand, Joe said, "What have you got on your mind, Chief Sequoia Pete?"

"We have two problems," Pete said. "One, how do we handle the arrowhead the FBI wants so badly?"

"Only two choices, buddy. You keep it or hand it over. No way they can simply take it from you and even though they are the feds, they're on Indian Reservation territory. They're outsiders here just like I am. So they got guns and badges and some degree of authority, but the national mood isn't going to let them work under any kind of Wounded Knee script."

"So?"

"Keep it until a better time shows up."

"Suppose they decide to search our hogan under other pretenses, like looking for drugs."

"Would they find any?" Joe asked him.

The answer was fast and short. "No way."

"You think they'd stick their hands down an outhouse retainer?"

Pete's mouth twisted in disgust. He nudged his sister and said, "You hang it on a string inside a sandwich baggie?"

"Good guess," Joe said when he saw Fox nod.

"Guess, hell," Pete snapped. "That's where she always hid her valuables. None of us were going to dive into that muck for anything."

"Then what's the other problem?"

"The impossible one."

Running Fox and Joe Gillian stared straight ahead and waited for Sequoia Pete to spell it out.

After a half minute, Pete said, "We need to find Miner Moe's cache." When the other two nodded, he continued. "*Big bird tree*. That's all we have to go on."

"I thought we had that figured out, pal. I was going to fly over the area and look for the damn thing."

Running Fox squeezed his hand again tightly. "It may not be a tree at all, Joe. Miner Moe is a real white native. He thinks like one of us and he acts like one of us. *Big bird tree* might just be a description, of something else entirely."

"Then what are we looking for?" Joe's voice was brusque with impatience.

"White-eyes," Fox said, "if he called it 'big,' then it was a big *something*. It could have been a riverbed shaped like a tree where a bird had a nest. It could be a rock outcropping where the person who named it saw a bird perched."

"That doesn't make sense."

"Not to you, but that's the way the original tribes thought."

"Then what do we look for?"

Pete and his sister exchanged a glance. "You'll know it when you see it," Pete said.

"Okay," Joe said. "So we get some air under us and look around for something big that's not a tree and might not even be there."

Overhead there was the faint propeller drone of a twin-engined plane. Joe's eyes picked up the glint of the sun off the reflective aluminum body and his eyes narrowed. That was Maxie Angelo's ship and it was getting ready to land at the reservation's one-runway airfield.

"The big fish is back in his pond," Joe muttered.

Both Pete and Running Fox nodded in agreement.

CHAPTER 11

Big Arms said nothing. His lips never moved, but his face spoke an eloquent language of hate egged on by a hunger for revenge. He knew there was no way he could challenge the white-eyes who had humiliated him again. Dying would have been better than having to live with the people all pointing him out as a fool. He could still tear the heads off any of them, but now the abject fear that once had held everyone in total subjection wasn't there any longer.

Now one of them could have a gun, or a knife honed to razor sharpness, and wouldn't hesitate to use it. Somebody, anybody, could come up behind him and with one sudden thrust, slide a blade between his ribs that the strongest of muscles couldn't stop. To that steel a muscle was only soft meat that it could slice easily. The needle point would penetrate the flesh, the fine edges of the metal would separate the tissue, and with no trouble at all the entire length of the weapon would stab into a beating heart and everything inside him would explode into horrible agony.

A warped frown twisted Big Arms' face into a grimace. He saw the old lady being helped out of an old pickup, and with a very deliberate twist of her head, she looked at him.

Big Arms swallowed and couldn't meet her eyes. He kept on walking and headed toward where a group from the local tribe in full historic regalia was dancing, the muted sounds of the drums keeping the tempo in full beat with that of his maddened heart.

Maxie Angelo was a person outside his sphere of recognition.

In his own world, Angelo was hated and feared and respected as only a mobster could be. Wealth and power bought him a form of respect he didn't deserve; he commanded it from all because he was known to wreak terrible vengeance on any who crossed him. Even from Ted Condon, who Maxie treated and tolerated like a court jester, allowing him to go to all sorts of extremes without reprimand.

Big Arms knew all of this. He realized that everyone else knew it too. They did business with Maxie Angelo because he paid immediately and in hard cash with no questions asked. The FBI knew all about Maxie Angelo, but they had nothing to slam him with and all they could do was play the cat-and-mouse game until Angelo made the slightest wrong move, then they could nail his hide to a Federal Prison wall.

Suddenly the great trafficker in crime was straight ahead, Condon beside him. When Big Arms walked up Maxie said, "He tricked you, didn't he?"

Big Arms simply glowered. A muscle twitched in his cheek. It was admission enough.

"You hear what the old women are saying?"

The muscle twitched again.

Ted Condon spat in the street. "He was kissing her. It was a long one, that kiss. The old women who saw it said it was a marrying kind of kiss. Her brother was all for it."

Everything Big Arms was feeling was written in his expression. Deadly rage. The dire need for immediate action. It was a wild, flowering deadly nightshade building up inside his chest and when it exploded into towering action there would be blood and the jagged ends of bones sticking out through ripped flesh and life would evaporate slowly, so that its loss could be appreciated and the revenge complete.

"They headed back to their hogan. If you leave now they'll be at the end of the Monster Teeth Hills."

Ted Condon knew what was going through Big Arms' mind and he said, "I punctured their gas tank. They should be dry by now."

There was nothing around Monster Teeth hills—no nourishment in the gray-yellow grass, so animals instinctively avoided the area. The jagged rock surface tore the tires from any off-road vehicles that tried to cross the odd desert anomaly.

Sequoia Pete had been so engrossed with keeping the pickup in the faint packed tracks of other vehicles that he had neglected to watch the gauges on the dashboard. When the engine suddenly coughed and bucked he glanced down, muttered something under his breath, and said out loud, "Damn, we're out of gas."

"You filled up before we left," Running Fox said.

Slowly, the pickup came to a stop, a silent giant bug dead in the desert. Joe said, "You have five gallon cans of gas in the back, haven't you?"

"It all went into your plane, if you remember," Fox said.

Joe had a grim look as he reached for the door handle. Outside, he stared back at their tire marks. There was no sign of wetness from spilling gasoline, but there wouldn't have been under that hot sun and with zero humidity. Next he looked at the twin tanks themselves. Nothing was dripping, but each tank had a nail-sized hole in it just large enough to leave them fuel enough to get well away from the village before having to stop.

Pete yelled, "What is it?

"Sabotage, pal. Somebody punctured your gas tanks."

Running Fox and Pete tumbled out of the cab to see the damage themselves. Pete shook his head in bewilderment. "Now what would anybody do that for?"

"Who's going to come along and give us gas?" Joe asked him pointedly.

"White-eyes, we're not going to die out here. We walked fifty miles before, we can walk back to our place from here."

"Can't you radio back for help?"

"Not today, Joe. This is our only yearly entertainment. Everybody, and I mean everybody, is at the powwow. They'll be singing and dancing and getting slopped with cheap booze and having one helluva time and nobody is going to be answering any radio calls. There's only one thing to do, so let's get moving."

"Okay with me. Let's leave Running Fox with the truck and the two of us can haul five gallon cans of gas back."

It was Running Fox who stopped that idea short. She said, "I'll go with Pete and we'll hook the small trailer to his Harley and come right back. We don't need any extra weight on that bike."

"But..."

"Flyboy," Pete told him before he could object, "you're a city type. You got city feet and wear city-style shoes with soles that are half broken down already. So play nice, guard the truck from any outlaws and count the lizards."

The two of them pulled the empty five-gallon cans from the truck, took two each and trudged off up the path.

Outside, it was blazing hot. With the windows down, the breeze came in in intermittent puffs, but it was too hot to be comfortable. Joe pulled out a cold beer from the cooler and downed it in two long pulls. He let out a belch and looked for Pete and Fox, but they had rounded a bend up ahead and were well out of sight.

He hadn't seen a single lizard.

By the time the sun had moved a good twenty degrees through its arc, he had finished the beers and two of the soft drinks, and taken off all his clothes except his shorts. He was wondering what kind of a skeleton he'd make.

Earlier he had started fanning himself, but even that became too much work. He looked at his watch and shook his head. Time seemed to have stood still. The only relief he had came from dipping his hand into the cooler and wetting his face. Even that was risky. If something happened to his friends that cooler was his only water source.

Joe kept wondering about old 819. She was squatting out there in the desert too, probably making weird noises as her metallic structure minutely twisted and reshaped itself in the glaring heat of the sun. But she wouldn't whimper, not old 819. She'd be patiently waiting too, her seat hot as hell, and he hoped none of the gauges were affected by the intense temperature. He wondered idly if he had left the canopy open, then remembered shutting it and sat back and leaned against the headrest.

Some foreign sound brought him out of his heat-warped serenity and he opened his eyes. On the outside of the truck all was still. Then he glanced in the rearview mirror and saw the cloud—big and brown and rolling slowly like a drunken dust devil. Then a dot showed itself at its base and kept growing larger, an almost outer space-like apparition that didn't belong in this wilderness at all. It began a series of erratic movements, being blotted out a second or so by the low spires of the teeth of the monster who abided in the hills, then it was back again and the sound was louder now and identifiable; and with a mighty roar the monster took it, shook it hungrily as it tossed it in the air, and watched while it came down with a ripping, thunderous crash on the road it had just left. The energy of the event dissipated the dust cloud while Joe slipped out of the cab and ran back to the wreck as fast as he could.

There was another sound too, a low moaning of something crushed, something injured, something needing help.

A piece of metal wrenched from the truck's body was by his

feet and Joe took it to pry at what was left of the cab. He succeeded in unjamming the twisted door, and, making sure the driver's head hadn't reached the frame, he got his hands around the post and pulled until he thought his joints would crack. His muscles and tendons stood out in raw relief against his naked skin and with an agonizing sound the door came free just as gasoline hit a hot pipe and flames shot out from the front of the wreckage, the heat of it blistering.

And there, looking up at him in the driver's seat, was Big Arms. There was no strength left in that mighty frame now. There was only recognition of his plight. His world had ended. All his physical might meant nothing at all. His white-eyes enemy could leave him to die and no one would know. Joe could feel the fire and knew that there would soon be an explosion. If Big Arms were still in the truck when it came… If Big Arms were fortunate, it would blot him out immediately. If not he would burn. Like meat on a spit.

Big Arms looked up at Joe and said, "Go."

Joe locked his arms around that great body. He said, "Like hell," and pulled with all his strength. The heat from the flames was scraping at his naked back and he leaned into it, wrenching, pulling the big man from the flames.

Once more, Big Arms said, "Go!"

Joe said, "Forget it," braced his feet, twisted the victim a half turn to the right, felt his enemy's body suddenly come loose from some constricting piece of framework, and with one great burst of energy, dragged Big Arms free of the wreckage just as the gas tank let loose.

Joe made sure Big Arms was comfortable, propped against a hillock of sand, before he ran back to Pete's vehicle. Behind the front seat there was a medical kit that he grabbed along with two bottles of soda from the cooler. He ran back and had Big

Arms sip at the soft drink while he salved and bandaged the burns and abrasions on his legs.

There was a dull roar from the burning wreckage as another pool of gasoline fueled the formerly diminishing inferno.

Overhead, the sun had completed its arc, but there was little cooling. The desert had absorbed all that energy and now was giving it back, but the encroaching twilight was at least relieving to the eyes. A hundred feet away from the smoldering wreckage of the pickup truck the two men sat quietly, thinking much, but saying nothing.

In the distance was a speck of light. It was moving fast, the probing finger of the headlight picking out the old tire marks to drive on. "Sequoia Pete comes back," Big Arms said with an odd quietness in his voice.

"Running Fox is with him."

"I know."

"Do we talk about this, Many Thunders?"

For the first time, Joe saw the big Indian smile.

"She has told you many things about me," Big Arms said.

"You did a lot of crazy things, kid. You hurt a lot of people."

"That wasn't me," Big Arms said. His voice was softer now, almost ashamed. "That was who I thought I was. Who I had to be."

"Invincible?"

Big Arms lowered his head and nodded.

"The British had a battleship by that name."

"What happened to it?"

"It got sunk, Big Arms."

"I would like it better if you called me by my right name."

"Okay, Many Thunders. Do we play nice now?"

"Yes."

"That's just us. What about Running Fox?"

"She is yours now," he said simply. "If anybody tries to stop you I'll..."

Joe put out his hand. "Let me handle that, okay?" He held his hand out and Mighty Thunders wrapped his fingers around it.

The Harley drove up, the trailer rattling behind it. Pete dismounted and asked Running Fox, "Do you see that?"

Even as he spoke, the two figures rose and walked toward them, limping, unsteady, but side by side.

Running Fox said, "Holy shit!"

"Watch the mouth, Sis," Pete said gruffly.

"Why?"

"Your husband might not like it."

"I'm not married, damn it!"

"You will be, little sister."

After a few seconds she said, "He hasn't asked me."

"That's a mere formality," Pete told her.

"Suppose I say no."

"You won't."

"Maybe he won't ask."

"He will."

As they came closer, Pete saw where the fire had touched the legs of Many Thunders and the glistening sheen of the ointment that had been smeared on him. The story needed little explanation, but there was still a big question unasked.

Before Fox or Pete could pose the question, Joe said, "I've been talking with our new friend here. Maxie Angelo instigated this cute scenario. He wants us out of the way no matter how."

"Why, Many Thunders? What has he got against us?"

After a few seconds, the huge Indian said, "I heard him say to Condon that you flew a plane, Joe."

Puzzled, Joe asked, "What difference does that make?"

Big Arms' eyes were half-shaded by thoughtful lids and he looked at each of them in turn. "He's looking for old Miner Moe's buried gold from the air. Doesn't want anyone to beat him to it."

"Does he know where it is?" Joe asked.

"From the air, it will show itself," Big Arms said.

"What do we do?" Fox asked.

"First we plug those holes in the pickup's tanks," Joe said.

"Then?"

"Then we stop Maxie Angelo."

In the early dusk, 819 stood out as something alien against the lighter shades of the sand. There had been little wind, so no abrasive particles had been blown under the engine cowling or into the brake pads.

Earlier, they had decided that Running Fox would fly back to the rez with Joe while the two men stayed with the truck.

This time Joe would land on the runway at the reservation where they could be picked up after they had a chance to talk to the station operator who, according to Pete, might not be inclined to help a white-eyes outsider but to Running Fox would give anything. Joe wanted a close look at Maxie Angelo's plane while the other two would check on Miner Moe and, if he was coherent, try to get more information out of him about what his cryptic remark about "big bird tree" had meant.

There were no runway lights on at the airport, but Joe made a low pass over the area with his landing lights on to make sure he was clear to come in, then banked hard, turned onto the runway and put down in a smooth three-point landing. There was no designated parking place, so Joe just braked and swung 819 around so that he was ready for a fast takeoff.

Inside the operations shack, they found the dispatcher sprawled out on a pile of feedbags, a pint bottle of cheap booze still in his hand, a quarter empty. The smell of the liquor filled the room.

Joe said something under his breath.

Running Fox said, "Joe…he doesn't drink."

"Even if he'd never had a drink in his life, that little rotgut wouldn't be enough to knock him out like that." He bent down to take a closer look at the old guy. Tobacco spittle had run out of his mouth and dried on his chin and, when Joe turned the man's head a little, he scraped the remains of a small pink pill out of the crease in his neck. He held it out for Fox to see. "They must've forced some down his throat. They missed this one."

"It's a pink duster," she said. "The kids get hold of them and pass them around when they're at their hill parties."

"What does it do?"

"It's a date-rape drug."

"I thought that was a big-city problem."

"This may be an Indian reservation, but people are people. There are good and bad and a lot you can confuse and corrupt."

"And Maxie Angelo brings this stuff in here?"

She nodded, sadness in her expression. "What can you do?"

"To kill a snake, you cut off its head." Joe's voice had a real bite to it.

"The snake isn't here," Running Fox said.

"His plane isn't on the runway or in the parking area either," Joe said. "You got any idea where he could go around here?"

Fox said, "He's been known to land out in the desert."

"Where? There aren't any strips on the sand."

"You found a place, didn't you?"

Joe nodded. A night landing would be out of the question, but if Angelo had a spot he knew about and had set down when there was still plenty of light he could well still be there now, waiting for dawn to take off. But why, he wondered—what reason would he have to stop overnight?

The answer was obvious enough. Maxie Angelo had found what he came for and all he needed now was to load it up and get away with it.

As if she were reading his mind, Running Fox said, "He got to Moe's stash." They radioed back to the pickup.

Pete answered. "You guys okay?"

"We're fine," she told him, "but Maxie Angelo's plane isn't here and the old dispatcher has been doped out of his mind. They did him one better than they did with Moe. Poured booze down his throat, then dropped a pink duster in for good measure."

Pete mouthed a curse and said, "Someone got to Miner Moe, too. Came in when there was no attendant. Left some pretty damn big bruises on the old guy."

"Where was Mama White Bird?"

"Out in the street with the others. A car was on fire in the middle of the road, but nobody was in it."

"That was a distraction, Pete."

"Well, nobody realized that when it was going on."

"Is Moe able to talk?"

"He's making sounds, but it will be some time before he's able to make any sense."

"We have to get in there," Fox told him.

"I'll tell you what to do. The dispatcher kept his old pickup truck behind the main building. It's under an overhanging roof. He keeps a gas can in the truck's bed in case it's empty. Come on in, okay?"

"You got it," Fox replied.

They located the exterior light and found the truck. It was a good fifteen years old and had been driven hard and put up wet, like the cowboys used to say. The key was in the ignition and when Fox turned it, the battery made a tired sound in turning over the engine, then it coughed, spit a few times, and shuddered into a worn grumble.

Joe said, "Can you handle this?"

She looked like she was going to give him a withering remark, then realized that he was truly concerned and instead said, "I was brought up on these crates. Besides, you think you could find your way back to the village?"

"Lady," Joe said, "you got the controls."

Thirty minutes away on the barely outlined road the light of the moon took on a shaded hue and a few stray clouds drifted by the half-full orb. There seemed to be a heaviness in the air and something was sucking the heat out of the ground. Joe noticed it, but said nothing until Fox pointed to the sky. "There's a storm coming in."

"Rain?"

"No rain. Wind and sand. It will strip the paint right off a car."

In the air, Joe could have avoided this situation. He would have had access to the government weather stations and picked up reports from other pilots and rerouted his flight to circumnavigate his way around the disturbance.

"How far out are we?" he asked.

"Fifteen minutes. Soon you'll see the lights in the village."

Her prediction was accurate. Beams were fingering out one area and several were flashing into darkened corners like long, probing fingers. Fox said, "Those are FBI vehicles. They're the only ones who have spotlights."

"Where are they?"

"That's Mama White Bird's place. Damn…if something else has happened to Moe…"

"I don't see any red lights from emergency vehicles."

When they got closer the moving bodies of men surrounded a still-glowing mass that spit off tendrils of steam as water was shot on it. Running Fox stopped the old truck a distance away and they got out and jogged to the scene of the fire.

Walker was in charge of the group squelching the rest of the flames with containers of foam and when Running Fox asked him what had happened, he shook his head in disgust. "Blasted car drove right up here and would have gone smack into Mama White Bird's place if the motor didn't quit. It almost looked deliberate, according to a couple of kids who saw it happen. The damn driver got out and ran for it."

"Any identification?"

"You think they'd tell us?"

"Whose car was it?" Joe asked him.

"Somebody said it was Big Nose Henry's?"

Joe looked at Fox curiously.

She said, "Big Nose kept it beside his trailer. He rarely drove it. Just kept it running so he could haul his cart full of junk out to the dump once in a while."

Looking toward Mama White Bird's house, Running Fox asked, "Anything happen in there?"

"The fire got everybody all excited. It's quiet now. Your brother's in there checking on the old man."

"Miner Moe?"

"Yes. He's okay."

The door on Walker's car was opened and the beeps on his radio were suddenly interrupted by a garbled squawk and a muffled voice.

Walker frowned and yelled, "Was that incoming?"

The other agent yelled back, "Yeah."

"Who is it?"

"Beats me, Chief. It's not our traffic."

"What the hell is a VHF signal doing out there?"

The young agent behind Walker said, "It's probably a bounce."

"A what?"

"A bounce."

"Now what's that supposed to mean?"

"Sir, I'm not a specialist in radio, but some places oddball signals turn up. Maybe there's something in the instructions..."

"Hell," Walker told him, "this is all new equipment. I wouldn't know where to start. You make any sense of it?"

"It's marine talk."

"Like what?"

"I think it said the cargo was loaded on the ship."

"So?"

"And they'll be casting off as soon as it clears up. That's seagoing chatter."

"We're not near a sea."

"I know. It's probably a bounce. You want me to..."

"Forget it," Walker said.

As they walked into Mama White Bird's house, Joe said, "A bounce my tail. If you have VHF equipment in your truck, Maxie Angelo could have it in his plane."

CHAPTER 12

Miner Moe was awake now, his eyes still looking drugged. When anyone spoke to him he'd absorb it, let the words sink in, then struggle for an answer. Pete stood beside the bed, Moe's hand held gently in his, and his conversation was deliberately casual, nothing that would disturb the old man. Big Arms sat on a handmade chair in the corner looking like a kid who's outgrown his potty stool.

"We got here just after the car blew up," Pete told them. "If it hadn't blown when it did, it would have taken the side right out of this building, Miner Moe and all."

"The FBI looking for the driver?"

"They'll never find him," Pete said. Then he nodded toward Big Arms. "But your buddy over there will."

"Oh?"

"Many Thunders put the word out. Somebody talks soon or he'll come after the whole damn batch of them. The kids in town are still scared stiff of him."

"How's Moe?"

"He wants to talk to you."

Joe took a step closer to the bed and patted the old guy's thigh. Moe managed a small smile. "They sure want me bad, don't they?"

"They're stupid," Joe said to him.

"All my stuff..."

"Yeah?"

"It's for the rez here. New houses. Real cooking stove.

Schoolhouse so…the kids won't have to travel so far. Mama White Bird needs a real…medical clinic."

"They'll get all that, Miner Moe."

"If you want…"

Joe looked across at Running Fox and said, "I already got what I want, buddy."

The wizened prospector nodded, pleased. "Good woman, she is." Then his eyes narrowed and he said, "All my goods…"

"How do we find the big bird tree, Moe?

"Ask Mama. She was born right beside it. She was named after it." And the old man's eyes fluttered shut.

Joe made a motion with his head and Pete followed him out of the room. They found Mama White Bird in the kitchen simmering something to feed her patient and Joe asked her, "What's the big bird tree?"

Joe saw her recoil, as though the question called up bad memories. "It's where I was born. Why do you ask?"

Joe said, "What is it?"

"It's the place where the old men said that the great bird men with the feathers in their heads died. The Ironheads killed them all, and then the Ironheads died there too. No one could explain why, what killed them."

"The Aztecs had feather headdresses," Joe said.

"And the Spanish had metal helmets," Pete said.

"I was born there because my mother gave me life very early. Very early."

"Where is it?" Joe asked.

"That," Mama White Bird said, "I don't know. I've heard the songs and the stories, but I have never been back since I was an infant."

Hearing this, Joe felt his heart sink.

✲

They watched the kids milling about the still-hot wreckage of the burnt car, thinking about what Mama White Bird had told them. Pete finally shook his head in exasperation. "The old men never made sense," he said. "They're stories from a century ago."

Joe reminded him that most fables seemed to have some basis in fact. "That iron hat business and feathers in their heads came from history. Distorted a little, but there's a similarity."

Pete waved his hands in disdain. "And they just 'died.' Poof, and the birds cleaned their bones. Great. So what do we do now?"

"*We*, meaning you and me, are going on a scouting expedition. We have a plane to find."

"Damn it, Joe, it's still night."

"We have to get back to the landing strip and gas up. By then it will be sunup."

They told Running Fox their plan, ran the motorcycle up the ramp into the back of the airfield dispatcher's truck, hoping it would stay together long enough for them to make it back.

It did. And when they arrived nothing had changed. The dispatcher was still where they had left him, breathing like an old drunk, a few mumbled words coming from between bubbly lips.

"Maxie Angelo did this?" Pete demanded.

"Nothing we can prove, but it fits. He doesn't like witnesses. Between him and Ted Condon they wouldn't have had any trouble taking the old man down."

They had to hand-pump the fuel out of the drums into the BT 13 and the sun was well up when Joe made his walk-around of 819. Unlike more modern equipment, the World War Two planes had far greater longevity and were made to stand the rigors of tough usage—more than the planes that were currently in use, Joe had found.

Satisfied that the inspection showed no apparent defects, Joe waved Pete into the rear seat, made sure he was buckled in and climbed into the cockpit. He adjusted his gas and prop settings, flipped the energizing lever and held it until the whine said it was ready to turn the prop, then flipped it over and watched the prop spin. The engine let a blast of smoke out the exhaust and roared to life. When he had a full magneto check he made sure Pete had his headset on, then released the brakes and taxied out onto the runway.

He leveled out at two thousand feet, circled the airstrip once, then picked up an east heading and changed prop pitch.

He heard the click of the intercom in his ears and when he looked in the mirror he saw Pete with the microphone at his lips and tapped his earphones for him to begin speaking.

"Flyboy, we going up to thirty thousand feet?"

Joe shook his head and picked up his microphone. "No way, Chief. This is no P-51. We don't carry oxygen on board. What are you worried about?"

"I don't feel like passing out, that's what."

"Five thousand will be our cruising altitude. No trouble there. You keep your eyes on the ground. We can cover a lot of distance from up here and on all that sand, a plane ought to show pretty well."

"Suppose we spot it?"

"A call to the FBI guys at the rez can get them to order a plane from a military installation in a hurry."

"Good luck," Pete answered. "The nearest base is in the next state. By the time anything got here they could be a long way off."

"Then we'll just have to think of something."

"Like what?"

"Damned if I know."

For an hour, Joe searched the area a sector at a time. They saw nothing but hills of sand and occasional weathered wreckage of old wagons. Twice, the sun-bleached bones of dead horses were like ghastly road markers pointing west. One even had the remnants of a saddle plainly visible around the skeletal remains.

Pete pointed out the edge of Monster Teeth Hills as it showed up dead ahead. From the air the ground had an even more jaw-like appearance, rocky protuberances jutting upward like deadly canine teeth. The ridge of nearly black stone was a good five miles long, stretching out in a two-mile width.

Joe touched the rudder pedal and nudged the stick and 819 banked into a right turn to cross over the dismal area. There was a sudden bump and Pete didn't bother using the mike. He yelled, "What was that?"

Joe lifted his intercom and said, "Thermals. The ground configuration changed and caused a disturbance. No sweat, buddy."

But he barely got the words out when 819 gave another violent shake and was sucked up another five hundred feet, buffeted all the while by the freakish air currents. He gave a quick glance at his instruments and what he saw made a chill run through him—the air speed indicator was reading a hundred fifty-five M.P.H., but the magnetic compass was spinning too fast to see the numbers go by. A glance showed the gyroscopic compass holding fast, but the altimeter started to make violent jumps from ground-level readings to ten-thousand-plus feet over the terrain.

In the back seat, Pete had seen the same thing and had grabbed the stick in a moment of terror, pulling on it in a manner that threw 819 into a violent, uncontrolled maneuver.

Very quietly, Joe spoke into the microphone. "Pete…Pete, get off that stick."

He could see Pete's face in the mirror he had adjusted to watch his passenger. Pete's eyes were wide with terror.

Once again, Joe said, "Pete…let go that stick or you're gonna lose this horse too."

Pete came out of it then. He let go, pulled his hands back and clasped them together across his chest. The terror was still there in his face. Controlled now, but still there. His mouth said "Sorry" soundlessly. Joe just nodded and concentrated on regaining control. 819 was bouncing erratically across the sky, but Joe pushed the throttle to the firewall, banked hard and blasted across the edge of the Monster Teeth Hills into stable air. He ran along the edge of the weird formation until he saw a huge V-shaped cut in the side of the jagged mountainside. Sticking straight up for a good hundred feet was a spire of blue rock like a giant's single bicuspid tooth.

He had no desire to go over the hills again, but made a pass closer to the spire so that the fingerlike protuberances on its sides could be plainly seen. Behind him he heard Pete yell out, "Joe! It looks like a stone tree."

And it would take a mighty big bird to land on that tree. Joe and Pete tried to talk at the same time, both having recognized the possibilities in what they saw. Someone gave that edifice a name long ago: *Big bird tree*.

Gently, Joe shifted the throttle and let the plane settle lower. When they got down to five hundred feet he saw what shouldn't have been there at all, parallel tracks coming out of the deep V of Monster Teeth Hills and where the tracks hit the packed sand, the deep imprint of tread marks were apparent.

Joe whacked the stick against Pete's legs and pointed out the tracks. Pete said excitedly, "Maxie Angelo's truck has mud treads like that. He's beaten us, damn it. He's gotten Moe's goods and is gone with them."

"It's a long way to a concrete road." Joe told him. "We can follow those tracks as long as he leaves them."

"Where could he be going?"

Joe thumbed the talk button. "He's got a plane parked somewhere."

"And we can't spot it from up here?"

"Not if it's camouflaged, Pete. We might be able to see *something* and pass right over it because we couldn't recognize it. The army has netting that could disguise a tractor-trailer from the air and Maxie wouldn't be passing up any possibilities at all. That plane is going to be under cover at the end of those tracks."

"Joe…there's hard ground about five miles ahead," Pete called out.

"Use your mike, pal."

He thumbed the button. "It's hard ground and a plane could land there. The old Tingo Road comes in there from the main highway and if Maxie could drive the truck out, Ted Condon could fly right off and meet up with Maxie later."

"You think Maxie would trust that kid with a load like that?"

After a minute's silence Pete said, "No. Maxie Angelo doesn't trust anybody. Period."

In ten minutes of flying the tire marks became dimmer. For short stretches they disappeared entirely and where the tracks cut in closer to the edge of the Hills, they disappeared completely for a full mile. Something drew Joe's eyes from the ground to his instruments and he saw the magnetic compass begin its wild gyrations again.

He couldn't sweat two strange situations at the same time so he dropped down until 819 was skimming along at 155 M.P.H. only two hundred feet up. Joe knew the nearly macadam-like earth would be devoid of tire marks in another mile or so and dropped even lower, trying to search out dust plumes or any signs at all of a vehicle's passage.

He didn't see anything.

But then he did.

The sun made it flash. A prism of color jumped out of what seemed to be the soil and when they flew close over the spot and the camouflage netting flopped from the prop wash, Joe knew they had stopped the escape of the goods Miner Moe had taken a lifetime to collect.

Pete was banging on his instrument panel before he remembered the microphone. He was yelling and pointing to the right of the plane and when Joe followed the direction his finger was pointing, he saw the body stretched out on the ground.

"That's Ted Condon," Pete said.

"Then where's Maxie Angelo?"

Joe gained a little altitude and banked to the right, keeping away from Monster Teeth Hills as best he could. He swept low again over the netting that had been stretched out to cover the Cessna, then spotted Maxie pushing his way through the fabric until he was out in the open. He was holding up a thick, ropey thing with one hand and pointing furiously at the fallen body of Ted Condon.

"What's he got there?" Joe said into the mike.

"Man," Pete said, "that's a rattler and it's a big one. Damn, Ted Condon must have been snakebit!"

"In that case, Maxie Angelo isn't going anywhere with his loot," Joe replied.

CHAPTER 13

The Cessna had a full complement of radio frequencies. Cost had been no object here at all. Joe's first call went to the nearest military base where he requested a patch to FBI headquarters and he was put through immediately. When an agent answered, he gave his name, read off his license numbers and requested a second patch to Mr. Walker on the reservation.

There was a delay of a minute and a half before contact was made with Walker and the call accepted, then the agent said calmly but with some impatience, "Mr. Gillian, this is Agent Walker. What is it?"

A look of relief touched Joe's face and he nodded toward Pete and made an *okay* sign with his thumb and forefinger. Then he touched the *send* button on the microphone and said, "Joe Gillian here, Mr. Walker. I think you'd better get out to the landing field at the rez. I estimate landing in fifty-two minutes with a cargo you'll be very interested in."

"Explain further."

"No time for that now."

"Why not?"

"Because we have a prisoner on board." He added, "Plus a couple of billion dollars worth of trade goods."

Walker's voice was strained. "What do you mean, *trade goods*?"

"You'll find out," Joe said. "Just be there."

Walker snarled, "What I want to find is that arrowhead! It wasn't in the latrine!"

"She told you where she put it?" When Walker didn't answer, Joe said, "I see, you dug but she had already moved it, hadn't she?"

Still no answer. Joe checked the clock on the instrument panel. "See you in fifty minutes, Mr. Walker."

Pete muttered, "You sure are going to piss that guy off."

"Big deal," Joe said. "You know that your sister moved that arrowhead? Those government guys must have had a time digging out that slop looking for it."

"Sounds like one of Fox's moves."

"Where would she have moved it to?"

"A place even I wouldn't look for it. She used to do that to me all the time when we were kids. It's a hole that's full of rattlers."

"Damn," Joe whispered. "You Injuns sure are mean."

"But not dumb, flyboy." Pete smiled at him in the mirror. "Meanwhile, I saw that magnetic compass trying to spin off its axis. You know what I think that means?"

Joe gave a silent start as the significance dawned on him, too. "Damn. Why didn't I think of that?"

"Me college educated," Pete told him. "Me put two and two together."

Joe picked up the mike and called the radio equipment car Walker was riding in. When he heard the click of the connection and the voice say, "Walker here," he said, "One more thing, Mr. Walker. If I were you, I'd also have a chopper handy with a geologist on board, and maybe some instruments a little more accurate than a Geiger counter." He hung up in the middle of Walker's demand for an explanation.

Behind him Maxie Angelo was making maddened sounds through the makeshift gag they'd slipped on him. His eyes were pure hate.

*

There was one thing about the U.S. Government. When necessary it could do things in one hell of a hurry. It could mobilize machines and manpower, build a Panama Canal, or turn a lousy old sand-bed landing strip into a packed-down runway an F-16 could put down on, complete with pole-supported flag markers to show wind direction in case the old wind sock didn't want to play that day.

A full dozen cars flanked the improvised runway, staying well back in case there was a ground looping incident or any mechanical failure. The doors of the cars were open, a man standing behind each in a full alert position, and Joe thought he saw handguns resting on the window ledges ready for a shooting emergency.

Joe's slow pass over the field was ostensibly to check for landing conditions, but it was also reconnaissance. When he pulled up into the landing pattern and rolled out onto the downwind leg, he knew they weren't all friendlies down there and he'd have to play the game close to the vest.

Behind him he heard a grunt, and said, "Now what are you thinking up, Pete?"

"I don't see Running Fox down there."

Joe glanced down quickly. "I don't see any of your cousins down there either."

He adjusted the controls and turned on to the base leg, pulled back the throttles again and dropped the nose. There was no cross wind at all and the flags and the old wind sock drooped sullenly, almost annoyed at letting a plane come in for a landing with no buffeting at all. The wheels touched down, Joe closed the throttle, let the nose settle, then turned into a parking position right beside the hanger.

Outside, at the line of cars, nobody moved at all.

The two men unhooked their headsets, unbuckled their seat belts and sat there. Pete said, "Spooky."

"They're waiting," Joe said.

"Why?"

"Regulations. They don't want to walk into a trap."

Joe pointed at the line of cars. They had started and the doors were closed. Windows were down and the noses of rapid-fire weapons were propped on the sills, all pointed toward the plane. They began to spread out in a pre-ordered formation until they made a semicircle around the Cessna, then they stopped.

Pete said, "Damn!"

"You can say that again," Joe told him.

The door on the lead car opened and Walker stuck his head out, half hidden behind a bullhorn. "Step out of the aircraft with your hands in the air," the bullhorn roared.

"Who the hell does he think we are, Joe?"

"Terrorists," Joe said softly.

"Us?"

"They're not taking any chances."

"Why?"

"While we've been away, they've been at the computers."

"So what?"

"The arrowhead, friend. They've been searching for an artifact like that one hell of a long time."

"Okay, we give it to them."

"The story doesn't end there," Joe reminded him. "I come in and accidentally land in rez territory. I find the arrowhead. The FBI is here to keep tracks on the big powwow. They do that at other reservations?"

Pete thought a few moments, then shook his head.

"They've had suspicions a long time that those strange bits

of mineral came from this area. So they keep this area covered. Hell, they weren't interested in your tribal customs."

"So what do we do now?"

"We get out of this plane with our hands in the air and get a full explanation from the FBI."

They came out like stick figures, arms straight up above their heads, the muzzles of six submachine guns aimed at their bodies. The faces behind the guns were bland, very professional, very well trained. Walker studied them a moment, then stepped forward, two others stepping out to flank him until they all were in perfect position for instant firing.

Walker made a hand motion for the two to walk a few steps, then pointed to one side and made an indication for them to separate. When they did, both felt a gun go into their backs, their hands get snatched and handcuffs slapped on their wrists.

Until then, all had been quiet, but Joe had had enough of the rough treatment and said sharply, "You mind telling us what this is all about?"

Mr. Walker holstered his Glock pistol, his face impassive. His eyes left the prisoners and he glanced over their shoulders. Joe and Pete turned their heads and saw Maxie Angelo being pulled out of the Cessna, all tied up, an almost doped look on his face. The head FBI man said, "What happened to him?"

"He pulled a gun on us," Pete said.

"How'd he get like that?"

"We outflanked him," Joe told him.

"In the plane?"

"Certainly."

"How'd you manage that?"

"Sitting Bull tactics," Joe said. Walker frowned and Joe added, "Before you read us our rights or do any of that TV routine, I'm going to give you a chance to get off the hook. Hell, you may even get a big fat promotion, but in case you don't believe me,

I'm going to remind you that I'm a well-informed individual, owner of a corporation, ex-military personnel of officer status, and have personal friends who are well-situated in congressional committees."

Walker's eyes stayed hard.

"You reading me, Mr. Walker?"

"I am reading you, Mr. Gillian."

Before Joe could speak again Walker nodded to two of his men. "Unhinge them," he directed.

From where he was sitting on the ground, Maxie Angelo was making strained sounds, not able to comprehend all that was going on.

Both Joe and Pete rubbed their wrists when the handcuffs came off. In front of them Walker said, "Go ahead."

"You haven't searched the plane yet," Joe said.

"We will very shortly."

"The cargo in that Cessna is very personal. It belongs to an old man who has spent a lifetime searching for it. This slob over here has been trying to kill him ever since he got wise to the situation. His partner is already dead out there in the desert where a rattlesnake knocked him off."

"Make your point, Mr. Gillian," Walker said, his tone showing his annoyance.

"Right now, in front of all these witnesses you've brought along, I want a written guarantee that the cargo I spoke of will be untouched, uninspected by your people, and declared to be totally owned by Miner Moe. I don't know his full legal name, but I'm sure my friend here—excuse me, my *brother* here—does. I'm also sure one of your people has a law degree and can draft up a legal document that will hold up in any court."

"Are you out of your mind, Gillian?"

"Nope." There was a very determined tone in his voice that made the FBI man stare at him.

"What makes you think the U.S. Government or any of us here would agree to anything like that at all?"

Joe grinned. It was a tantalizing kind of grin that was almost a smirk and he said, "Because what we have to trade is worth more than ten thousand times...no, make that a million times more valuable than what's in that plane."

It didn't happen quickly at all. Walker's face stayed cold and firm while his mind went over the details of what had happened in the very few days he had seen go by and the implications dawned on him. The furrows in his cheeks went away and the ice around the pupils of his eyes seemed to thaw. He looked at Joe, then at Pete, and said with an incredulous throaty whisper, "*You found the source.*"

The nod Joe gave was barely noticeable.

Walker turned to the nearest man to him and said, "Go bring up Marty Johnson and Kooperman. Tell them to get their briefcases. And get the portable laptop out of my car."

"One more thing," Joe said.

"What?"

"Where's Running Fox?"

"In detention at our camp."

"Get on the radio and have her released."

Walker whistled and pointed to a middle-aged guy standing by a car, still cradling his rifle. He put the gun inside the car and came up to the plane. Joe nodded briefly and said, "You aware of the potential in that arrowhead?"

"Yes, I am."

"What would a mountainful be worth?"

The man stammered. "A pickup load could stabilize the world situation right now."

"Also make a pretty good weapon, wouldn't it?"

The geologist nodded and said nothing.

"Supposing the other side got some too," Joe suggested.

"Be a standoff, I guess." He paused briefly, then added, "At least for a little while."

"And anything's better than nothing, right?"

"What's this all about?" the geologist asked him.

"We're about to give you a whole mountain-load," Joe told him.

The geologist's face went absolutely white.

"Are you speaking rhetorically?"

"Not at all," Joe said.

"We're not on a level high enough to make a deal like this," the geologist said. "Congress will have what's left of our heads after the newspapers get hold of it!"

Joe said, "Man, you haven't even heard the details yet."

"But…"

Walker came up behind him. "Shut up."

But the geologist went on. "If this is for real, do you know the power we'd have in our hands? Why the world…"

Walker said, "We're not interested in what the world would do, my friend. The world has already knocked down the Trade Towers in New York, blown up one of our destroyers, bombed our embassies and taken a mess of our citizens prisoner. Right now the ball is in our court and we are going to play it our way for a change."

Almost silently, the FBI geologist whispered, "*Who are you going to trust when the digging starts?*"

Walker's tongue ran across his dry lips and when the agent came up with the laptop computer he walked away, propped it on the fender of a car and began typing. For fifteen minutes, nobody said a word and the faint tapping of the computer keys sounded like far-off gunshots.

Somebody coughed and everybody turned to see who it was.

Maxie Angelo's body was shaking visibly. It was all too much for him. He wasn't thinking about any world crisis. All that was in his mind was how the hell he was going to make it through a long prison sentence.

For the first time, Pete said, "Where do we go from here, buddy?"

"First," Joe said, "we sign some papers that guarantee ownership of certain properties."

"You think they'll stand up in court?"

"You'd better believe it, kid. This affair is going to involve an awful lot of Native Americans who can vote and own property and will have the sympathy of the good old U.S.A. behind them."

"No offense, White-eyes, but we've heard it before."

"It'll be different this time."

"Then what?"

"Then we take our government geologist up for a plane ride and let him watch the magnetic compass do its dance."

"You suppose he'll believe that?"

"Oh boy, he'd better believe it. He'll know damn well what's down there and any greater scientific evidence is only icing on the cake. Now, let me get hold of Walker."

The FBI man was snapping the laptop shut when Joe reached him. He said, "The authorization went through—provided I get positive evidence."

Joe nodded. "Good." Then he asked, "You have any twin-engine-certified pilots with you?"

"I have three."

"One will do. Now, while we get the cargo out of the Cessna, I want somebody to bring Running Fox out here. During that time, we'll load the cargo into several of your cars after a careful written inventory and you'll take it all back to Mama White Bird's place and have it unloaded there. Make sure Miner Moe sees it all, and you guys keep a damn good watch on it until we get the tribal police to take over and arrange for a transfer to a bank vault off the rez."

"Anything else?"

"Nope."

"You enjoy being the big boss, don't you?"

"Yup."

"You're a pisser, Gillian," Walker said. "I hope some of my guys turn out like that."

While they awaited the arrival of Running Fox, Joe took the FBI geologist up in the Cessna. He sat next to Joe; Pete was strapped into the rear seat. Without the load of cargo, the Cessna flew like a great bird, light, maneuverable, instantly responsive to any touch on the controls.

The anomaly that was Monster Teeth Hills was visible on the horizon, then as they headed into its mouth, a nervous tension filled the cabin.

Joe said, "Keep your attention on the magnetic compass and don't be surprised at what you see. The effect isn't minute. It's damn near explosive. You don't need any exotic equipment to see the power we're going over."

The geologist nodded curtly. He knew something was going to happen, but he didn't know what. He had never believed in speculation or trusting other people's opinions and had to see for himself. Frankly, he expected to see some nervous jumps from the magnetic compass, but these things happened when a plane flew over areas where there were great concentrations of iron ore. He had even seen deviations on ship compasses when they sailed over a sunken ship in the Great Lakes that was laden with an iron-rich cargo.

He had never seen a fluctuation like this though.

Joe pointed his finger as they went over the jagged innards

of Monster Teeth. The magnetic compass jumped as if it had been touched by a two-twenty-volt electric cable; it began spinning, the markings on its face only a white blur. Quickly, he turned the Cessna in a one-eighty, got outside the range until the compass slowed down, then went back in and did it again.

"Want another run?" he asked.

The FBI geologist shook his head. Shakily, he said, "I'm convinced."

"Of course, you'll double check it, won't you?"

"Of course," he repeated. "Can we go back now?"

"That wasn't much of an inspection tour," Joe said.

"It was enough for me," the agent replied.

He saw her when he was on the approach leg. She was standing apart from the cluster of men, her ebony hair swirling in the sunlight, ruffled by the breeze. A form-fitting skirt outlined her with curves and ripples and the multicolored silk blouse did things that even made a pilot react long before the wheels touched the earth.

She was waiting. She was waiting for him. Nobody dared get near him as he stepped off the plane. But it was not because of what they had for each other. It was because Big Arms, Many Thunders himself, was standing there, ready to protect his people. His face was fierce, but he was hiding a smile.

The FBI team worked with absolute efficiency. Mr. Walker handed Joe a folder of papers that had come off the computer and, after scrutinizing the signatures, Joe swallowed hard and said, "Where are the originals?"

"Delivered to your main office..." he checked his watch "...an hour ago. You may use one of our phones to confirm, if you wish."

"I'll take your word for it," Joe said. "Did the cargo get to Mama White Bird's place?"

"The tribal police are covering it now."

"Good."

"You'll be available for further interrogation by our people, I assume."

Joe let his eye reach out to Running Fox. She just stood there and let the wind tell its silky-soft story as it played around her. "Don't let it be too soon, though," he said.

"Right. Now one question."

"Shoot."

"Why did you want another certified twin-engine pilot?"

Joe looked at Walker, smiled, and looked back at Running Fox again. "Because he's going to fly that beautiful squaw over there and me back to old 819 out in the desert where we depart in a two-seater for parts unknown."

"Why?"

"Because I'm going to propose to her. She's going to say yes and I'm going to marry her. A big Indian on the rez will tie the knot and who do you think will be the best men?"

"*Men?*" Mr. Walker said.

From the side, Pete said, "I'm one, but..." Then a big grin spilled over his face as it dawned on him what Joe had meant. He watched as Joe walked toward the Cessna and took Running Fox's arm under his and turned her around. Before they got into the plane, she raised her face and her tongue ran over her lips very lightly and Joe's mouth found hers and, for many long drawn breaths, they stood there before they climbed aboard.

Beside them, Many Thunders walked up. He put one giant hand on Joe's shoulder, one on Running Fox's.

"I'm the other," he said.

THE
END